RING OF
CONSCIENCE

James Stoddah

First Edition 2014
2QT Limited (Publishing)
Tatham Fell, Lancaster. LA2 8RE.
www.2qt.co.uk

Release Partner: OUTLET PUBLISHING GROUP
Bulloch House, 10 Rumford Place, Liverpool. L3 9DG.
www.outletpublishinggroup.com

Requests to publish work from this book should be sent to:
press@outletpublishinggroup.com

This book is a work of fiction.
Any resemblance to actual events or persons, living or dead, is entirely coincidental.

www.jamesstoddah.com

Cover design: Kyle Wilson, Gothalicta adapted from Miki Rose initial concept.

ISBN – 978-1-910077-03-0

PLEASE NOTE

All the clues in this book work and the website melodema. com exists. This is an interactive book so feel free to think along with the characters and try to follow the clues for yourself.

Or better still – beat them to it…

For Marilyn

The creator of all my possibilities

ACKNOWLEDGEMENTS

I am eternally grateful to all the people who have helped me find the time, space and sanity to write. Firstly, my immediate family: Marilyn, Jake, Harley, Kyle and Annette for putting up with my strange ways and giving me emotional support. The professionals: Karen Holmes, Emma Pritchard, Bruce Nicholson, Steven Greening and Hilary Johnson for their technical help. Also the network of other helpers, who have helped with logistics, research and design: Catherine Cousins, Kyle Wilson, Andy Wild and Miki Rose.

RING OF CONSCIENCE

The end of the beginning

The dawn introduced the early morning light, as if it already knew the secrets the future would leave as a legacy on this day. Donald Chadwick stared out of the window, his pride dampened only by nostalgia.

It was the end of a long week at the close of a dank and depressing British summer. It was little wonder that he was missing Las Vegas. In contrast to the desert heat and dry sands of 'Sin City', his wife was happy to be back in England. Cornwall, to be precise. The picturesque peninsular of her homeland was a little nation in itself. Most of her forefathers had refused to venture beyond the Cornish border but Violet Chadwick was part of a rebellious generation.

Violet Chadwick was the only living link to her ancestors' Cornish heritage. Their land had been chipped away over generations until Tregarwen Manor House, with its twenty-two acres, was all that remained.

Donald Chadwick always knew that his retirement was going to bring him to England. He wouldn't have wanted to retire in Las Vegas. Cornwall was beautiful and he was happy to spend his remaining years in England with his wife. If only it would stop raining.

It was a special day, too. Four-thirty in the morning and they were both up, having finished breakfast. They had to make the long and tedious drive to London. They could have stayed overnight in a hotel but Violet didn't like to leave the dogs. They were her pride and joy; two prize golden retrievers, Sam and Stardust. The dogs had already had a run out in the three-acre gwel. This was their own field, their own run-around, with a small wooded area and beck. Usually at this time of year the beck was dry but, after so much rain recently, it was overflowing. The dogs needed drying off before Donald and Violet could put them in the car and set off on their journey.

Jason Chadwick had moved to London a year earlier. He was their only son and had already achieved great success in his career. Today, Jason was to be honoured by the London Institute of Technology for his services in developing internet communications. Jason was probably amused as much as he was flattered by such a quirky award but Donald and Violet were still proud of him, even after all these years. They *had* to be there.

The rain eased a little during their journey. The main road was quiet. Donald listened to a selection of seventies' Motown from the local radio station as they headed east, in his Mitsubishi Shogun, past Bodmin towards Launceston. The daylight was still trying to penetrate the clouds.

Violet rested her eyes. She was not asleep, merely absorbing the motion of the journey while The Supremes attempted to summon up the new day.

Donald became aware of a light behind him. It approached fast and he wasn't sure if it was a motorbike or a car with only one working headlamp. In no time at all, the vehicle – it *was* a bike – caught up with them. The road was a dual carriageway and Donald expected it to pass but it remained behind them for several miles. Finally the biker made his move to overtake. It had only just passed the bonnet of Donald's Shogun when it cut inside sharply. Donald swerved to avoid it. He vented his frustration by banging on the steering wheel to activate the horn.

'Damned cheek!' Violet muttered.

The biker moved out again and then slowed, cutting up Donald once more. He was about to express his anger but then saw the biker point what looked like a revolver in his direction.

Donald panicked and swerved to his left. The car hit gravel and he could not regain control. The Shogun tumbled down an embankment. He could hear his wife scream as they were tossed around like laundry in a tumble dryer. Then the car stopped.

Donald was upside down and disorientated, and his movement was severely restricted. He felt battered and bruised but in no great pain. The dogs were whimpering and he was aware of them scratching the back of his seat. His wife didn't look too good. She was conscious but had blood streaming upwards past her nose. He tried loosening his belt but couldn't manoeuvre himself to reach the catch.

Just then, Donald saw a dark figure approaching. He yelled for help and the figure stopped. From his position, he could only see the stranger's legs and waist. The man was dressed in black and looked like he was wearing leather pants.

Donald yelled again and banged his fist on the door as hard as he could. One of the dogs began to howl. The man stood there, motionless. In a moment of sudden clarity Donald noticed a light - flickers of orange light! *Oh God no!* he thought.

'Hey, help!' Donald yelled. '*Help us please!*'

The man stood for a few seconds longer, then turned and walked away.

The fire took hold quickly. Donald could feel his legs stinging and burning. He twisted frantically, trying to find a way out, but he could feel his skin starting to shrivel in the heat. The light was so bright now. The only sounds were loud spits and crackles.

He looked over at his wife. Her eyes were shut tight and

she was wailing softly.
    There was nothing more that he could do.

CHAPTER 1

Ten years later

It was merely a passing comment, that was all: Jason Chadwick's words suspended on a delicate fibre of time. He could never have predicted that his casual words would prove so fatal.

Four weeks prior to Jason's suicide, Amy Pearce had been helping him to prepare his forthcoming lectures. The office was noisy. The incessant drilling on the pavement in Chancery Lane had made rational thought impossible, so they had taken a short walk along Holborn High Street and landed themselves the comfy leather seats upstairs in Starbucks, overlooking the pigeon-spoiled red brick of High Holborn.

Amy remembered the afternoon well; it was a rare occasion when Jason allowed himself to show emotional vulnerability. He became diverted from their work and somehow the conversation side-tracked. He told her a childhood story, something about his father building a bridge of straws. She didn't take in the details; she was too busy savouring the occasion. Although she'd worked for Jason for over seven years, since leaving school, she still knew very little about him. Yes, she understood that he was a famous scientist, and was in awe at him having his own dedicated Wikipedia web page, but she'd learned little about the person within. Now, as he appeared willing to talk openly to her, she said as much.

'I don't suppose anybody really knows me,' Jason said. 'It's not that I try and hide myself, but I don't really open up much.' He grinned, watching her tongue fight the froth from her cappuccino. 'Maybe I'm lazy,' he joked. He was juggling with the last crumbs of his blueberry muffin, inelegantly teasing them into his mouth with the cuff of his royal-blue Armani shirt.

Amy smiled.

'Funnily enough, it's something that I've become aware of lately,' he continued. 'And there are silent days, when I'm back in Cornwall, when I seem to be too aware.'

Jason leaned forward and looked so hard into Amy's eyes that she could almost feel his stare burn into the back of her skull. 'If anybody *really* knew me,' he said, in little more than a whisper, 'they would *understand* me, and that could be worth a fortune to them long after I'm gone.' He sat back in his chair, giving Amy a wink, and she watched his face disappear behind a grande macchiato.

It was a strange comment, even by Jason's standards. He was always deep, often cryptic. He would have made a good politician, forever answering questions with questions – but she loved his way of speaking. With it came a sense of humour and, even on his darker days, there would be something in a one-line comment that would make her smile, giggle or laugh until her lungs were sore.

They stayed in Starbucks for several hours. Amy made frequent trips to the counter for more designer coffees and as many to the bathroom to make way for them. They were oblivious to the people around them, so the man who approached them took them by surprise. He was young, dishevelled, unshaven; he looked as if he had the battle-scars of an army veteran. He grabbed Jason's hand and squeezed it hard.

'I know you better than anyone,' the man muttered. His

voice was rough, an angry whisper. Then he let go of Jason's hand and hastened downstairs.

Jason jumped to his feet, ready to pursue the stranger, but he had left quickly. By the time he and Amy had packed up and left the coffee house, the man was out of sight.

'Are you OK? What did he say?' Amy asked, concerned.

'He reminded me that I should have stayed at home,' Jason joked. But his eyes were wide and Amy knew he was nervous. She scowled. This time she wasn't amused at his attempts to distort the situation with humour.

'He said he knew me better than anyone,' Jason said, looking upwards to the sky, possibly for some divine explanation.

He probably wasn't joking after all.

Strong as ever and pretending, for Amy's sake, that the incident didn't matter he had accompanied her back to the office. Nothing more was said about the episode.

✱✱✱

Little over four months later, Amy was sitting outside the Swallow Café in London's Regent Street, soaking up the spring sunshine with her cappuccino, when she saw the man again.

As she watched him, knowing instinctively that it was the man who had accosted Jason, she began to panic. He was in his mid-twenties, with a long thin face and high cheekbones. The scars on his cheeks cast shadows, making his face look somehow unclean. And there was something about his eyes… He was sitting five tables away, angled towards her with his feet up on the grey aluminium chair opposite, pretending to read *The Sport*. She was aware that he was looking in her direction. His face seemed angry.

She could sense the fear building in her. She recalled the conversation in Starbucks; she thought about Jason's line that you had to know him to understand him. She remembered how the man had suddenly appeared, and his words to Jason… Maybe Jason *was* murdered after all; maybe this man intended to kill her too. *Why me? Why Jason?*

Amy looked around then casually stood up. Although she didn't look directly at the man, she was aware of his movements and could sense his stare. As calmly as she could, she walked inside the café and paid for her drink, then asked where the toilets were.

'Downstairs,' the waitress smiled as she pointed towards the door behind the counter.

Amy made her way down the stairs, hoping to find another exit. Instead of turning towards the ladies' toilets she noticed a small passageway leading to what looked like a laundry room. It was darker downstairs, damp and musty. A fire exit door was directly ahead. Amy let out a sigh of relief as she moved quickly towards it but before she could reach the handle, she heard a voice.

'No! No! Not in here!' She looked to her left and saw a small, rather plump young man wearing a white apron, hurrying to block her path.

'I need to leave,' Amy said, panic in her voice. 'There's a man following me.'

'No! Not here!' the man repeated again and burst into a voluble stream of some unfamiliar language.

'I have to!' she snarled, about to push him out of the way. The man, obviously one of the waiters, put his arms out to stop her and backed into the door. As he did so, he pushed the bar which opened it. He quickly turned to close it but Amy noticed movement on the outside. It was the man from Starbucks.

She moved swiftly and crouched down behind a wooden bench on which there were wire baskets of tablecloths. The waiter turned around, looking startled. The woman had disappeared and a man was running through the fire exit towards him.

'No!' the waiter cried. 'Cannot come…' His voice tailed away as the intruder reached inside his jacket pocket, pulled out a handgun and smashed the handgrip against the side of his head.

Amy watched the waiter crumple to the floor, unconscious. She gasped, but thankfully the assailant didn't hear her. He spun round and ran back through the fire door into the street.

Amy waited a few seconds before running upstairs to alert the staff. She was hysterical.

'Call an ambulance!' she said, the moment she saw staff. They looked at her, shocked. By now the hysteria had taken over and she struggled to get her words out. The manager came over to her and held her shoulders gently, trying to calm her. A waitress investigated downstairs, then returned quickly and shouted to call an ambulance immediately. Amy was in tears and terrified. The manager led her to his office. She wanted to be out of sight.

She felt sick and could barely catch her breath. She had never experienced danger before. She was shaking, aware of every noise, every movement around her, anxious that the man would walk back through the doorway at any second.

The wait seemed to last an eternity. Eventually a woman police officer entered the room and Amy burst into tears.

She was safe.

CHAPTER 2

Detective Sergeant Lucy Bridges awoke at seven thirty. She had slept reasonably well, considering the events of the night before. Relationships within the department were strictly out of bounds but, having been promoted and working with Detective Inspector Thomas Riley for nearly two years, her emotions were becoming too strong to ignore. Especially now that she realised that he felt the same way. Riley was in line for the chief inspector's job; there was no way she would jeopardise that and she, too, was career driven.

Lucy had always considered herself strong, professional, but that kiss – twelve lingering seconds of passion – had weakened her. They had not taken the kiss any further but she had wanted to, so badly. She and Thomas needed to talk about what was happening. She had two options as far as she could see: transfer or leave the force. Whatever option she chose, she had to be with Thomas Riley.

At the station, they avoided each other all day. When the call came to go to the Swallow Café, it was the first time that they had been forced to spend working time together.

Thomas drove. Lucy wanted to say something but couldn't; it was the wrong time. As they pulled up outside the café's Regent Street entrance, Thomas glanced towards her and smiled. 'We'll talk tonight.'

She thought that she was probably still blushing as they

entered the café.

When they arrived, the café was closed. Paramedics had already taken the injured man to hospital and Amy was en route to Charing Cross police station. The manager was clearly flustered. A short man, wearing a pinstripe suit and yellow shirt with a gold fish-neck button brooch, he certainly didn't look as if he was used to getting his hands dirty in the general running of the place.

He showed them the crime scene. Lucy noticed that he wasn't too concerned about his injured member of staff; his priorities seemed to be getting the café reopened and the police out of sight as quickly as possible. Thomas wasn't too pleased by his attitude; he called for the Scene of Crime Officers to check the area for prints and get prints from the staff, too. He instructed the manager to remain closed until they had statements and a full forensic examination had been carried out. The manager turned away in disgust, kicking an aluminium mop bucket as he returned to the kitchen to inform his staff.

Thomas and Lucy glanced at each other before descending the stairs to the basement. They helped secure the crime scene before taking a walk out of the basement door on to Air Street. It was clear that the attacker could have gone in any direction.

'He's long gone. Let's speak to this woman and get an image of the guy,' Thomas said.

'You think that she could have done it?'

'It seems unlikely but let's hear what she has to say.'

The pavement was busy on Regent Street. There was a ceaseless river of tourists, while the tempting windows of London's finest stores drew them in, like iron filings to a magnet. Most people seemed oblivious to the fact that the Swallow Café was surrounded by police.

Two men stood across the road, watching the activity from the first floor window of Drapers' department store. They watched Riley and Bridges leave the café.

'I think I better lay low for a while,' commented the

scruffy young man to his father, Oliver Carsley.

'Yes, Ashton, you must. You've already done too much damage.'

****

Amy had always rejected the claims that Jason committed suicide. When the police called at her flat in the early hours of that Sunday morning, her world collapsed. She remembered peering through the blinds and seeing the two officers at her door; she knew immediately that something was wrong. Wearing her olive green Thai silk pyjamas, a Christmas present from her boyfriend Gerard, she grabbed her dressing gown before opening the door.

Amy invited the officers into the flat. The open-plan kitchen-lounge was a mess; she was embarrassed and remembered apologising. The officers explained that her boss and good friend Professor Chadwick had been found dead in his house in Cornwall. They told her that they did not believe there were any suspicious circumstances but they were still investigating.

Amy didn't say a word at first. She was shocked and summoned every ounce of self-control to stop herself from breaking down completely. *No suspicious circumstances?*

'He wasn't ill. Was it a heart attack? Did he collapse?' she asked, her voice just short of hysterical.

'It appears for now that he took his own life.'

Suicide? 'No!' Amy said. 'There's no way... There must be a mistake. He has lectures on Monday in Birmingham. He wasn't depressed, he had too much to live for. There's no way that he would have taken his own life.' She took a deep breath, still fighting the tears.

The police officers looked at each other.

'Well, Devon and Cornwall Police would like to talk to you as soon as possible. Maybe you can explain this to them.'

'Yes. Yes, definitely. This can't be. I know Jason, there's no way.'

The officers offered their condolences and turned to leave. She tried to stop herself breaking down. She had never felt such pain.

As the door closed, she stood still, leaning against the wall, waiting for the tears to fall. Then she threw herself onto her sofa and buried her head in the cushion and … nothing. She was numb, emotionally mutilated, and the tears would not come.

'No fuckin' way!' she shouted, 'Never!' She sensed anger rising inside her. He would not have done this to himself. He would have not have done this to *her!* She would make the police see…

Overcome with a new energy, Amy catapulted herself off the sofa, stamping her feet as she began tidying the flat. She scrubbed every surface, violent emotion behind every movement, lecturing herself with every task. Her hands were raw, her knees bruised.

She dissected every conversation that she'd had with Jason in the past six months, every joke and every decision. How *dare* he take his own life! He didn't; he wouldn't!

She was still wearing her dressing gown when there was another knock on the door. By now it was one thirty; she hadn't realised the time.

She opened the door reluctantly and two men, dressed in dark blue double-breasted suits and white shirts with cerise-crested ties, introduced themselves as DI Matthew Bennett and DS Alistair Scholt from Devon and Cornwall Constabulary. They were from the Major Crime Investigation Team.

'I'm sorry to have to talk to you at short notice, I understand it must be difficult for you,' DI Bennett said, as they sat at the dining table. 'With Mr Chadwick being a wealthy, high-profile scientist, we needed to discover quickly if there was anything suspicious about his death.'

'He was in no frame of mind to take his life, I know he

wasn't. He was making long term plans.'

'I see. Had there been any disagreements with his family or at work lately?'

'Nothing at work. I know that he was worried about his eldest son, who lives in America. He wasn't depressed about it, just disappointed.' The detectives seemed quiet and pensive, and their silent gaze made her feel uneasy. 'What makes you think he took his own life?'

DI Bennett took out his notebook and read a suicide note that Jason had allegedly left on his computer.

If you find this letter then you will know that I have succeeded in my mission to move on to the next world. I know many people will be shocked by my decision but it is not one that I have taken lightly. I have been very fortunate and have lived a happy, albeit lonely, life. I have achieved many great things but I regret that I have failed in the areas that matter: love and parenthood being the most important. This is not the reason I have made such a sacrifice, though.

I have always been a spiritual person and I have many beliefs that I have studied for many years. Simple things give me simple pleasures. I know if I move on now, I can take my skills, my creativity and my love of life to a new dimension. I know I am not wrong; anybody who really knows me will understand this. Please don't mourn for me, welcome me in your prayers to my new world.

Amy was stunned. The words seemed unreal; it was like listening to Jason talk but it wasn't Jason. He had never been 'spiritual' but there was something familiar about his words: *anybody who really knows me will understand this*. That was Jason all right.

Amy had a lump in her throat and could barely speak. This time the tears didn't hesitate. The detectives consoled her and poured out a glass of water. There was little more she could add, but she couldn't believe it.

Within days the police concluded that he had indeed taken his own life. There seemed to be no motive or interference from any outside parties.

He was gone.

***

'Is that man going to be alright?' Amy asked as Riley and Bridges entered the room at the police station. The room reminded Amy of her headmaster's office at St Luke's High School in Chelsea. It was small and minimalist, painted white. The black nylon carpet looked as if it were fused with wire that would shred the feet of anybody who tried to walk on it with bare feet. Everything else in the room looked, and smelled, as if it had come out of an office showroom. It certainly didn't look like a room used for questioning witnesses or victims of crime.

'He's conscious for now. The medical staff hope he will pull through but this was a serious attack,' Bridges explained. 'Did you see what happened?'

'I saw everything! The man was after me, though, I'm sure.'

Amy explained what had happened at the Swallow Café. She also recalled the incident at Starbucks four months earlier. Riley and Bridges asked a lot of questions about her personal life and background. Amy assumed that they were trying to assess whether she was a genuine witness but they made her feel uncomfortable. *Unless they suspected her.*

She found DI Riley arrogant. He was attractive enough – he looked like he'd walked off the set of an old movie, with his slim physique and dark eyes. But he delivered his questions coldly and Amy felt threatened in his presence.

She pleaded with them to examine Jason's alleged suicide. Riley was silent for a short while, as if he were evaluating her story. Eventually his mood seemed to change and he lightened. He told her that they would contact Devon and Cornwall Police and explain what had happened today, but he couldn't promise that it would lead to a further investigation.

'I need a full statement from you and your fingerprints. My main concern now, if your story is true, is for your safety. Do you think the attacker is likely to know where you live?'

Amy shuddered. She hadn't thought about what would happen next and, as Riley asked the question, she realised the seriousness of her situation. There was a man with a gun out there, and he could be targeting *her*. She stared fearfully at Riley, close to tears.

'Maybe you should stay with a friend or relative for a while, until we catch this man,' Lucy Bridges suggested, passing Amy a tissue.

Amy nodded, trying to compose herself. She was escorted out of the room by a WPC. It was time to give her fingerprints and a formal statement and try to supply a photofit of the attacker.

CHAPTER 3

Amy's father, Arnold Pearce, picked her up from the station shortly after seven o'clock. She had considered ringing Gerard but resisted. He was too volatile and she felt that she needed compassion and sympathy, rather than more questions. She would call him in the morning.

She was relieved to see her father. Arnold was a giant, six foot seven and two hundred and thirty pounds, but surprisingly slim because of his love of playing sport. To many people, he oozed power, not just because of his size but the way he dressed, the way he spoke and even the way he stared. To Amy he was a giant teddy bear; she loved and respected him and in return his bond with Amy was set in stone.

When he received his daughter's call, he'd just returned from court. He had been representing a landowner who was fighting to keep the rights of passage to land he'd once owned and collected ground rents for. Arnold had been fighting a losing battle and he was exhausted but he left immediately for Charing Cross police station to collect Amy.

His frightened daughter hugged him like she did when she was a tiny child in his arms. For a few seconds, he remembered the true value of parenthood and, in spite of his daughter's tears, he cherished the moment.

***

'Pull over a second,' Amy demanded, as they passed Jason's old flat. Jason had lived less than ten minutes' drive from Amy's parents on the outskirts of Kensington and as they passed his home, she recognised Jason's son, Brandon. He was carrying boxes out to a van. Amy had only met him two or three times but he had his father's eyes and a similar way of moving. She had last seen him at Jason's funeral with his younger brother.

She wound down the car window. 'Hello. Brandon? Is that Brandon?' she called out to the man.

'Who are you?' he snapped. Amy realised that he didn't recognise her and she sensed that he was less than happy to be approached.

'I'm sorry, it's Amy. I was Jason's PA. I was just passing and I thought I recognised you,' she said.

'Someone has to do this,' Brandon said, placing another box into the van.

'Suppose so,' Amy agreed. She was surprised that he still hadn't acknowledged who she was. 'Have you cleared out his Cornwall home too?' she asked.

'Of course. What's it to you? Looking to sponge some more off the dead guy are you?'

Amy was shocked. He glared at her and she felt uneasy. Her father moved uncomfortably in the seat next to her and leaned over to look at Brandon.

'No, I haven't had a thing. I thought… I mean… I don't want anything, I was just making talk to be polite. I'm sorry, I'll go.' Amy began closing the window, trying to remain dignified without letting him see her growing anger. *How dare he suggest such a thing?*

Brandon suddenly called out to her. 'Here! Have these,' he said. 'I was going to throw them. They mean nothing to me. Maybe you want to give them to the university or something.'

Brandon held out two boxes to Amy. Arnold opened his door to help her put them in the back seat.

'Thank you,' said Amy, quietly. 'For what it's worth, I

really cared about your father. He was a good man.'

'So everybody says,' Brandon muttered as he turned away and went up the grey steps leading to the main door of Jason's apartment block. He closed the door behind him.

'Come on, it's been a long day. Let's get home and have some food.' Arnold put the car into gear and they drove away.

***

It wasn't strictly true that Amy hadn't received anything. Two weeks earlier, a letter arrived from Jason's solicitor explaining that Jason had left her his ring. It was a gold signet ring with a symbol on it, a letter 'M' engraved to look like a beamed semi quaver. The ring was too big for Amy so she'd bought a chain and wore it around her neck.

It had been a long day. As Amy took off her necklace before getting into bed, she stared at the ring. Jason had told her once that it was his 'Ring of Conscience'. She couldn't recall what the symbol meant but the story of the ring always amused her. When Jason was in his teens, his family had visited England on holiday from their home in Las Vegas. After a day trip to the Tower of London, Jason had dreamed that he'd stolen the Crown Jewels. In the dream he was caught because he had somehow dropped a distinctive ring which carried this symbol and the police had traced him. The dream gave him the idea to have a ring made up. He called it a Ring of Conscience to remind himself not to try anything stupid because he'd get caught.

The tale seemed a bit contrived and the making of the ring exceptionally virtuous to Amy – who didn't do bad things sometimes? But that was the sort of man Jason was. He always strived to do what he considered was 'right'. It was the only mitigating circumstance that Amy could find for Jason's suicide. He must have genuinely believed that he was doing the right thing.

But if he'd been murdered.

Amy couldn't sleep.

***

After they'd interviewed Amy and she left the police station it was shift-change time. Riley and Bridges left the investigation to the night staff while the forensics team did their work.

They returned to Thomas's house intending to talk but talking soon gave way to passion. The time they had together was too precious, and reason and guilt gave way to pleasure. When they returned to work the next morning, the complications of their relationship bore heavily on their conscience.

They were brought up to date with the investigation. Relatives of Vito Rolanski, the Polish victim of the Swallow Café attack, had been traced. Hospital reports indicated that he'd suffered a fractured skull and bleeding had caused pressure on his brain. He had to undergo surgery to drain the fluid to ease this pressure. Vito was drifting in and out of consciousness but he was still critical and the doctors were becoming increasingly concerned.

The fingerprints lifted from the door only matched the staff, and the attacker's coffee mug had been brought in from outside by staff who cleared the tables and washed up.

The only lead they had for now was Amy's photofit of the attacker which was circulated to the other police stations in the Metropolitan Police area as well as the *Evening Standard* and the London *Metro* newspapers.

Thomas Riley saw Lucy differently now. He watched her through the glass partition as she spoke with the Devon and Cornwall police. Her caramel-coloured hair dipped over her cheeks and bounced delicately with her breath as she spoke. She had a glow about her today; her eyes glistened. Her skin was flawless bar a tiny mole on her cheekbone not far from her left eye.

In all the months that he'd spent with her and fantasised about her, he never thought of making a move. It just happened. Now what should he do? Chief Inspector Roland Moore was moving on and Thomas had applied for his job. If he got the promotion, Lucy would be working with him much less. Even so, relationships within the force were off-limits and there was no way they could hide this. He didn't want to jeopardise her career, either. They *must* talk about it.

For now, though, he had to get through the day.

✳✳✳

Lucy Bridges replaced the receiver and entered DCI Moore's office.

'I spoke with Devon and Cornwall police about Amy Pearce and they'd like me to fax her statement about the incident at Starbucks. They had considered Jason's death to be a cut-and-dried suicide. They'll need serious convincing if they're to investigate further.'

'Do it. The girl must have reason to believe this man was after her. Yesterday's attack seems unlikely to be a coincidence. Unless you think she was responsible?'

'No. There were enough witnesses who saw the man follow her and he definitely didn't return.'

'OK, then,' Moore said, leaning back in his chair and not letting his eyes move from Lucy. 'I don't suppose,' he continued speaking slowly, as if choosing his words with caution, 'that you and Inspector Riley have anything to tell me?'

'About what?' Lucy stared back, panic in her heart but her face impassive.

'Office rumours, that's all – probably.' DCI Moore looked down at his desk. 'Plus, I saw the way he was looking at you. You do understand this can't happen?'

'Oh, I see. You think … no, don't worry. Everything is

fine. We're both professional, we wouldn't get involved, if that's what you mean.' She smiled, hoping that she sounded convincing.

'Good!' Moore said. Having got his message across, it was onwards and upwards. 'Now let's find this bugger!'

An hour later, DCI Moore received a call from St. John's Hospital. Vito Rolanski was dead.

Chapter 4

Jason Chadwick's solicitor, Frank Duffy, left his office in Chelsea and headed for his car. Redearth and Partners Solicitors, were based above a shopping precinct in the heart of Chelsea's Kings Road. The car park was underneath the shopping complex.

It had been a long and tedious day; he was ready to go home to his family. But as he unlocked his car he felt a sharp poke in his back.

'Don't look around and do as I say. There is a gun in your back, so choose your answers carefully. OK?'

Frank froze. The car park was busy, he knew that he could draw attention to himself but he wasn't sure whether to risk it. He heard a click as if a gun's safety catch was being released. *No, he didn't want to risk it.*

'I understand. My wallet is in my right pocket. Just take it,' Frank replied, though he didn't think for one second that this was a simple mugging.

'I don't want your wallet, sir, I need information. If you give me what I need then you and your family won't get hurt. Do we have a deal, Mr Duffy?'

'Yes, I understand. I'm listening.'

***

DCI Moore called in Riley and Bridges for an update. Despite some reservations, he'd put them together again on this case. They worked well as a team, there was no drama with them and he always felt as if he could feed off their energy. They were motivated and he liked that.

There had been no sign of a break-in at Jason Chadwick's house in Cornwall. It didn't appear that anything had been stolen and there was nothing suspicious about his death. Devon and Cornwall police had forwarded the autopsy report to Charing Cross police station. It revealed that Jason had died from a single gunshot wound through the roof of his mouth. The gun's position was relative to his fall and his prints were the only ones on the gun. He had left a suicide note. There was no reason to believe that his death was anything but self-inflicted.

'Find out what you can about Jason Chadwick,' DCI Moore ordered Bridges. 'I want to know everything. He was born a US citizen, so see what you can find out there too.' He turned to Riley and asked him to speak again with Amy Pearce. 'She seems convinced this man was after her. Look into her background and go through her statement on yesterday's attack. She may be able to recall some more details now she's had time to think.'

***

Amy had spent the evening with her mother and father. Recently she'd only managed to see them once a month, though she phoned them regularly. Their conversations were always about practicalities; she had rarely spoken to them about emotional issues before. But last night it all came out: her feelings for Jason, her love of life, stories of places she had been, things she had done since leaving home – all the things she'd never discussed before. She told them about the 'convenience' boyfriends she'd spent time with to hide her true feelings for her boss. She knew that she and Jason could never have a relationship – he was more than twenty years her senior – but it didn't stop her longing for him.

She talked, they listened and, when they were all exhausted in the early hours of the morning, they went wearily to bed.

Amy didn't sleep well. The day's events played in her mind like some horror movie. *What if the man had caught up with her? What did he want from her?* In the morning, after reluctantly eating breakfast, she collected the boxes of notebooks and papers that Brandon Chadwick had given to her.

Back in her room, she opened the first box. Books were neatly stacked inside. Amy smiled, wondering whether Brandon had inherited his father's regimented organisation skills. She flicked through the top book and attempted to read through Jason's scribble and spider diagrams. She assumed these were his college or personal study books; the content was unintelligible.

She decided to go through them over the coming weeks and see if there was anything that might be of interest to a university. She knew that Jason had been actively involved in the development of the World Wide Web. She had attended several of his lectures and been awed by his work, but looking at the information in these notebooks, she couldn't tell whether this was his development work or merely college notes from his days at Massachusetts Institute of Technology.

Towards the bottom of the first box, Amy randomly pulled out another book. To her surprise it was a journal, a day-to-day account of his life in 1980. Jason would have been seventeen years old then.

Amy started reading. He had documented everything, from what he was doing, what songs he was listening to, girls he 'loved' through to 'quotes of the day'. The diary covered his final days at school in Las Vegas, when he found out that he had been accepted into the prestigious MIT. He seemed so happy yet so young.

One of his good friends at the time was a girl called

Emmanuelle Sexton. Jason had spent a lot of time with her, though their relationship appeared to be platonic. They had obviously remained in touch because Amy recalled meeting her once; she hadn't realised that their friendship went back that far.

Amy became engrossed in the journal. This was his real life. He had used these pages to document his feelings, fears and ambitions. She hoped that there were more diaries in the boxes.

One entry told of his crazy dream, the one that inspired the ring of conscience that she now wore around her neck. Jason wrote that he had a paralysing fear that he might do wrong. As she read, Amy realised he'd made the ring up not only as a deterrent against wrongdoing, but also as a way of absorbing any evil thoughts and deflecting temptation. The ring actually meant something to him. He'd obviously spoken in depth about this to Emmanuelle. *Maybe I should get in touch with her*, Amy thought. *Does she even know about Jason's death?*

As she wondered what to do, her mother escorted DI Riley into the room.

'Hello,' Amy said, dropping the journal from her lap as she stood up. She was surprised to see the inspector. 'Have you found him?' she asked immediately.

'No. I'm afraid I have some bad news, though. The young man at the Swallow Café died from his injury,' Riley replied.

Amy was stunned. 'I witnessed a murder and the victim should have been me.' She sat down slowly, staring at the floor.

'We need your help,' Riley admitted. 'I need you to go through everything once more. I need every little detail you can think of about what happened yesterday afternoon. Can you think of any reason at all why this man would be so interested in you?'

Mrs Pearce offered them coffee and left them to talk. Amy solemnly went through her story again, adding little more. She felt so guilty. She couldn't help thinking about the victim's family.

Riley took notes as she told him about her encounter with Brandon Chadwick the previous evening. She mentioned Brandon's off-hand comments about her wanting to 'sponge more from the dead guy'.

'I thought that was odd,' she said. 'I've never sponged off Jason. The only memento I have is his ring. He left a note in his will that it should come to me.'

She showed the ring to Riley and he studied it as she explained what she knew about it and the story of how it came to be. Riley sketched a rough copy of the symbol into his notebook.

'I don't know what the symbol stands for, or its origin,' Amy said. 'But when he was very young, Jason somehow adopted it as his own stamp.'

Riley stared at the pattern for a while in silence. Then he asked if she thought the ring had any connection to the Crown Jewels.

'I don't think so. I don't know much about the Crown Jewels other than that they're priceless. Weren't they stolen once?' Her thoughts were drifting. 'I wonder if they were ever recovered?'

Riley brought her back to the present. 'Do you know any other details of Jason's will? Did he ever discuss his estate with you?'

'No. It was never mentioned. The ring was a surprise.'

'Maybe Brandon assumed that Jason had left you more,' Riley suggested.

'Maybe.' She shrugged.

Amy told the inspector all she could remember about the time just before Jason's death, but there seemed to be nothing out of the ordinary.

'Maybe the ring has some significance,' Riley said. 'It's one line of enquiry for a motive for the incident at the café yesterday. The only thing we know for sure at the moment is that Vito Rolanski was an innocent victim.'

***

On his way back to Charing Cross, Riley stopped at Jason's apartment to see if Brandon was still there. He rang the buzzer but there was no answer. Luckily another occupant of the block was just leaving and Riley slipped inside as the main door opened.

He climbed the stairs to Jason's flat on the second floor and knocked on the door. Nobody answered. A woman came out of the opposite flat and asked if she could help. Riley showed his badge.

The woman liked an audience. She introduced herself as Cara.

'I've known of Jason for years but I didn't really know him, if you see what I mean. He was always polite but he kept himself to himself. He's helped us out from time to time with the odd computer crisis.'

'Did you see anyone here yesterday?' Riley asked.

'You mean Brandon? Yes, I had a few words with him. He's nothing like Jason. He's like quinine – he leaves a bitter taste in the mouth. A real arrogant Yank.'

Riley smiled. 'Any idea where he was staying?'

'No,' Cara replied. 'We barely exchanged greetings. But he's not come back today, so he must have cleared all of Jason's stuff out yesterday.'

Riley asked if there had been anybody else in the flat since Jason's death.

'Only that solicitor chap, shortly after Jason died. And the estate agents have been showing people around.'

'Can you remember the name of the solicitor?' Riley knew he could find it through the probate registry – but that meant more time wading through red tape.

'No, sorry. He did tell me when I first met him, but it didn't sink in. It reminded me of a cartoon name though.' She giggled. 'Daffy Duck, maybe.'

Riley smiled and thanked Cara. He gave her his card.

36

'Give me a call if you remember that solicitor's name.'

***

Back at the station, Riley was greeted by Lucy Bridges. She had been investigating Jason all day.

'OK, this guy was a legend!' she said, perching on his desk, looking at her notes. 'He was born Jason Lewis Chadwick, May 5th 1962, in Las Vegas. His father, Donald, developed security systems in Las Vegas and was generally regarded as "Mr Security" there throughout the seventies and eighties. Jason went to the Massachusetts Institute of Technology when he was eighteen. He married Penny in 1984 and had two sons, Brandon and David. He split with his wife in 1988 and stayed in Boston, helping Tim Berners-Lee develop what we now call the World Wide Web. He even worked with Al Gore and apparently came up with the term "information superhighway". Can you believe it? Jason left America in 1996 when his parents retired and moved to Cornwall, where his mother had lived as a child. Both parents were killed in a car accident ten years ago. Jason stayed in England and lectured in universities all over the world. He's helped a lot of major names, including Google and social networking sites, with their research and development. He spent weekdays in London and weekends back at the country house in Cornwall.' Pausing for breath, Bridges turned the next page.

Riley smiled; she had a passion for detail but she got carried away and spoke so fast that he'd only absorbed half of what she had said. But he didn't stop her and Lucy continued. 'He lived alone. No current girlfriend but was loved and respected by everybody – apart from his ex-wife.'

'…and kids,' Riley interrupted.

'Not necessarily so.' Bridges smiled with an *'I know something you don't know'* expression on her face. 'Brandon and David Chadwick made contact with Jason about three

37

years ago. Jason has been sending money over to Boston for David's college and they've met on several occasions.'

'That's odd,' Riley said, confused. 'I've spoken with two people today who told me that Brandon was arrogant and they had the impression that there was very little bond between him and his father.'

'I'll look into it. Do you think Brandon has anything to do with what has happened?' Bridges asked.

'It's possible. He is in England right now. Do you know who Jason's chief beneficiary was?'

'I'll find out,' Lucy promised.

* * *

After Riley left, Amy returned to Jason's journals and read through the comments he had written about his ring. Curiosity got the better of her and she used the internet to try and track down Emmanuelle Sexton. She knew that Emmanuelle ran the history department at one of the Boston universities. Luckily it didn't take too long to find her email address so she left a quick message:

> *Hello Emmanuelle, this is Amy Pearce, I was Jason Chadwick's PA. I'm sorry if the news hasn't got through to you yet, but Jason died a few months ago. It's been a big shock to us all.*
>
> *I have some questions I would like to ask you about him. He left me his ring and I have some old journals. I was wondering if you could get in touch.*
>
> *Many thanks, AMY.*

A long and emotional call to Gerard followed. Amy had met Gerard at a Halloween party at the Hippodrome Club in London. Their relationship was based on companionship rather than emotional intensity. Gerard was an IT technician at Oxford University and he'd recently separated from his wife. Amy was reluctant to get involved at first, logic warning her that he was probably on the rebound. And he was ten years older than her. However, seven months on, Gerard seemed stable, not yet a divorcee but not pining for his ex-partner either. They usually met at weekends in London, depending on his commitments.

The conversation, as she had predicted, did not go well. Gerard's instinct to take control of the situation was too much for Amy and she ended up in tears. She knew he was trying to help and respected the rage that he felt towards her attacker but his aggression about the man was so intense that his anger leached into Amy too. She felt that, in his eyes, she carried part of the blame. She didn't need this right now. She asked him not to call for a while and said that she'd be in touch with him when she was ready.

Amy spent the rest of the day reading through Jason's eighteenth year. She discovered more journals in the second box. They became a distraction from the terror within her and the concern that she may well be the killer's next victim.

Chapter 5

'We have a missing solicitor!'

These words greeted Lucy Bridges as she entered the office. She'd not seen much of Riley at work yesterday and had to visit her family in the evening. They were working an early shift today; it would be another day of disguising their desires and hoping for an opportunity to talk.

'Really?'

Riley handed her a slip of paper. The brief fax explained that Frank Duffy of Redearth and Partners, Solicitors in Chelsea was missing.

'A tenner says that's our mystery solicitor at Jason Chadwick's flat. He never turned up for work yesterday and nobody has seen him for twenty-four hours.'

'Can we investigate?' Bridges enquired.

'Kensington and Chelsea are on it now. We'll get the nod if we're in.' Riley winked at Bridges; he could read her mind.

***

Amy had drifted off to sleep early in the evening while reading Jason's journals. The events of the past two days had finally taken their toll. She awoke around midnight and dragged herself into bed without washing or removing her makeup and slept solidly until five-thirty, when something woke her. It sounded like a sharp bang, as if somebody had thrown a stone at the window.

She sat up. The room was silent, except for the distant rumble of traffic. She remained still for a couple of minutes then, feeling nervous, she carefully manoeuvred herself out of bed and edged towards the window. Early shards of daylight were forcing themselves through the curtains. Amy made a gap in them, small enough to look below.

Her parents' home was a recently renovated two-storey apartment, inset from the road with small segregated garden areas to the rear. Amy's room was at the back of the building. She couldn't see anybody outside and was tempted to open the curtains further, but common sense stopped her. If her assailant was out there, he had a gun. He may not need any more than a glance of her to shoot. A movement caught her eye and she jumped away from the window.

Amy ran to her parents' room. Her mother stirred. 'Amy?' she whispered, startled to see her daughter.

'Wake Dad, quietly. I think that there's somebody outside.'

Arnold Pearce rose quickly, leaving the lights off. He told his wife and daughter to wait and grabbed his mobile phone before slowly descending the stairs. All seemed quiet. He checked every room for signs of a disturbance but it didn't seem as if anybody had entered the apartment. The blinds in the kitchen-dining area were not fully closed so he looked carefully through them. There was a sound outside, a crack, as if a twig had snapped under foot. He moved around the oak chest that separated the two windows and again peered slowly in the direction of the noise.

There was a shadow at the far end of the window, which quickly disappeared in the direction of the garden. Arnold ran to the sun lounge at the back of the house and saw a figure in black run behind the shed and clumsily climb over the wall. As Arnold ran back upstairs, he dialled 999.

'Get dressed. The police are on their way. Whoever it was has gone but he may be back.'

'You saw someone?' asked Amy, concerned.

'Somebody ran into the garden and over the wall,' Arnold explained.

'I think I know what they want from me,' Amy said slowly. 'I think it's Jason's ring, but I don't know why.'

Within ten minutes of Arnold's call, two police constables arrived at the Pearce household. For Amy it seemed an eternity. Her heart was racing; she didn't feel safe. She retraced her recent movements in her head while waiting for the police to arrive. Had she been followed in the past few weeks? She saw the faces of strangers every time she closed her eyes.

The family explained everything that had happened in the previous days to the constables and explained about the attack on Amy in Regent Street.

'We need to call in CID from Westminster,' the older of the two officers said. 'They can assess whether or not your intruder is likely to be part of their murder investigation.'

Riley and Bridges arrived at Amy's parents' house within half an hour of DCI Moore dispatching them to Kensington. In the car, conversation between them had not once strayed from the case. Although they were both eager to talk, neither was brave enough. And this wasn't the time.

Arnold met them at the front door. He had called work to tell them he would be late in and told his secretary to cancel his early appointments. Luckily he was not due in court.

He took the two detectives around the garden and showed them the wall behind the shed where the intruder had escaped. There were clear footprints and scuffmarks. Lucy followed the footprints and looked for similar ones around the house.

'This is wrong,' Arnold said, looking at the shed door. 'This has been forced open.'

Riley examined it. The panels at the bottom were out of line and chipped, as if somebody had tried to prise the door open by lifting them. The door opened easily. Inside it didn't look as if anything was missing.

'What's that?' Riley pointed at an A5 envelope with

'AMY' written on it in black marker pen. It was clearly visible on top of a toolbox right in front of them.

'No idea.' Arnold looked puzzled.

Riley put on gloves and carefully reached for the packet. It was quite thick and looked new, not like something that had been in the shed for a long time. They returned to the apartment with the package and Amy gave permission for Riley to open it. He opened the bottom end of the envelope using a kitchen knife.

'OK,' he said, very slowly, peering inside. 'We have money.'

He squeezed the sides as he upended the envelope, allowing the contents to fall onto the table. Everybody remained silent for a moment, staring at the contents of the envelope. 'I'd say five thousand pounds, maybe more.'

Riley used the knife to shuffle the money a little. At the bottom was a piece of paper. He grabbed another knife and used the cutlery to unfold the paper. The note was handwritten and they all leaned forward to read it.

Amy, you may be in danger. Take this money and go away for a few weeks. Try to remain as anonymous as possible and let the police do their work. It was Jason's wish that I help you if you are in danger. Show the police this letter and they will be able to trace me, I was his solicitor. I too may be in danger and that is why I will also be a missing person while I carry out my own investigations...

Take care, good friend, and remain safe.

It wasn't signed.

'So the intruder was trying to warn Amy,' Riley suggested, breaking the silence. 'That's probably why he headed for the shed as his escape route. He wanted to be seen.'

He motioned to Lucy as she passed the front window. He told her what they'd found in the shed and decided to call DCI Moore. They needed his advice.

After a brief wait DCI Moore phoned back. 'Get over to Redearth and Partners in Chelsea and help investigate the disappearance of the missing solicitor, Frank Duffy. It looks like there's a connection to Jason. I think that's your intruder. I'll come over to the house and talk to Amy. We'll decide what to do from there. This is getting too complicated – we may need assistance from Scotland Yard. One thing's for sure now, there's no doubt that this has everything to do with Jason Chadwick. I'd better get on to the Devon and Cornwall Police, too.'

Chapter 6

It took ten minutes to drive to Redearth and Partners; it would have been quicker to walk from the Pearces' apartment. The receptionist called for Brian Denman, senior partner and a close friend of Frank Duffy. He invited the detectives into his office and explained what he knew.

When Frank had not turned up for work, Brian had called his house. Frank's wife said that he'd left for work as normal the previous day but didn't return at night. This did occasionally happen with work, but he would always call. Nobody had seen or heard from him for nearly twenty-four hours. Frank's appointments were mainly routine meetings but he *had* handled Jason Chadwick's will.

'Would it be possible to see the will?' Bridges asked.

'Yes, I can copy the file. We're still handling Jason's estate. We already have a buyer for his Cornish property and interest in his flat, but as of yet the assets haven't been consolidated properly.' Brian added, 'Jason's sons were not happy with his will. They flew over from America. They were furious, as you'll see. He only left them one hundred thousand pounds each, yet he was obviously worth a lot more.'

Denman passed the file to Bridges.

'Quite generous, I would think, considering the ex-wife denied him access throughout their childhood,' Lucy said.

'Quite,' Brian replied. 'There was a letter of instruction

that is mentioned in the will and is included in the file. Reading it through this morning, it may have something to do with Frank's disappearance. He could have been approached or threatened for information and now he's lying low. Obviously his family need to know that he is safe.'

'Yes, I think that's what has happened,' Bridges said. 'We found a note warning Jason's PA, Amy Pearce, of danger – it had money with it, advising her to lay low for a while.'

'There you go. He has obviously followed Jason's instructions, then. Thank God for that. I'll tell his family right now. Is there anything else you need?' he asked, as if he now wanted rid of them.

'Can I see Frank's office?' Riley asked.

Brian Denman opened the office. There was little to see: filing cabinets, law books and numerous bound documents. One bright orange folder stood out, a spot-colour of life in an otherwise lifeless room. It was hardly inspiring, thought Thomas, but practical. Strangely, the room was devoid of photographs. Every office in the station had at least one photograph: a family member, a girlfriend/boyfriend or at the very least a dog. Frank was a family man, so it seemed odd.

'How well did Jason know Frank?' DI Riley asked.

'Frank knew Jason's family for many years. He came to London from St. Ives in Cornwall, must be about twenty-five years ago now. His father had a practice there and they handled Jason's mother's family estate for decades. After Frank's father died, he decided to move to London to be near his new wife's family. The Hudson family remained loyal to Frank, though, and he handled their affairs from a distance.'

The detectives thanked Denman and left for Charing Cross. Back at the station, DCI Moore was still out. Riley and Bridges used the large desk in his office to examine the file. Firstly, Lucy found the will, written as a letter and witnessed by the firm. As she began to read, Riley braced himself for her bionic reading skills, hoping to absorb her words at the same speed that she delivered them.

'*This is the last will and testament of Jason Lewis Chadwick dated the fifth day of May 2005 and supersedes all others beforehand. I hope to die an old man, leaving my mark on history in a way that my father did before me. I hope this will serves as a legacy for my own children and that I will die a man who has been loved as much as I have loved. However, if this really is my last will then I will have failed. I may be happy, I am certainly a lucky man and I take none of my success for granted. However, my only regret is that I have never in my life felt truly loved and nobody truly knows the man I really am.*

Wealth is a commodity that helps us maintain a standard of living in which we can feel secure and comfortable. I have much wealth but I have worked hard all my life, as did my father. Perhaps I have sacrificed too much living to reach a goal that I don't even understand myself, but it has not been fuelled by money – much more by ambition. Anybody who has access to my wealth after I have moved on should also have to earn it.

Anybody that truly understands me, that truly loved me, will have learned how to claim my wealth. If this is earned through my legacy a hundred years from now, they shall be just as worthy as anybody who finds it now.

I appoint Frank Duffy, currently of Redearth and Partners Solicitors, as chief executor of my will and administrator of finances according to an accompanying letter, which should be presented, together with this will, for probate. Upon my death, the sum of one hundred thousand British pounds should be paid directly to the following people: my son Brandon, my son David and my dearest friend Emmanuelle Sexton. To my PA, Amy Pearce, I leave my gold signet ring with the engraved musical-M symbol. Other fixed assets, including the family house in Cornwall, flat in London and technical equipment and objects of value should be sold and held according to instructions left with Frank Duffy, the proceeds of which, net of inheritance tax, are to be held in secure trust. Personal effects such as clothes, journals, photographs, etcetera, are to be shared with friends and family, with first option going to my sons.'

'Ambiguous,' Riley said. 'I would be confused if I was his son. It would make me want to ask questions. But I suppose, considering they hardly knew him, a hundred grand is still a tidy sum.'

'Let's see what was in that letter to Frank then.' Bridges took the letter and was about to read it when Riley snatched it from her and said, 'My turn.' Bridges gave a friendly scowl.

'Frank, my dear friend. I hold you and your partners as executors of my will and I instruct you to act in good faith to manage my estate.

I suspect that there may not be harmony amongst my kin but hopefully they will have the sense to accept it and maybe understand why I have distributed my estate in this way. I hope and pray that this does not put you and your partners in any sort of danger but if that happens, I hope to have a contingency plan at hand. God forbid this will ever BE my last will, but events over the past few months have caused me to be extra cautious.

1. *I have registered a web domain using a company name that I have set up using a global accommodation address so that it cannot be traced on a 'whois' search. Please make sure that this is constantly renewed. It is held with the Domain Registry of America and access through their website: Username: Indigo. Password: f0rc3. Domain name: melodema.com. The website is a stepping stone for any person to understand me*

enough to be able to claim my legacy. I would imagine there will be much curiosity about my wealth so I hope that somebody might make the connection to the existence of such a site.

2. *The website is hosted on a US secure government server via MIT. I very much doubt that this will ever be offline but if technological advances require data to be held on any external server, please make sure that the site remains online.*

3. *Should Redearth and Partners close down, please make sure that the estate remains managed according to my instructions, even if it takes generations for my legacy to be rightfully claimed. I therefore ask that the decision to pass on execution rights to my estate be carefully considered.*

4. *After the sale of my assets, please deposit all funds, net of inheritance tax, into the account below: National Bank of America: account: 90911106 Branch ID: 104598. Instructions will be held within the bank as to what to do with them.*

5. *It is very likely that somebody within the firm will be asked about this letter, as it is mentioned in my will. I trust that everybody will be professional and say nothing. However, on the off chance that such an approach is made with any threatening intent, then please ONLY mention that the letter mentions a website called melodema.com and that my funds are to be deposited into a US bank account. Hopefully this would be enough information to stop anybody getting hurt. If such an approach happens, and, God forbid, serious injury or worse happens as a result, I have an investigative scenario, details of which I keep in the study of my apartment in my desk drawer in an orange folder. Common sense should be used here.*

6. *Frank, I hope that the above will never happen and feel confident that it won't; it is just a fail-safe.*

However, I leave a key to my apartment with this letter. I suggest that you let yourself in and claim this orange folder immediately and keep it safe in your office, just in case. Please make sure that Amy Pearce is safe; if she is in any danger at all then please make sure that she is looked after. I thank you Frank for all your help and support.

To cover all ongoing Redearth expenses, please take £50,000 from the sale of assets, which I hope will more than cover costs.'

'What did he know back then, I wonder? It seems like a will from a man who knew he was going to be killed,' Lucy said.

'There was an orange folder in Frank's office. We should go back there. This explains why the neighbour saw Frank at Jason's flat,' claimed Thomas. 'It seems as if Jason played out some quixotic fantasy role-play with his own death. Maybe it was suicide after all.'

'I doubt it,' Lucy retorted. 'He knew he was in danger. That will was made two years ago. He had planned something. We need to check out this domain.'

She moved across to the computer. Thomas watched her fingers race over the keys as she logged on, verified her password and launched the internet browser. It seemed that she could type as fast as she could talk.

'melodema.com requires a password,' she said, confused.

Riley looked over her shoulder. The screen was yellow, with a small box requesting a password but there was no more information. Lucy tried f0rc3, the password that was suggested for the domain in Jason's letter, but it didn't work. She tried 'force', 'Cornwall', 'Amy', and 'Emmanuelle', including every possible alphanumeric combination by replacing numbers for vowels as in 'f0rc3', but still had no luck.

'We've hit a brick wall already,' she mumbled, the

excitement of the challenge already defeating her.

'Don't worry,' Thomas said. 'I doubt it's important at this stage. Let's get that file from Frank's office.'

'We should check out this Emmanuelle Sexton, too. Jason also left her money.'

✳✳✳

The orange file was empty. Brian Denman looked as puzzled as the two police officers standing in front of him. The folder was stamped with the Redearth and Partners logo and dated, but there was nothing inside.

'This isn't like Frank at all,' he said. 'Copies or scans of all the firm's important documents are usually kept in the company safe, in case of a fire or force majeure. Frank hasn't filed any copies. I don't know what he was playing at.'

'Maybe the file contained the money for Amy,' Lucy Bridges suggested, looking at Brian for some indication that the possibility may be worth considering.

'Maybe,' Brian agreed, looking pensive. 'You would have thought there would be a monetary provision for Frank, too. Frank wouldn't just disappear without saying anything to anybody. He must have been frightened, maybe for his family.'

'Or,' Thomas interrupted, 'there's a clue here that's been deliberately left for the police to find. After all, Frank was keen to let us investigate his disappearance. He would have known that we would return for the orange folder. It was left clearly in view, after all.'

They spent a further hour in Frank's office, looking for anything that could be useful to their investigation – appointment diaries, telephone message pads and computer schedules – but they found no indication at all about where he might have gone. As they left, Brian Denman took their card and said that he would carry out his own internal investigation. He promised to look into Frank and Jason's previous dealings to see if there was any hint of where Frank might be.

* * *

The moment Riley and Bridges entered Charing Cross, they were summoned to DCI Moore's office. He closed the door behind them.

'Our Super wants assistance from Scotland Yard,' he began. 'We have two suspicious deaths, one missing person and around fifty million missing pounds.'

'Fifty million?' Riley and Bridges said in unison.

'Indeed. That's Jason's estimated worth. As well as his work in helping develop the World Wide Web, he was sole beneficiary of his parents' estate after their deaths. His father developed and ran the entire security system for casinos in Las Vegas. He sold his company prior to his move to England. Somebody knows where his money is, someone else wants it, that's my theory. I don't know what this has to do with Amy Pearce, and I'm convinced that she doesn't either. I've just spoken with DCI Alderman at Scotland Yard and he suggested handling it from there, especially as there's a Polish national involved. So he is putting together a team there too. I've just explained this to Amy Pearce.'

Riley was annoyed, he didn't know why. He loved a challenge and the professor's eccentric behaviour had excited something inside him that he hadn't felt in a long time. It was different from the usual crimes they dealt with.

'Are we still on the case?' he asked.

'That's going to be Alderman's decision, but right now no.'

Riley couldn't hide his disappointment. 'I could do with more time on this, I like this case...'

'Inspector Riley, are you listening to me?' DCI Moore interrupted. 'This is already too much for our limited resources, we are already dealing with multiple forces, liaising with Poland, and more than likely multiple American police departments while we locate this money and check out Jason's son.' He continued without looking away from Thomas. 'You make yourself available when needed. You prepare the case notes for Scotland Yard and you make yourself available for DCI Alderman if he wants you. Meanwhile, you do what I tell you, and you do not argue with me. Do you understand?'

Lucy shrugged, motioning to her partner. 'Come on,' she said softly, 'let it go.' She turned to Moore and told him that she would write a report on their efforts to date and hand the file over by the end of the shift. Riley glared at her before turning round and walking out, slamming the door with such a force that the whole room shook.

'Good work, DS Bridges,' Moore added as she turned to leave his office. 'Both of you. He'll come round. We can't guarantee that we can keep Amy Pearce safe without the Yard's help.'

Lucy Bridges understood, but her heart still sank.

Chapter 7

Amy cursed as the door went again. She was so tired. Three times she had had to explain what had happened in the early hours of the morning and after DCI Moore had left, all she wanted to do was to crawl back to bed. Arnold took the rest of the day off too. They were eating lunch and discussing the idea of a power nap when the buzzer had gone. The caller was persistent but Arnold reluctantly answered and moments later returned to the kitchen with Gerard. Amy tried to curb her anger, having asked him to leave her but he looked visibly shaken.

'Sorry Amy, I've been worried sick for you,' he said, holding out flowers to her and then lent forward to kiss her cheek. 'I shouldn't have made you feel like that, I wasn't angry with you.'

Amy was stunned but respected that he had come to see her, and his apology in front of Arnold was certainly brave. She had to compose herself to let the anger subside before thanking him. She offered him a coffee, they went to the sun lounge to talk and she explained everything that had happened. Gerard wanted to help but there wasn't much he could do. He offered for her to stay with him but she declined.

'You liked Jason, didn't you?' Gerard said, looking subdued.

'Yes, I suppose so,' Amy admitted. 'Not in a romantic

sort of way, I don't think. I don't know, Gerard. He's gone, there's nothing I can do about it. I don't know what to do now. I'm in danger. Even his solicitor must have known I was here so maybe the killer does too.'

'Will you go away somewhere, like the note suggests?'

'DCI Moore told me that Scotland Yard will be in touch. Some team there is going to make some decisions. I can't really do anything until they do.'

'I'm staying in London this week. If you need any help or somewhere to stay, just call me. Do consider Oxford though.'

They sat in subdued silence for a while. Amy needed to think about what to do. She may not have been safe but felt safer for having her father around.

Gerard had to leave. She was pleased and relieved that they'd been able to speak properly and respected that he had called, but she didn't feel comfortable with his offer.

After he left, Amy attempted her nap but fear and confusion made her restless. She was so tired.

***

Thomas Riley sat alone in the lounge of his Pimlico police house, the cream and red walls absorbing his sombre thoughts. For the first time in his career he had become too involved in a case.

He knew part of his problem was Lucy; his emotions had finally got the better of him. He saw the disappointment in her eyes when Moore told them he was handing over the case. To make matters worse, DCI Moore was sure to reprimand him in the morning for storming out.

Alone with his thoughts, every sound in the room was magnified. The ticking of the kitchen clock was driving him mad. He was hungry but he couldn't be bothered to eat. This is what love does, he thought, it makes you crazy.

A week before, he had been happy, secure, motivated, enjoying his work. Since that kiss, the foundations of his cosy existence had crumbled. He questioned himself, he questioned his work, indeed his whole future. He thought of Jason Chadwick and he empathised with the man he'd never met. He did not want to die a lonely man.

The phone didn't ring. Thomas hoped that Lucy would call, just a sign that everything was going to be all right. He checked his computer in the hope that she was online. Lucy was an internet geek, introduced to MSN Messenger by her younger sister, and all her family used Skype or social networking sites to keep in touch. She wasn't online. He stared at her Skype name on his contacts list, desperate for it to turn green.

Curiosity finally broke through his inertia and he opened melodema.com. The blank yellow page seemed such an anti-climax. How was anybody going to know its password? What would the password lead to, anyway? He tried random words, all without success.

Thomas felt a strange affinity with Jason. He wondered what it must have been like to be part of the development of something as important as the World Wide Web. Jason had left a real legacy; he had stood shoulder to shoulder with Al Gore and listened to him speak his own words – he must have felt so proud. Why would a man like that want to end his life?

Jason couldn't have cared that much for money or material things. His apartment in London was small and practical; he looked after his mother's country house in Cornwall at the weekends but he could have done so much more with his wealth. He wasn't a socialite, he was driven by ambition and creativity. Jason didn't appear to need anything else.

Thomas shut down the computer. The darkness outside had invaded his sitting room. He forced himself into the kitchen, not particularly tempted by the prospect of frozen lasagne but knowing that he must eat.

Another silent hour passed, the phone still didn't ring. He couldn't even find the motivation to attempt his daily ritual of *The Times* crossword. An early night was the only response to the malevolent hush; he needed to put this day behind him.

Sleep, however, wasn't ready for Thomas. He couldn't get Jason out of his head. He wanted one more day on the case, just one more. Was Jason's suicide as cut and dried as it appeared to be? Did the Devon and Cornwall police even question his death as suspicious, or did they take the easy option the minute they discovered his suicide note? What was melodema? What was the significance of the word?

The more Thomas asked himself questions, the more he resented the investigation being taken out of his hands. Jason was a scientist: digital science was his life; '*Anybody that truly understands me, that truly loved me, will have learnt how to claim my wealth...*' The words echoed in Thomas's head, a barrier against the sleep that he craved.

Finally he got out of bed; he wanted one last look at melodema.com. What if Jason had left a hidden message? He stared at the page, moving his mouse around the screen in case it picked up any invisible links. The page was blank. He remembered that one of Jason's achievements was helping Tim Berners-Lee develop hypertext module language (html), the language that houses the content of internet web pages. Thomas looked at the toolbar on top of his internet browser and opened 'view page source'. This opened the web page in simple text and characters. There was nothing obvious in there, either.

He spent the next hour reading up about hidden messages and encryption. Eventually he found a website about steganography. Steganography was originally used 2500 years ago by the ancient Greeks, who would hide messages on wooden tablets coated with wax, or tattoo messages on the scalps of messengers, which were hidden as their hair grew back. Nowadays the main use of steganography is to hide messages within the fabric of images or audio, using defects in eye-to-brain and ear-to-brain signals. Some messages can only be viewed with a secondary source, for example a video camera or mobile phone.

Thomas looked at the 'view page source' again. The only image was called 'yellowbutton.jpg'; this was obviously tiled over the page to make the whole page view as yellow. He isolated the image; it was merely a yellow square. He copied this square into Photoshop that he used to view and edit pictures from his digital camera. He played around with the filters and effects but again, there was no message.

He stared at the screen a bit longer, wondering why Jason had used a .jpg image rather than simply put a background colour (hex) code, which would have been much easier. He decided to use the image to recreate the page, maybe trying a different colour. He used the 'paint fill' effect to turn the yellow image black. As he did so, he realised the tolerance level was too low: his image, instead of instantly turning to black, merely turned the edges black. What he was left with was blurred but definite yellow text, which read:

V1ct0r14

Thomas's adrenalin levels surged as he returned to the page to try the password. It worked! 'Yes!' he shouted clapping his hands above his head, proud of his investigative skill.

He sat down to read Jason's message.

My name is Professor Jason Chadwick. I am probably dead if you found this web page, because you will not have discovered it on any search engines. However, to be sure **click here** *and submit your email address. If you do not receive an email reply inside an hour, then you can assume that I have passed away.*

If you knew me personally then I hope that my death was not too much of a shock and that my closest friends are not missing me too much. My will may have been disclosed by now and has probably caused a commotion. I apologise to my sons that I did not leave them more money but I hope that what I did leave them has made a difference to their lives.

The remainder of my estate (probably, not far short of $100 million after tax) will hopefully be claimed one day. In order to find it, you will have to get to know me and understand the person that I was. Hopefully you will enjoy the simple things, like I did. If such a sum is tempting, then I suggest that you start here because every man is an architect of his own fortune and on Diana's hand sits the nest to my own.

Thomas's excitement changed to enlightenment. 'He left a bloody treasure hunt?' he said out loud. He read through the message again and again, trying to make sense of it. He didn't know if he felt angry or elated.

It was three o'clock when Thomas closed down the computer. His shift began at eight and he needed his sleep to prepare for the day ahead. But sleep eluded him again.

This could be his chance to solve all of his problems. It could also be why Amy was in danger.

Curse DCI Moore.

Chapter 8

By five o'clock in the afternoon Amy had given up on trying to nap and joined her parents downstairs. The house was quiet. They huddled together in the silence for a short while before Arnold went into the kitchen to help to his wife cook.

Amy fetched her laptop to check her emails, Emmanuelle had replied and she seemed eager to help:

Hello Amy,

Sadly I am aware that Jason died. It was a big shock and I will miss him with all my heart. I regret not being able to attend the funeral.

I do remember the ring well; he called it his 'Ring of Conscience'. The ring originates from a dream he had when he was younger. Long story. What do you want to know about it? I'm surprised he left it to you, to be honest. He obviously cared about you.

Any friend of Jason is a friend of mine. I hope you can keep in touch.

Em.

Amy let it all out to Emmanuelle – a long, long email explaining everything that had happened to her in the past few days and her theory that Jason had been murdered. She hesitated briefly before pressing 'send' but considered

Emmanuelle a strong enough friend of Jason's to be an ally. She clicked the mouse and the email disappeared from her screen: decoded and transported instantaneously through a mass of fibre optic cables and placed on a server ready for Emmanuelle to read as soon as her computer logged in to request it. This was possible, in large part, to the work of her boss and good friend Jason Chadwick. She missed him so much.

After dinner, Amy went to her bedroom. She was tired but she grabbed Jason's journal and ended up sitting on her bed while reading about his time in Boston.

Jason had set up home with friends outside the campus. A friend's father owned a large house just the other side of the Charles River. Jason met his wife-to-be, Penny, within a few weeks. She was an art student and he met her during an evening stroll in Fenway Park. She was sitting on a bench, reading Homer's *Odyssey,* and he'd struck up a conversation about the Trojan War. His knowledge seduced her and he invited her back to the house to look at his collection of prints of pre-Raphaelite paintings.

Jason's father had once caught him staring at a poster of Hylas and the Nymphs when he was sixteen. He'd assumed that Jason was taking a healthy interest in Victorian art and bought him a number of prints of works by Waterhouse, Millais and Morris, which he brought with him to Boston. In reality, Jason had been staring at Hylas and the Nymphs because he adored the half-naked beauty of the Nymphs. To hide his embarrassment, Jason had taken out several books from the library and started reading about Greek mythology. To his surprise, he became passionate about the subject.

Jason and Penny hit it off from the beginning. He'd known right then and there that she was the one. Reading his journals, Amy could see that Jason's love for her was special. Amy was jealous, and also curious. How could a love that seemed so strong fall apart? When she'd known him, Jason had very little to say about his ex-wife; he had rarely mentioned her, and only then in the context of his sons.

Later, Amy returned downstairs. Her parents were watching the television but they turned it off as soon as she entered the room.

'It's OK' she said. 'You just carry on doing what you'd normally do. I'm OK, honestly. I feel a lot safer now the police are on the case. I just wanted to collect my laptop.'

Her mother smiled. 'As long as you're OK. It's been a worrying few days for you.'

Amy took her laptop from the table and went in to the sun lounge. Emmanuelle had replied; she seemed genuinely relieved to hear Amy's views about Jason's death and equally worried about Amy's safety. She couldn't even begin to think why Jason would want to end his life or risk putting Amy in danger. Her best theory was espionage: it could be something to do with e-commerce-related warfare. She knew Jason was assisting leading search engines develop a faster and more comprehensive search facility. Maybe there was a problem over royalties or copyright, something that an internet Mafia organisation had handled. But even if that were true, what would they want with Amy? She was only Jason's PA.

Emmanuelle ended her email by inviting Amy to Boston. Maybe the break would help her, and it would get her out of the killer's range for a while. Amy was tempted but held back on a reply until she had time to sleep on it.

'Espionage? I doubt that,' she muttered.

By now the tiredness was taking over, she had to at least try. Thankfully her mind surrendered to the chaos and let her sleep.

***

Amy awoke early next morning. She looked out of her window, listening to the birdsong that heralded the new day. She had slept a little but yesterday's five-thirty rise had triggered a new routine. She was wide awake, still in her dressing gown, but drinking her first coffee as she observed the garden from her bedroom window. It was tranquil outside, bar the occasional flight of a magpie or sparrow.

A new day seemed so full of hope, as if all the yesterdays were filed away under 'history'. Her worry now was that her tomorrows were uncertain. The changes in her life over the past few months were totally unexpected. She had become complacent; her old life was regimented but uncomplicated. She had dreams and hopes but was young enough not to have to chase them with any sense of urgency. Now she was caught in some indeterminate state, a prisoner in her parents' home and being hunted without any idea why.

She had to get away. She considered Emmanuelle's offer of a holiday in Boston. The more she thought about it, the more she was tempted but the idea of travelling alone was frightening. She would need permission to leave from the police. Maybe she should speak to DCI Moore or Scotland Yard. Maybe they would even chaperone her to Boston.

Amy sat back on the edge of her bed. The pink and white embroidered blanket, made by her mother when she was thirteen, was all that seemed familiar to her. She reached down for Jason's journal and sat back to read about his time in Boston.

Jason seemed just as full of life back then as he was until the last day she saw him. She read about a weekend trip Jason and Penny made to Buffalo. Jason was one of the last of his circle of friends to get his driver's license. After he was given his first car by his father, a Land Rover Jeep, he made that trip his first proper outing. He described the weekend with the detail and tenderness of a romantic novel and Amy felt her eyes well with tears.

There had been moments that Amy considered sacred to her and Jason. In particular, she remembered a day about two years ago. Jason had been lecturing in the north of England where he was a speaking at the University of Manchester.

He was moving on to Hallam University in Sheffield on

the Monday, so they spent the Sunday together in the Peak District. She remembered the winding road over Snake Pass. Jason stopped his car at the summit and they looked down at the glory of the Derbyshire Pennines. They stopped at Castleton and explored the Blue John caves, ate genuine Bakewell tarts under the Bridge of Wye, and sat for hours at the foot of the Weir at Monsal Dale. OK, she thought, it was hardly Niagara Falls but it was still special, and so much fun. They laughed at the irony of drinking Buxton water at the foot of the source from the £1.79 bottle that they were sharing. The spray from the falls hypnotised them. At one point in the late afternoon, the sun poked through the canopy of trees, framing the waterfall with a rainbow. Jason seemed genuinely happy at that moment.

'That's what we are, you know,' he said quietly. 'Rainbows and waterfalls. I'm the waterfall, tumbling effortlessly into an abyss; you're my rainbow lighting my way, beautiful colours embracing my fall.'

Amy was stunned. She wanted to tell him that it was the most beautiful thing anybody had ever said to her but then he winked at her and stood up, dusting himself down. Amy had said nothing, but she cherished the moment. She felt so happy but she couldn't let it show; he was her boss, it was never an option for her to think of taking their relationship further. That tender moment, deep in the forest of Monsal Dale, had never left her.

I wonder if he said those words to Penny that day at Niagara Falls, she thought as she continued reading. *No, they were for me.*

Chapter 9

Thomas Riley had barely fallen asleep when the noise of his phone's alarm alerted him to the new day. Initial dread gave way to courage. He would put aside the frustration of the previous day and tackle whatever the new day presented. If he couldn't work Jason Chadwick's case in the office, he could still follow the clues at home.

His mind drifted as he got dressed. Sometimes, as his feelings had grown for his partner, he'd fantasised about them starting their own investigation agency. He wasn't disillusioned with the force and he enjoyed the work but the internal politics and the station banter were as draining as the crimes he was solving. There was an introverted side to his nature that meant he could never feel comfortable at the station. He knew he was driven and ambitious, he knew he had an ego that was often motivated by competition, but in many ways it was a mask he wore.

He took a deep breath before leaving the house and psyched himself up for the day.

DCI Moore called Riley in as soon as he walked into the station. Bridges was already in his office. She gave Thomas a warm smile as he entered the room. *It's going to be alright,* he thought.

'Sorry about yesterday, boss,' he said, the second Moore caught his eye. 'You're right, we can't handle this alone. I'll be happy to assist in any way the Yard wants. I was wrong to show my anger. I was disappointed, that's all. We have to find this guy quickly before he gets to Amy Pearce.'

'Good,' said DCI Moore, holding back the smile his position of authority shouldn't allow in these circumstances. 'Because another outburst like that and I'll have you up in front of the Chief Super. Understood? '

'Loud and clear, sir,' Riley said, glad that he'd got in his apology first.

'Now, the reason I called you in,' DCI Moore said, still looking in Riley's direction. 'Frank Duffy took a plane to Las Vegas. He paid for an open ticket. Las Vegas Police Department are going to alert Scotland Yard when he is seen or if he returns to McCarran airport. Though he might have information essential to the case, he isn't considered a suspect yet. DCI Alderman is letting Las Vegas Police Department handle it for now.'

'It looks like he is deliberately setting a trail for the police to follow. It's probably better to follow his actions than simply bring him in right now,' Thomas said, probing his own theory. He took a breath, ready to say something about his own investigation, but something stopped him. Maybe it was pride, but he was keen to see how far the Met's Cyber Crime Unit could get with the melodema.com clue – and see if he could stay one jump ahead of them. It was obvious that Jason had sought to leave his fortune in some unorthodox way. Thomas's progress so far wouldn't necessarily help the investigation.

Lucy looked at him; she must have caught his hesitation, but she said nothing.

'From hereon then,' DCI Moore stated, staring directly into Riley's eyes, 'DCI Alderman calls the shots on this case. You make yourself available as they require but we move on.'

'What about Amy?' Riley enquired.

'Somebody from the yard will see her today. They'll decide what happens next, OK?'

***

Amy finally got up at nine. She had had been drifting in and out of sleep, thinking about Jason, and her father had already left for work. Shortly after breakfast two detectives arrived to speak to her. DCI Moore had spoken to her about requesting help from Scotland Yard and DCI Paul Dawson from Scotland Yard was now sitting opposite her and her mother, with his partner writing notes as they discussed Amy's story and options.

'Why am I in danger?' Amy asked. 'What have I done? If someone wants the ring, they can have it. It's not worth putting us all in danger. One person is already dead because of me.' Her eyes started to well up again.

DCI Dawson couldn't offer an explanation but suggested that she remained at her parents' house. The police would put twenty-four hour surveillance on the property. In the meantime, if she could give them a couple of days to assess the situation and speak with Devon and Cornwall police before she went outside the house… That should give them enough time to make a decision about where she should go next.

He studied the ring hanging around Amy's neck. 'Do you mind?'

Amy removed it and passed it to the inspector. 'Very strange, isn't it? I wonder if the symbol has a meaning? Did he ever mention it to you?' he asked, running it through his fingers, looking for any abnormalities.

'Only that he called it his Ring of Conscience to remind him not to try and steal the crown jewels.' To her surprise, Amy expelled a single nervous laugh that she tried to disguise as a cough.

Dawson motioned to his partner, who had been writing notes and hadn't spoken a word. He took several photographs of the ring then ripped out a page from his pad and used a pencil to rub an impression of the image. He made the process look very technical but she remembered doing the same thing herself at junior school, using a penny. They promised to investigate the symbol for her.

Amy mentioned Emmanuel's offer to let her stay in Boston for a while. The inspectors looked at each other.

'This might be an idea, I will need to discuss it with my Super but in the meantime, stay indoors. We're setting up an investigation team to work on this.'

Amy was relieved that things seemed to be happening. She hoped they would let her travel to Boston; she felt as if she was under house arrest. The two detectives left shortly afterwards and promised to keep her updated. It was a waiting game now.

Amy stared at the ring. She knew Jason would never intentionally put her in danger. *There must be something else.* Maybe the symbol itself meant something. She decided to investigate online, but couldn't put the symbol itself into any of the search engines as it didn't have a name. *Ring of Conscience* had no relevance either. Eventually she gave up and returned to Jason's journals.

***

No longer in the guise of a Scotland Yard detective, Nathan Hammond studied the paper in front of him. The rubbing he'd made from Amy's ring was quite clear but the image itself seemed of no immediate relevance to his investigation. He made a call. 'Don't worry, this is perfect, but we need to move fast.'

***

Thomas and Lucy left the office with orders to investigate a fatal incident at the Café Crypt in St. Martin's Church.

Thomas was silent and Lucy felt uneasy. She broke the ice as they climbed into the car. 'Is it me?' she asked, dreading the answer.

He hesitated before switching on the engine. 'I don't know,' he replied. She noticed a crack in his voice, as if he was about to implode. 'It's a classic dilemma, isn't it? Juggling desires with common sense. I've lost focus. Plus,' he continued, finally looking her in the eye, 'I really wanted this case. The detective work is what I enjoy. I want the chief inspector job so badly, but I keep screwing it up with Moore.'

'Maybe you're too eager, but that's not a bad thing, is it? Moore knows that,' Lucy said, offering some words of comfort, together with the soft hand, she placed gently on his.

Riley smiled and started the engine. The warmth in his smile melted her. She could understand his frustration yesterday but she was also afraid that he would pull away from her. He didn't phone her last night. Was he upset with her? And his show of distain towards DCI Moore was uncharacteristic.

They had to talk properly; it would kill her otherwise.

Chapter 10

After their shift had finished, Lucy Bridges found the courage to ask. She didn't want another lonely night spent in limbo. She hadn't called Thomas last night because she was worried what he would say. She was relieved that today had gone well and he seemed to be his normal self again. But they couldn't put off the inevitable: they *had* to talk.

She invited him to her house for dinner but he declined, inviting her to his place instead.

He had something to show her – a secret.

***

The talking was delayed until after they finished their meal at Garfunkel's. Neither had eaten properly during the day and they both fancied a high protein fry-up – without the queuing. Garfunkel's was perfect.

As soon as they entered the house Thomas apologised again for the previous day's outburst. He offered her bourbon but she declined, opting for a coffee instead.

'What are we going to do?' he asked her, dreading the answer but knowing decisions had to be made.

'I only wish I knew,' Lucy said. 'I confess, I love being with you and if I partner you at work, that's better than nothing. If I partner you here, then one of us has to change career. I know how much you want Moore's job. If I transfer, my contract restricts me from working within eighty miles so I'll have to give it all up. One thing I know, we can't just carry on like this. Moore already suspects something.'

They stared at each other. Thomas knew that even if they broke it off now, things would still be awkward, especially if he got the chief inspector's job. His role would be office based and he would see less of Lucy.

'We're in big trouble aren't we?' Lucy said, looking down at the dregs in her coffee, swirling them around a little to form a circle at the base of her mug. 'The truth is, I really want us to be together if there's a way. I'll miss being partnered with you when you get Moore's job.' She smiled, still watching her whirlpool. 'Oh God, your ego! You really *will* be better than me then.'

Thomas looked at her. He didn't want this to end any more than she did. He tried not to smile at her joke. He knew he had an ego, but it was playful competition with her and very much in jest. He knew it wound her up and he loved her reaction. He thought hard before saying his next words.

'What if there was a way?' he began. Lucy looked up, curious, as he continued. 'What if I could raise money, big money, the sort of money that would allow us to start our own private investigation company?'

Lucy looked confused. 'Really? Are you serious? Have you won the lottery?'

Thomas laughed. *Now that would be ideal,* he thought. He hesitated, wondering if he should tell her or try to find Jason's money himself.

'Well, yes I am serious but it's complicated … and unethical.' He looked at her, wondering how shocked she would be by his plan.

He led her to the computer, opened up melodema.com then explained his thought processes that led him to identify the password. She seemed genuinely amazed, especially as he was talking her through his Photoshop discovery. Thomas opened the page and let her read it.

'Oh wow!' Lucy knelt down beside him to take in Jason's instructions again. 'It's an online treasure hunt! No wonder there's all this secrecy and intrigue.' She looked up at Thomas. 'Does anybody else know about this?'

'No. I wanted to see how long it would take – or rather if – Scotland Yard could suss it out. I didn't really think that me knowing this much would make a real difference. It became obvious from Jason's will that he had set up something like this.' After a pause, he added, 'Plus, I don't have a problem with this morally. If I, or rather we, can solve the riddles along the way then we will be as worthy as anybody. Let's face it, they already have the number of this bank in the US and they will have instructions from Jason. The Yard or even the FBI would have the power to locate the money, surely? I assume that everything has been done perfectly legally.'

Lucy stopped to think. Her adrenalin levels were so high that she was thirsty to the point of nausea. 'What if the guy that's after Amy already knows about this? What if he's got further than you, and Amy has something – maybe a clue, maybe the ring itself. This is why she could be in danger. We *have* to tell Moore.'

Thomas looked down. He was worried about Amy but he still felt that Scotland Yard was capable of figuring out the clues simply from knowing that melodema.com existed. He'd been thinking about it all day and wondering whether Amy had any idea what was going on. Maybe she was playing it cool but his gut feeling was that she knew nothing. She seemed completely unaware of any details relating to Jason's will.

If he *did* take up this quest for Jason's millions, he would need access to Amy. How else could he understand Jason properly? Maybe she knew the identity of this Diana that Jason mentioned in his message. Was that a clue? If so, where did the clue begin?

He read it through again: *every man is an architect of his own fortune and on Diana's hand sits the nest to my own.* It looked like the focus of the riddle but what would be next? Would it be another clue or the details of how to acquire Jason's fortune?

Lucy stood up. She'd read Jason's words half a dozen times now. 'Let's pretend,' she said, 'that we're doing both. We're approaching this with the view of potentially helping Scotland Yard find a link to Amy, but if we actually uncover the treasure, then we make a decision. Let's see if we can get somewhere with this tonight.'

She smiled, pushed him aside and shuffled herself onto his seat. He was relieved by her sudden enthusiasm but resisted the urge to hug her, afraid that it may distract them from the busy evening ahead.

OK. Let's pretend.

***

It was shortly before eight o'clock in the evening when Amy received a call from DI Riley. By now she was confused. Two more detectives from Scotland Yard had arrived in the afternoon and she had to go through the events of the past few days again.

She was exhausted. This afternoon's interrogation was almost identical to the one earlier with DCI Dawson and his partner. She must have seemed exceptionally hostile to her visitors today. When DCI Jim Alderman asked to see her ring, she threw it at him and told him to keep it until this was over. For a while she had hated Jason; she'd never thought that would be possible.

Alderman considered Emmanuelle's invitation to Boston but asked Amy to stay locally for now, reiterating what DCI Dawson had suggested, that they would discuss her safety with the Boston police. So she was still a prisoner in her parents' home. There seemed to be a lack of communication between departments as DCI Alderman seemed unaware of the earlier visit.

Amy vented her frustration on Riley as she explained everything that had happened in the past twenty-four hours. He seemed sympathetic. He seemed to care too, asking a lot of questions about Jason, trying to understand more about his work, the people he was connected to and about his past.

Amy explained about the journals that she was reading. They documented a period of four or five years. She told Riley about the story of Hylas and the Nymphs, and Jason's love for Penny. The phone call lasted over an hour and by the end of it, Amy felt that she finally had an ally, somebody she could speak to without worrying about protocol.

Thomas left her his mobile phone number and told her she could call any time. He explained that he was not working directly on the case, as major decisions would be handled through Scotland Yard, but that he and DS Bridges were still helping the Yard and handling a lot of the database investigations.

When the phone call ended, Amy watched the sun set as she sat on a cane chair in the sun lounge. When the phone rang again, it was Gerard. She told him about the visits and said about Emmanuel's offer to spend time with her in Boston – thankfully he thought it was a good idea.

Amy ended the day much happier. As she prepared for bed and closed the curtains in her bedroom, she saw an unfamiliar car parked directly outside. She could see the uniforms of the police officers inside. She felt much safer.

✳✳✳

'That was clever,' Lucy remarked as Thomas replaced the phone after his conversation with Amy.

'Hopefully that was a one-off,' Thomas replied. He was already feeling guilty and also nervous: *had they now crossed the line?* 'There may well be information we need. It'll be good to keep her happy – and maybe safer too.' He was pleased with his diplomacy. 'Plus, I feel that we're still working the case in some way with this.' He finished scribbling notes from the conversation then looked up at Lucy. 'Amy seemed clueless at the mention of this Diana. Her voice didn't falter when I mentioned the name. I honestly think that she's unaware of the clues on melodema.com.'

'I was wondering, as you were talking, if Diana was a nickname Jason had for Amy. It would make sense that the attacker would want the ring, if that were the case,' Lucy suggested.

'I thought about that when I first read the clue but now I've spoken with her, I'm not sure. Maybe her attacker thinks that, though – assuming he knows as much as we do right now.' Then he added, 'Frank Duffy knew Amy was in danger. How did he know? Is it because a clue leads to Amy or did he simply suspect that she could be in danger because of something that was said to him?'

Lucy smiled. 'Or maybe it's for the same reason that we know she's in danger: because she's likely to know more about him that anybody else.' She paused, watching his face. 'You love a puzzle like this, don't you?'

Thomas grinned. Yes, he did. This was the reason he'd joined the police force in the first place. He was driven by the chase and the conquest; a case like this was a dream.

'You know, as a child, I collected puzzle boxes. I used to keep notes inside for my future self. I used to read Wilbur Smith books and about the discoveries of tombs in Egypt and dream of finding treasure. A challenge like this is like all my childhood fantasies rolled into one.'

He rubbed his hands together and began to go through the telephone conversation with Amy. Lucy made bullet points on Thomas's computer, something they could refer to later for clues.

Amy had explained about his early relationship with Penny and suggested to Thomas that they look into this, as she couldn't see how a relationship that seemed so perfect could deteriorate the way it did. Lucy wondered whether there was another woman involved. Diana?

Lucy opened the melodema.com website again, using the password v1ct0r14 to access Jason's message. She was deliberating whether a clue was held within the password; it was obviously an alphanumeric translation of 'Victoria'. Or were the numerical values in the password significant? She made notes on Thomas's computer along the way. We make a great team, Thomas thought.

Thomas was deciphering his own notes and writing down information from the phone conversation that he thought might be relevant. 'It's worth putting the clue into a search engine and seeing if there's any information that shouts at you,' he suggested to Lucy.

She opened a new window and tried. 'Nothing of relevance. Hold on, I'll split it,' she said. 'That's interesting' she mumbled a few seconds later, just loud enough for Thomas to look up and pause. *'Every man is an architect of his own fortune* is a famous quote.' She continued to read the computer screen as Thomas came over. 'That's strange. It's famously quoted twice.' She looked up at Thomas and pointed to the screen. 'A Roman historian named Sallust is reported to have originated the saying around 50BC in relation to the Catiline Conspiracy. However, the saying is also said to have originated two hundred years earlier from a Roman politician named Appius Clauius Caecus.'

Thomas looked puzzled. 'Roman origin? That's strange. Amy mentioned that Jason had a strong interest in Greek mythology but nothing about the Romans.'

They spent the next hour searching reference sites. Firstly they looked into the origin of the quotes from both Sallust and Caecus, attempting to connect them with 'Diana'. They read about the Catiline Conspiracy, about the Roman politician who was implicated as a human rights' terrorist, but there was no reference to any Diana. It eventually became clear Sallust himself was referencing Roman censor Appius Claudius Caecus.

Lucy hypothesised that one of these two historians would somehow link to Amy's ring to become the focus of the clue, so she looked for as much information as she could find about the ring or the symbol. She didn't have much luck – the symbol needed a *name*. Ring of Conscience also showed no direct results in her search.

Thomas continued examining his own theory that this was an historical clue. He found it hard to believe that Jason would have left Amy a vital part of a clue, if he believed that his legacy could take a hundred years to solve. He must have also known that this would put Amy in danger. He suggested a back-to-basics approach by cross-referencing 'Romans' and 'Diana' in the search engine to see if there was anything relevant.

Lucy punched the words into the search bar and the second the results came through she exhaled an excited low breath.

Thomas stood up to read over her shoulder but she shuffled the chair back so they sat side-by-side, transfixed by the computer monitor.

Diana was the name used by the Romans for the Greek Goddess of Hunting and of the Moon, Artemis. They read through various websites on the subject. The Moon Goddess was a warrior, obsessed with her virginity, and yet she was also the protector of birth. Artemis was the vicious and powerful, daughter of Zeus and Leto and twin sister of Apollo. She murdered her hunting companion Actaeon after he had apparently caught sight of her bathing. Artemis also shot her hunting companion, Callisto, a nymph who was seduced by Zeus. Knowing that Callisto guarded her virginity fiercely, Zeus disguised himself as Artemis to get close to her and then raped her. Artemis was also responsible for casting Orion into the stars where he could still be seen as a constellation.

Lucy typed the name Artemis into the image browser. The goddess had been the subject of many famous paintings and sculptures. In almost every one, she bore her bow and hunting arrows and in the most famous statue of all by Leochares, housed in the Louvre, she was leading a stag.

'Could it be that simple?' Lucy asked, trying to restrain

her excitement.

'I think we must be on the right lines here. Nobody knows who Diana is and you would have to *know* Jason to even begin to understand the clue.'

'I agree but maybe that was the easy part. It's what we do with this information that complicates matters.'

Lucy updated her notes and printed out two copies, which they read over another drink on the comfort of Thomas's sofa.

Chapter 11

Nightfall descended, leaving an array of pink and orange over the mountains above Henderson. Frank Duffy looked out from the twenty-seventh floor window of his MGM Grand hotel room. This is the time that Las Vegas comes to life, he thought.

It had been a long journey. He was tired; the additional eight hours to the day were telling his body to rest but the smell of the hotel, the noises and the lights had awakened a curiosity that thrilled him. He could feel the pull of Las Vegas's dark side– but that was not why he was there.

Frank unpacked his holdall then washed away his fatigue. He hadn't packed much, merely a suit, some casual slacks, a habotai silk shirt and some underwear. He didn't want to take much. He thought about Jason: he was a good friend, a good man. The company, together with his own father's firm, had handled much of Jason's UK business. Frank had known Jason's mother well and grieved for her after the accident ten years ago.

Frank visited Jason's Cornish home after he died. His company had to put it on the market but he'd taken time to privately pay his respects to his friend. Jason would never have meant to cause this much anxiety and probably never envisaged such chaos. Moreover, Frank thought, there was no way he would have taken his own life.

'Watch over me, dear boy,' he said, his hands clasped

together in a parody of a prayer. Frank realised how much he would need some divine help in the next few days, if nothing else but to give him courage.

He took out Jason's letter again, the one from the orange folder, and refreshed his memory of the instructions. He thought back to the previous morning at Amy's parents' apartment; he hoped he'd done enough to attract their attention and that she had been given his note. He hoped, too, that she had taken his advice to get away. Hopefully the police were on to him but he didn't want them to find him, not just yet. He needed to track down the ex-mayor of Las Vegas, Beverley Johnson.

In spite of his tiredness, Frank decided to take a walk. The path to The Strip was through the main casino and he took it all in en route: the chattering of the roulette ball jumping in and out of dream numbers, tormenting and thrilling the punters. Businessmen, here for tax write-off conferences, found solace at the craps' tables, their whooping and yelling juxtaposed with the moans and groans of poker players at the card tables. Crazy women were shrieking, having hit the $1000 Wheel of Fortune in the slots. Everybody's hopes and dreams were on public display; everybody looked happy, even when their luck was down. After all, this was Las Vegas.

Frank passed an enclosed lion habitat and stopped briefly to watch the handlers entertain the crowd by grooming the golden beasts. They played like giant kittens, rolling on their sides, lapping up the fuss. Only in Vegas, he thought, making his way up the escalator leading onto The Strip.

The first thing that Frank noticed on Las Vegas Boulevard was the heat. Even without the direct sunshine, the air was a searing blast that made him pause for a second, allowing his senses to rebalance and absorb the magnitude of the picture before him. Nothing he'd ever read or heard about Vegas prepared him for that second. This was not just a light show; it was like stepping into a parallel world.

Directly in front of him, a bridge over the busy boulevard invited him to New York, New York – a Manhattan skyline lit up in blue, green and pink, together with the Statue of Liberty and scaled-down Hudson River. Winding above him, weaving through the replica buildings, was a giant roller-coaster. There stood a massive electronic billboard advertising the Coyote Ugly bar. He saw the turreted spires of Camelot Castle and huge glass towers lit up in every colour. There must be a hundred million lights, he thought, taking his first steps over the bridge.

He stopped and looked north from the bridge over the Boulevard. The traffic, like the walkways, was heaving. Every other car was a limousine and the majority of the remaining cars were Ferraris, Aston Martins, Dodge Vipers or Lamborghinis.

It was hard to be cynical. Some might call it tacky but it was too lavish to be considered cheap. It was as if the city were built on every childhood fantasy yet was strictly for adults-only access. No virgins in Vegas, for sure.

He continued across the bridge and onto The Strip, taking in as much as he could. He jostled for pavement space and was accosted every few yards by young men brandishing cards showing ravishing beauties together with their phone numbers. You didn't just talk with these girls on the phone; you met them and, if you were rich enough, you enjoyed their company all night – together with unlimited access to their perfect bodies.

Frank could see The Bellagio in front of him. It was a stone's throw away, he thought, but Las Vegas was deceiving. The hotels were so big that he was losing perspective. Ten minutes later, The Bellagio did not seem any nearer. Eventually he reached a moving walkway, framed by giant pillars and lined with palm trees. He stood still and looked over at the most glorious sight he'd ever seen: the dancing fountains of The Bellagio were entertaining a crowd of thousands. Synchronised to the theme from *Titanic*, Celine Dion's vocals were translated into aquatic beauty. Every crescendo lifted the jets more than a hundred feet into the air. Time could stop now; who needs what tomorrow brings?

That evening, Frank forgot his troubles and fears. He even forgot about his family and buried himself in the parallel world before his eyes. *Time could stop now.*

***

It was getting late. Thomas Riley and Lucy Bridges were on the early shift again and it was fast approaching midnight. They were pleased with their achievements with Jason's treasure hunt but disappointed that they were no nearer piecing together information relating to Vito's killer – or even knowing what to do with the information that they now had. Neither had they made any decision about where they should go with their own plans. They knew they wanted to be together but it was not possible if they wanted to keep their jobs.

Thomas was back at the computer looking at the clue one more time. He wondered why Jason was confident that melodema.com was not traceable through search engines. He went through a similar routine as he'd done with the opening page. The Internet address was www.melodema.com/page1.htm. He clicked the toolbar at the top of the page to 'view page source' to open the text version of the page, but this time there was no yellowbutton.jpg for the background. It looked like the whole page was one image: page1.gif.

'That explains why you can't find melodema.com on search engines like Google,' he said to Lucy, who was putting on her shoes ready to leave. 'The page is a single image and the text we read is typed as part of that image. The search engine robots can only read html text and embedded tags. Even an image search like Google Images won't pick it up because he simply named the image 'page1.gif' – no mention of melodema. It would only be viewed by people placing 'page1' into the image search – and since there are probably a million or more 'page1' images, the search engine would only show the popular sites. It's very clever.' Thomas watched Lucy as he spoke. 'You can stay you know,' he continued, looking disappointed as she prepared to leave.

She walked over and kissed him on the forehead. 'It's OK,' she said quietly. 'For now, let's just keep things like this. I've enjoyed tonight and I can cope with this much, until we can sort ourselves out.' Lucy held both of his hands gently and continued. 'Just knowing that you feel the same way that I do is a foundation for us to build a future at our own pace.'

Thomas smiled. It was what he needed to hear. 'And I really *do*, Lucy, I think I've known for a long time.' He brought her hands to his lips before releasing them. 'Come on then, I'll walk you back.'

Lucy didn't live far from Thomas. The Pimlico police houses were widely used by the Metropolitan force and two estates ran adjacent to each other. Lucy kissed Thomas goodnight outside her maisonette and they parted. He was aware of her climbing the iron stairs to her front door, her shoes clattering on each stair and echoing in the quiet night air. He watched her enter the flat before he turned back towards his own home.

As he began walking back, he noticed a dark blue sedan parked on the corner. The headlights were dimmed and a man seemed to be writing notes and looking towards Lucy's maisonette. He shielded his face as Thomas approached. Thomas tried not to make it too obvious that he'd seen him but he was worried. As he passed the car, the man was talking on his mobile phone. Thomas's paranoia eased as he made his way back home.

He was relieved that the day had ended so well. He was tired; lack of sleep from last night's investigations and this evening's adventures with Lucy had left him exhausted but his mind was active.

What do I do with the clue? The realisation hit him as he turned the key to let himself back in the house. He rushed to the computer and wrote www.melodema.com/page2.htm in the address bar at the top of his internet browser. Since the previous page was called page1.htm, maybe it was as easy as that.

Straight away a sky-blue page came up with a password box, just like the first page of melodema.com. Thomas chuckled. 'So simple!' he said to himself and typed 'stag' into the password box. This time, however, there was no progress and the page simply remained as it was. He tried 'bow', 'arrow', 'bows' and 'arrows', 'stags', 'hunting dogs', 'Artemis' – every combination of numbers replacing letters, as Jason had done with v1ct0r14 and f0rc3. Nothing happened. The blue page appeared again with an empty password box.

Thus began the ritual of probing the web page for further clues. This time 'view page source' had a background colour code but also one image: bluebut1.gif. Once again, Thomas isolated the .gif image and played with Photoshop, looking for a steganographic clue but this time his trick didn't work. The image seemed quite grainy, not as sharp. He wondered whether the missing pixel dots would give a clue if he zoomed in on the image to magnify it – but again, there was nothing obvious.

He stared at the image for about ten minutes, about to give in to the sleep his body craved. Why a .gif this time instead of a .jpg? He searched information about .gifs – they were primarily used as animated images – but there was no animation with this, just a plain blue image. Or was there?

He remembered that Photoshop had an animation plug-in. He looked on his computer, located 'image-ready' and opened the .gif in this software. He couldn't believe his eyes. Nine boxes opened. A plain blue image appeared in the first box but a transparent letter appeared in each of the subsequent boxes. He grabbed a pen and paper and wrote the letters F O L L Y S K Y. He stared for a few seconds. 'Folly Sky?'

He returned to the computer and placed the letters in the password box but again nothing happened. He searched for Folly Sky but nothing obvious stood out so he retraced his steps. Why two sets of clues? He remembered that the image that contained Jason's instructions on page 1 was also a .gif file. He isolated this image and opened page 1.gif in his animation software. This time the main message appeared six times, and at the bottom of the image was a black bar. In the corner of each image there was a different letter.

Thomas grabbed his pen and paper and wrote U N D E R A. He stared at them for a minute, trying to separate the letters: *under a folly sky*. He tried this as the password, 'Please work!' he shouted as he pressed enter. Again, he had no luck.

He became more frustrated and, in his weariness, found it increasingly difficult to rationalise his reasoning. *Maybe 'under a folly sky' referred to the Artemis clue?* He cross-referenced 'folly sky' and 'Artemis' but once again there was nothing of relevance.

Thomas felt that he had come so far, only to fall at the last hurdle. It must be simple he thought to himself – that was Jason's way.

Eventually he closed down the computer. It was nearly two o'clock and he had to be up for work in four hours. For once, he really didn't want to go to work. He had his own work to do and nothing else mattered.

He would make a decision in the morning.

Chapter 12

'It wasn't what you think,' explained Beverley Johnson. Her office boasted an enormous glass frontage looking out over the Las Vegas basin. It would have resembled a conference room rather than an office but for hundreds of leather-bound files covering three shelves that spanned the entire length of the room. The extensive greenery in the room included Chamaedorea Palms and a Braided Ficus Tree, which must have stood almost six foot tall.

'I was being blackmailed. Donald Chadwick was used. The Hammonds set the whole thing up, I'm certain of it.'

She was a powerful woman. Simply being in her presence made Frank Duffy feel uneasy. She looked solemn.

'Are you aware that Donald and his wife lost their lives in a car accident in 1997, a year after they moved back to England,' Frank asked. He tried to assess her reaction; she looked horrified. 'Until a few years ago his son, Jason Chadwick, accepted that it was an accident. But something happened to make him question their deaths and the more he investigated, the more he became convinced that they were murdered.'

Beverley looked genuinely shocked. 'I had no idea. We were very close, Donald and I.'

Frank saw her eyes fill as she stared out of her window. 'Donald was based at The Bellagio. He designed, installed and ran the security system for nearly all the hotels on The

Strip. When I was mayor, we worked hand in hand with the hotels and Las Vegas Police Department. Donald was highly respected. Some of his ideas were visionary, he even worked with NASA at one time – I believe he helped develop technology that could zoom a camera image to hundreds of times its size and still retain the detail. And remember, this was right at the beginning of the digital photography era. NASA developed his algorithmic ideas into the designs of their Near-Earth Asteroid Rendezvous probe missions. I gave a reference for Donald and was even asked to be present together with his lawyer at one of his meetings with them.'

'You told me that the Hammonds set the whole thing up,' Frank stated. 'Set what thing up?'

'That photo you came to show me,' she said, tapping an envelope on the table lightly with her manicured nails. A snapshot inside from a surveillance camera showed Beverley handing over a package to Stock Hammond. 'I met Stock Hammond, that's true, but I wasn't dealing. I was giving him money there, yes, but that's because I was being blackmailed. I wasn't receiving any hand-outs and I certainly wasn't getting involved with the case.'

'Obviously Donald Chadwick thought you were – maybe he had been told,' Frank suggested.

'Yes, set up. That's what I said. He never called me after the case. I resented that, I knew he must have either seen me or been manipulated.' Beverley looked flustered, the memories of a difficult time haunting her. Her bright red lipstick stood out over perfectly shaped lips. Something flashed in his mind: Dali's Mae West, she had Mae West's lips.

'Have you seen Stock Hammond or any of the family since they came out?' he asked, wondering how far he could ask her to help in uncovering the truth about Jason's death.

'No I haven't. Stock is still in jail I believe. I heard that his brothers Paul and Nathan were released a few years ago but that's all I know.' Beverley looked up at Frank. 'Why are you here, Mr Duffy? I am pretty sure you didn't come all this way to simply try and destroy my name after all these years.'

'I needed to talk with you. I need your help,' Frank confessed. 'Jason Chadwick died a few months ago, suicide apparently.'

'I'm sorry to hear that,' Beverley responded. 'You are certainly the bearer of bad news today,' she added. 'You think he was murdered?'

'I'm certain of it,' Frank replied. 'Jason prophesised his death and left me a letter of instruction in his will should anything happen to him.' He looked across the wide table at Beverley Johnson. The sunshine behind her had moved slightly and reflection from her fingers, heavy with gold rings, made him squint as he spoke. 'He left me that photograph, asked me to contact you and ask for your help. The letter told me that you were set up and that his father moved to protect you.'

She was obviously shocked. 'I don't know how I can help. It's been so long.' She offered him a coffee and continued talking while pouring Columbia's finest. 'Stock Hammond was a bully. The family placed themselves in prominent positions in society and managed to drain five-million dollars a year from the casinos – right from under the casino owners' noses. Donald was on to them and they knew it, but they had top lawyers in their pockets. Stock's brother, Paul, was a lawyer. They manipulated people to make it look as if Donald's evidence was not credible. They tried to turn the tables on me, too. That meeting in the photo was stage-managed. I thought it was weird at the time to have an exchange in public, it was sure to be picked up. I don't know what they were saying to Donald about me but it sure wasn't good.'

'Can I ask?' Frank, lowered his voice a little, unsure how much Beverley would open up, if at all. 'Why were they blackmailing you?' His eyes didn't leave her face.

'They wanted me to intervene in the case, get on their payroll as such, maybe discredit Donald. I didn't take the bait and they made it clear they would get to my family.

They knew they couldn't buy me or get me to stop Donald so instead they wanted money. It was peanuts. I knew what they wanted. They wanted political power.' She took a breath and looked at the photograph again; it was the first time she had really studied it. 'I guess this photo must have been sent to Donald with some story about me being directly involved with them. Maybe, instead of investigating me, he sold the company and moved away, leaving the facts as evidence. He wasn't called as a witness. I heard that he'd moved to England. Stock and nine others, including his brothers were convicted, primarily on evidence that Donald's team collected.'

Frank listened, trying to piece together a puzzle which seemed to have no sides. Was he to investigate this himself? If the Hammonds had something to do with Jason's death, was that why Amy was in danger? He'd assumed she was being hunted because of Jason's money. This new information had more to do with what happened to Jason and his parents.

When it became obvious Beverley had little more to add, he thanked her and she escorted him to the lobby. She reiterated her sadness about what had happened to Donald and confessed her relief, after all these years, that he had not simply abandoned their friendship.

'For what it's worth,' Frank said as he shook her hand, 'your Vegas is a wonderful city.'

Beverley Johnson smiled and nodded as she watched him leave the building. It was *her* Vegas; she turned back to her office allowing a brief moment of pride to balance her sadness.

Chapter 13

It hadn't rained for weeks so the pounding of raindrops on the window, driven by the southerly gale, was a welcome relief. Amy awoke. She was jittery at first until she recognised the harmless sounds outside.

Her mouth was dry and she needed a drink, so she crept quietly downstairs trying not to wake her parents. A brief glimpse at the hall clock informed her that it was ten past four.

The wind was howling through the trees. Amy peered outside. Rain and wind lashed against the glass with increasing ferocity. Amy wondered if there was still the police surveillance outside; she felt sorry for the officers if there was – and a little guilty. She decided that she would phone Scotland Yard in the morning and thank them.

Her mind wandered to Emmanuelle. She would love to get away to Boston. Amy had never been to America but she had always wanted to go. Jason had once promised to take her to Las Vegas. He painted lavish pictures of magnificent structures and themed hotels that rivalled cities. Morally, the place was so ugly that it was beautiful – but he always claimed that if you could ignore the gambling, the place was a genuine education. Not that she expected the same of Boston. She knew it was a playground for the greatest young minds in the world. It housed universities that every parent desired for their children.

Emmanuelle was right at the top of the brain-chain. She ran the Boston University Department of History; Jason had always been fascinated by her knowledge; there didn't seem to be anything that she didn't know. Jason's teenage journals documented Emmanuelle's lust for facts. He used to prepare weekly quizzes for her, researching them at the central library in Las Vegas. From the little that she knew of Emmanuelle, Amy thought Emmanuelle sounded fascinating – and a genuinely nice person too.

Amy returned to bed, listening to the rain and retracing the past few days in her head, attempting to find a path to guide her future. A wave of self-pity overwhelmed her and she cried herself back to sleep.

* * *

Thomas bolted upright from a deep sleep. A second bang confirmed his initial fear – something was wrong. The wind outside rattled the gutter but he was used to that. No, the noise came from downstairs.

He turned on the light and moved to the door. On the landing, he looked over the banister and saw that the kitchen light was on. Somebody was inside the house. He returned to the bedroom and threw on a pair of jeans and a black fleece, then slowly crept down the stairs, his heart beating hard. He was used to being in potentially volatile situations at work but he felt vulnerable in his own home, especially right now, with the way this case was developing.

Another bang! Thomas froze, then called out. There was no response. He ran down the remaining few stairs and turned towards the kitchen. He slowed his approach but the noise that reverberated through the room the second he walked in paralysed him with fear. He stopped dead in his tracks.

It took him a few seconds to realise that there was nobody there. The back door, open in the wind, was swaying and banging on the corner unit. He ran to the door and the rain hit him like a cold shower. There didn't seem to be anybody outside.

Thomas moved into the living room and quickly scanned the room but there was no sign of any disturbance. He returned to the kitchen, heart still thumping, acutely aware of every noise and movement. Somebody's been in here, he thought. The kitchen door lock had been tampered with.

The only visible footprints on the kitchen linoleum appeared to be his own. Maybe whoever it was had been disturbed. Maybe the wind had pushed the door open with such a force that the intruder ran.

He tried closing the kitchen door but it wouldn't shut properly; the wind, plus the damage to the lock had caused a shifting in the mechanism. For now, he wedged a broom underneath the handle to stop it from flying open again.

Thomas looked around, trying to make sense of what had happened. Was this connected to the Jason Chadwick case or just an opportunistic attempt at a break in? He put the kettle on and considered his next move. The remnants of the evening's investigations were all over the living room: paper strewn all over the floor, scribbles and guesses for the clues, his notes from Amy's conversation, the printout that Lucy had put together detailing what they knew about Jason. He didn't want to justify any of it to his colleagues. Maybe he should keep this to himself.

He made a coffee and went to sit in the living room. As he left the kitchen he felt a blast of fresh air – the front door was now open.

Thomas hurried down the corridor. There wasn't any damage to the door: it had been opened from the inside.

'Christ!' he said out loud. His panic levels rose again. Switching on all the lights, he checked every room and every cupboard until he was convinced that there was nobody inside the house. And it didn't look as if anything was missing.

Damn! he thought, I really *must* report this now.

He called Lucy first. It was only five-thirty but she was

awake, unable to sleep because of the wind. She was shaken to hear what had happened but agreed that he must report it to Moore. He might suggest getting forensics down to check the place. The intruder had put the kitchen light on; maybe he left a fingerprint.

They agreed not to tell anybody about medolema.com for now, so after his call Thomas collected all the evidence from the floor and filed it away in his cabinet drawer before calling the station. Somebody arranged to come down from Belgravia station.

To Thomas's surprise, when the knock on the door came an hour later, it was DCI Jim Alderman from New Scotland Yard. He arrived with two uniforms. Thomas had met Alderman a number of times over the past few years. He was a high-profile detective; he wouldn't be here to investigate a break-in, so he had to be looking for information.

DCI Alderman was tall, grey haired and softly spoken but his stare was so intense that he was intimidating. His words were sharp and he was deeply focussed. Thomas nervously explained exactly what had happened.

'I didn't catch a glimpse of the intruder, but he must have been experienced to get inside the house and remain unseen the way he did. I think he was unlucky – the wind woke me otherwise he could have gone through the place I can't believe that this was simply an opportunist break-in. Maybe he was looking for something in particular.' He paused for a moment then asked, 'Do you think it might be related to the Jason Chadwick case?'

'We can't rule it out,' Alderman responded. 'I was hoping you might be able to tell me. What might somebody be looking for?'

'Maybe the same thing they were looking for with Amy. My feeling is that this is all about Jason's money. Amy had a theory it might have been connected to the ring that Jason gave her,' Thomas added, looking for a reaction.

'Okay, I'll tell you where our investigations have led us so far, then you can see if you can fill in any missing pieces from what you know,' DCI Alderman suggested, without glancing away from Thomas.

Maybe it was just the guilt but Thomas felt uneasy – trapped, even.

'We've been in touch with various US police departments and the FBI is involved now. They followed up that bank account in the US that was cited in Jason's will; they know about his money and that it's secure. There's no sign of any foul play or laundering. They've interviewed Jason's ex-wife and she has no knowledge of anything that might shed light on Jason's death. The FBI checked her financial activity and there are no irregularities. His eldest son, Brandon, hates his father and has a serious gambling problem. In fact he has so many problems that he's the focus of the FBI's current line of investigation.'

'Is he still in England?'

'No. But Brandon has been in England a number of times since his father's death. He stayed for a week after his father's funeral, came back to go through personal effects last month, then returned here to clear out the flat this week and returned to Boston yesterday. Boston Police are following his every move at the moment.'

'Was there anything suspicious about Jason's death?' Thomas asked, wondering how much of his own information he could share with the Scotland Yard man.

'Nothing at all. Light bruising on the top of his index finger was documented in the autopsy report but that could have been caused by the recoil of the gun. That's the only slightly doubtful evidence and it's so slim, the Chief Super won't allow the manpower to investigate.'

'How far have you managed to get with melodema.com?' Thomas asked. He needed to assess whether he should mention his own investigation. Secretly, he hoped that they had made little progress.

'Well, I was going to ask you the same thing,' Alderman replied. 'We've tried to access the ftp index, the online folder that houses the site, but each folder is password protected, as is the opening html page on the website. What we did find out is that *melodema* is a Latin word used in scriptures to mean a psalm. In Rome, on the base of one of the Vatican City's southern pillars, there is the *Melodema Stone*. Legend has it that it was taken from inside the Sistine Chapel and that if you touch the stone you can hear the heavenly choirs in your head. It's also been used as a healing stone. A small carving on the stone is a slanting semi-quaver with a drop bar, making it shaped like the letter M. It looks like Jason both adapted and adopted the symbol for himself and had it embossed onto his ring – Amy's ring.'

'That explains a lot then,' Thomas said. He considered how much he could tell the DCI. 'I tried to look at the site a number of times but there is just the password box.' He paused to see the Alderman's reaction. Selfishness, possibly fuelled by his love for Lucy, stopped him going any further. He figured that if he told Alderman then he would tell Amy and, as a result, Amy would not be able to be used for information. *Used*, he thought, *I* am using Amy.

'I do have a theory,' he continued. 'I think it's pretty obvious that Jason has set up some sort of treasure hunt for his money. What if the ring is part of a clue and Jason's killers, or even his family, are prepared to go to any lengths to try and find the fortune?'

'We touched on this back at the Yard.' Alderman's stare fixed on Thomas like a missile locking on to its target. And then it hit. 'We've been able to monitor hits on the site and there has been recent activity. Most of it has been through proxies which are impossible to trace, so it would make sense that it's connected. Another IP led to this address.'

Thomas felt sick. He had to think fast and choose his words carefully. IP addresses could identify the location of internet access and information about the service provider, even devices used to access sites. Criminals used proxy addresses that provided fake randomly generated IPs that were untraceable.

'Yes, I was checking it out as we were preparing our files

for you,' Thomas said carefully. 'I couldn't get beyond the password but I'm still convinced that this is what Jason has done.'

'If that's the case, the problem now is this,' Alderman said, sitting back slightly. 'If your break-in this morning is connected to Jason Chadwick – what has it got to do with you?'

Thomas hoped that Alderman was buying his story. He couldn't say anything else now; he would be in trouble if this ended up as evidence that he was withholding. The break-in seemed too organised to be opportunist. Maybe somebody else had also tracked his IP activity.

'I'm honestly not sure,' Thomas replied. Alderman's gaze didn't leave him for a second. 'Unless somebody also tracked down my IP and thinks I know more than I do.'

Alderman sat up a little straighter and surprised Thomas with a change of direction. 'Amy has been invited to stay in Boston by Emmanuelle Sexton, an old friend of Jason. She's a lecturer at Boston University. Boston Police Department are checking her out but it seems a genuine offer. I read the email correspondence between the two of them,' Alderman added as he rose to leave. 'It might be a good idea, while we continue our investigations here. It depends whether Boston PD feel they need to keep surveillance open – and if we feel she needs a chaperone. In the meantime, we'll see what we can find here. You'd better sort out new locks.'

'I'll get that organised now,' Thomas said. 'If I have any more information or theories over Jason's case, shall I come directly to you?'

'Yes. I'm coordinating the investigation. Here's my direct number.'

'If you need a chaperone, I'd be more than happy to escort her,' Thomas added.

'We'll see.' DCI Alderman passed Thomas his card as he left.

Thomas felt nauseous. His nerves were shattered. He didn't know if he was in trouble, or if he'd done enough to deflect attention away from himself. They were certainly on to him.

He was in too deep now. What had he done?

Chapter 14

Frank Duffy took a taxi back to the MGM Grand after his meeting with Beverley Johnson. He sat in his hotel room, looking out of the window trying to think what to do next. He looked back through Jason's instructions, which had been left to him inside the orange folder that he'd recovered from Jason's flat. When he'd last spoken to him, Jason was questioning his parents' accident and was concerned that whoever killed his parents might have wanted him dead too, especially since Brandon and David had come back onto the scene. He had been doing his own investigations.

Frank knew that Jason had sensed trouble after he thought he recognised the name of a man that Brandon owed money to. Jason suspected that the people Brandon had been hanging around with were connected to a crime organisation that Donald Chadwick had broken up in Las Vegas. Jason certainly didn't want his estate to be left to his sons so he'd talked to Frank about his idea of leaving the bulk of his legacy in a treasure hunt, and asked questions about how to set it up legally.

Jason had been so pleased at first when his sons made an effort to track him down. At that point he would have probably done anything to help them. However, after they'd stayed with him in Cornwall for Christmas, the only time they contacted him was when they wanted money. David was going to college and seemed to be making something of his life, even though he seemed rather distant and difficult to bond with, but Brandon was a different story. Initially he'd asked for small amounts of money, the odd hundred dollars for clothes. But then his demands had increased. He told Jason that he'd taken a trip to Atlantic City with a friend and got carried away on a personal side-bet. He owed fifty thousand dollars to a guy who was threatening to kill him. Jason bailed him out and Brandon promised to stop gambling and come over to the UK where Jason would teach him about computer technology. Brandon never came – and never gave up the gambling, either.

One day Jason had received a call from a man named Anthony Strong, claiming that Brandon owed him half a million dollars and that he would claim it from him if his son didn't pay up within ten days.

Jason phoned Brandon. The young man seemed blasé about the whole thing, as if he expected Jason to pay up. When Jason refused, Brandon became aggressive. Jason phoned Penny but she couldn't help; since Brandon got in with these heavies from the estate brokers Coopers-Herald, he'd gone off the rails and she hadn't spoken to him in nearly a year.

Jason was worried and confused. He started his own investigation online to see how genuine the threat was. He cross-referenced Anthony Strong with Coopers-Herald and found that Paul Stringham, who managed the company, had a brother called Anthony in Atlantic City. Anthony Stringham also had a ten percent share in the company. Jason had a theory that Anthony Strong was actually Anthony Stringham and that Brandon's friends at Coopers-Herald were using him. He phoned Brandon, who totally rejected Jason's claim. He'd known Paul Stringham for nearly two years – Paul had taken Brandon under his wing – like a *real* father. It was Paul who had initially helped Brandon track down his father.

Jason looked further into Paul Stringham and Anthony Strong and that's when he discovered that Stock Hammond's brothers Paul, Anthony and probably Nathan, too, had assumed their mother's maiden name – Stringham. Again Jason rang Brandon, even suggested that he might be in danger but Brandon refused to believe it. Brandon had somehow paid the half a million dollar debt to Anthony Strong and now he wanted nothing more to do with his father.

Frank read Jason's letter again:

My Dear Frank,

There is £25,000 in my safe, the combination is 73819881 – make yourself invisible and let the police investigate my death. If Amy Pearce or Emmanuelle Sexton is in danger because I mentioned them in my will, get them out the way for a while. Make sure they have enough money to survive at least while you begin my investigations.

My father was a good friend of the Mayor in Las Vegas, Beverley Johnson – something bad happened, my father sold the company and moved to protect her name. I know now that she was set up – she needs to know this. If you or any of my friends have been approached, then the chances are you are being watched and may be in danger.

As you know, my wealth is to be claimed via clues I have set up online. It's supposed to be a fun and exciting hunt to leave a personal legacy to anybody who takes the time to understand the real me. If you get as far as this letter, you'll understand that something has gone wrong. I hope that my legacy has not left a trail of destruction.

I think the same people responsible for my parents' death have now connected with my sons. These people placed themselves in responsible positions in society – lawyers, police workers, councillors. You can't trust anybody; they are capable of assuming new identities and could probably take up residence in any country.

Frank, I trust you. You are one of the most intelligent

people I know. Go to Las Vegas, find Beverley Johnson and you'll hopefully be able to figure out what to do next. Be careful when discussing any of my business with my sons. I have a strong feeling they are being manipulated into believing that they will be heirs to my estate.

Good luck and thank you.
JASON CHADWICK.

Jason had confided to Frank that he believed his parents were killed in revenge for breaking up a multi-million dollar fraud operation run by the Hammond family in Las Vegas. He believed that the family, many of whom had already served time for their part in the fraud, were manipulating Brandon and that they were using him to get to Jason's money.

At the time, though, Frank was unaware of these names and still unsure what to do next. Hopefully, he'd left enough clues to let his family and the police know where he was. He hoped that they'd have enough presence of mind to monitor his movements rather than simply arrest him. He'd deliberately left the empty orange folder in a place where it would stand out. Right now, he felt very much alone.

Chapter 15

Amy's mother had left her to sleep and she eventually woke at ten. The rain had cleared but there was still a strong wind. She looked out of her window and, to her relief, the police vehicle was still there.

Her mother greeted her as she walked wearily into the kitchen. 'Sit down, darling. I'll make you some breakfast.'

'Thanks, Mum,' Amy replied, kissing her mother's neck as she passed by her. 'I couldn't sleep last night, I felt so guilty. Those poor officers sitting out in the rain. I wonder how long they're going to be camped there? I'll phone the police today and find out how they are getting on.'

Amy sat at the table, brushing her hair with her fingers as she waited for breakfast. The phone rang and she answered it, not expecting the voice at the other end to ask for her. It was DCI Paul Dawson from Scotland Yard, giving the green light for to Amy to stay with Emmanuelle in Boston. She would be accompanied to the plane, greeted at the other side and taken to Emmanuelle's house. The police had made all the arrangements but she would have to leave by midday to catch her flight. They'd cleared it with Emmanuelle.

Excited, Amy ran upstairs to start packing. Then she remembered her passport, which was back at her flat. Her mother took Amy's keys and hurriedly drove over to collect it. The traffic was busy and she was away for over an hour, but she returned just as Amy had finished filling her suitcase.

Amy wrote a quick email to Emmanuelle, letting her know that she couldn't wait to come over and thanking her for the invitation.

At exactly midday a navy-blue Mercedes MPV arrived. The detective constable accompanying her to Gatwick Airport introduced himself as DC Joseph Woods. After loading the car, Amy kissed her mother goodbye. Her father was in court but sent a text message to wish her a safe journey.

As the vehicle left with Amy, the driver flashed a badge and spoke quietly with the police officer on surveillance duty at the Pearces' apartment. DC Woods accompanied Amy to check-in and into the departure lounge. He told her that she would be collected at Logan Airport and taken directly to Emmanuelle's house.

Amy sat in the departure lounge feeling free for the first time in nearly a week. What a week it had been, a week she would rather forget.

***

It was past eleven when Riley finally arrived at the station. News of his break-in had circulated rapidly through the station, together with speculation and the odd joke — apparently he had wet himself when he heard the kitchen door bang against the cupboard. Riley was thick-skinned enough to rise above it. 'Good job you lot do all my dirty washing!' he said as he walked into the office.

Lucy chuckled along with everyone else, but she was concerned. 'Are you OK?' she asked quietly.

'I'm fine,' he said with a grin. 'I'd have been here an hour ago if the locksmith hadn't made such a meal of changing the locks. I made more progress last night,' he added in a whisper. 'I'll tell you about it later.'

Lucy suddenly felt excited. She'd enjoyed last night and marvelled at Riley's enthusiasm over the puzzles. She couldn't wait to hear the update, but for now they had another mess to handle: a youth had been stabbed at the Empire Nightclub – a thousand potential witnesses and no leads. It was going to be one of those days.

***

The seven-hour flight to Boston went without hitch. Amy enjoyed herself – simply being free from the house was a great feeling. She'd brought some of Jason's journals with her, thinking that they might be good for Emmanuelle to read. They could drown their sorrows, toast his memory together and share their own memories of him tonight.

The plane finally halted at the terminal. It seemed to take an eternity for Amy to get through customs, which included digital fingerprinting and a retina scan before she could get to her luggage. She felt claustrophobic at the carousel, waiting for her suitcase; hundreds of agitated passengers were jostling for space, apologising to fellow passengers for obstructing them or landing their cases on their toes.

Eventually a khaki suitcase with luminous pink tape on the handle made its way towards her. Amy smiled – her mum was right. In all that chaos, a piece of pink tape was enough for Amy to instantly recognise her own case. She grabbed it and made her way out to the main terminal building – she was in America at last.

***

Shift was just ending. Riley and Bridges hadn't made much headway with the nightclub stabbing so they left the evening staff to examine the CCTV footage at the entrance to the venue. They visited DCI Moore's office as they were leaving to update him on their progress.

'Garfunkel's?' Thomas asked Lucy as he opened the door of the police station.

'Why not?' she asked with a smile. She was tempted to link arms with him but resisted, tugging at his sleeve instead to lead him across the road.

They ordered their usual – and a bowl of salad to alleviate the guilt. Thomas explained his discovery last night, the next page and the new clues. He also told her about his conversations with DCI Alderman and how they'd uncovered the information about the Melodema Stone in Rome.

'That's interesting. But do you think he knows how far *you've* got?' Lucy asked.

'No, I don't think so. Though we'll need to use a proxy server ourselves if we continue. I think we need to. We should at least see if we can get far enough to make a connection for the case or a decision about the money.'

They sat waiting for their food, trying to make sense of *Under a folly sky*. They thought that they should look into 'melodema' a little more online. That could be the key. The ring symbol was called melodema; could that have any reference to the first clue – the Diana clue?

'What if…' Lucy spoke slowly '…the Folly Sky clue refers to a painted sky, like you'd find in a theatre production, for example. Maybe there's a statue of Artemis inside a theatre.'

'Or amphitheatre?' said Thomas, adrenalin levels beginning to rise again.

They finished their food quickly, both eager to get started on another evening of investigation. When they arrived at Thomas's house, it was dusty from the locksmith's drilling and the forensic examinations. Thomas vowed to clean up tomorrow; it was the weekend after all, and he could afford the luxury of a lie-in.

Lucy claimed the computer first. Thomas smiled and went to pour the drinks. She was willing to help him finish the rest of the bourbon tonight. He took out his notes from the drawer.

There was little mention of melodema or even the

Melodema Stone in the search engines. It was as if it were a forbidden secret. Thomas wondered how DCI Alderman had found his information. They did find several vague references to the Latin meaning 'Psalm', but very little else. A cross-reference of *melodema* and *Diana* produced no results at all but with melodema there was at least another Roman connection. They felt certain that they were on the right lines.

Lucy cross-referenced 'folly sky theatre' and 'false sky theatre' and found only the Akron Civic Centre in Ohio; there wasn't any melodema reference or any mention of Diana or Artemis. She then typed *Artemis False Sky* into the search box. There were many references to her moon-goddess status but little to go on.

Thomas wondered about the wisdom of talking to Amy again but resisted. Something told him to hold back; he was still hoping that DCI Alderman would ask him to chaperone her to Boston.

A frustrating hour passed by. There was much reading, many theories, but no progress. Lucy was showing signs of exasperation and her head was aching. When Thomas suggested some fresh air, she was grateful for the idea.

They walked up Belgrave Road, away from the river, resisting the temptation to take their investigation into the numerous pubs that they passed. The evening was pleasant, the winds had now receded to a gentle breeze. Thomas always loved dusk; there was something magical about the street lights as they warmed up to their familiar orange.

Conversation never strayed from the clue. *A folly sky.* They felt that they were so close but missing something obvious. How could they *understand* Jason? What did they know about him? Maybe Diana was a person after all.

They reached Victoria Place and simultaneously remembered the v1ct0r14 clue. Victoria … Diana: girls' names. Maybe each clue was related to a girl's name. Maybe they were all former girlfriends.

'Do we know anything about Jason's former partners,

before he met his wife?' Thomas asked 'Amy didn't recall anybody by that name but what about in his childhood, back in Las Vegas?'

'I don't remember noticing it. I doubt Amy would have known much about his old girlfriends. It's worth investigating, but how? All of his immediate family are dead.'

They continued walking and thinking. Lucy looked distant. She had not said much for a few minutes so Thomas asked what was on her mind.

'I was wondering about Las Vegas. I seem to remember, when I was cross-referencing *Diana* with *folly sky*, that there were a few references to Las Vegas. Maybe I've missed something. I think I'd forgotten about Jason's connection with the place.'

They decided to return to Thomas's house down Vauxhall Bridge Road. As they crossed the road, a dark-blue BMW slowed. Thomas looked up as the car turned right and sped away.

'That's strange,' he said. 'I think that car was parked outside your block last night.'

'Do you think we're being followed?' Lucy asked, concerned.

'I'm not sure but I think I should mention it to Alderman. I wonder if it has anything to do with my break-in this morning.' Thomas tried to remember what he'd seen of the registration number as it drove away.

Back at Thomas's house, Lucy immediately went to the computer. She cross-referenced 'folly sky' and Las Vegas. The first few pages offered little. She was just about to try something new when she noticed a reference to Artemis.

'Hold on, I might have something.'

Thomas joined her, watching her open a piece about travelling to Las Vegas. Lucy was quiet, trying to take in information.

'Caesar's Palace in Las Vegas. It says here that their forum shops have a false sky that lights up a twenty-four-hour cycle every hour. Looking at this picture, there are many Roman statues – I can't find reference to Diana or Artemis though.' Lucy continued reading, clicking the odd link and referring back to the page. Eventually she found a photograph of a statue that had been annotated: *This statue is Artemis, known as Diana by the Romans – the Moon Goddess.*

'Oh my God!' They both said simultaneously, reading the caption. The photograph of Artemis had an eagle on her hand.

'That makes sense. Try it!' Thomas ordered. She was already typing the letters e-a-g-l-e into the password box.

'Bingo!' a new page opened. He hugged her and she smiled.

Chapter 16

Thomas took in a lot of information within a second of the new page opening. The page was called melodema. com/tellmewhy.html. It had an olive green background with a single image on it: a photograph of a bridge in a valley. It looked more like a viaduct, set among lush greenery. There was a river flowing underneath the bridge and the picture looked as if it had been taken from the hillside. He right-clicked the image with his mouse to look at its file name – it was simply called *justapicture.jpg*.

They wrote down the details and Lucy updated her notes on the investigation. She printed out the picture twice and they moved to the sofa, sipping bourbon and wondering what to do next.

'It's my turn to uncover this one,' she joked. 'You're already two ahead of me.'

'So Diana is not a real person. We're already beginning to understand our professor.' Thomas couldn't recall feeling this excited in years. 'We overlooked Jason's use of the word, *nest*.'

'True. I wondered if it was metaphorical for *nest-egg*?'

When Thomas's mobile phone rang, they both jumped. He was going to ignore it but he'd given his number to Amy. He looked at the front display and it just said *work,* but he answered it anyway.

It was DCI Moore. Something was wrong.

'We think Amy Pearce is in trouble,' DCI Moore stated. 'I've just had a call from Jim Alderman at Scotland Yard. Amy has flown to Boston, having been given the nod from the Yard to visit her friend – only the Yard never gave the nod.'

'O...K. Well that doesn't make sense,' Riley said, wondering where this might lead. He felt disheartened. He was hoping to have built on last night's conversation to enrol her help again.

'Apparently, somebody posing as an inspector from Scotland Yard arranged her flight and escorted her to the airport. They even fooled the surveillance team into believing that her trip had been officially authorised. It was only when Jim Alderman phoned Amy to update her on their progress that they realised she'd gone.'

'Have you caught up with her?' Thomas asked.

'The plane we believe she travelled on landed in Boston fifty minutes ago. Boston PD will hopefully intercept her but I'm waiting for news.' DCI Moore replied. 'According to Mrs Pearce, you spoke with Amy for a good hour last night. Is there anything that she said in that conversation that they need to know?'

Thomas shuddered. He had not told DCI Moore about the conversation last night because it was hard to justify it professionally. He knew he was in trouble.

'Yes, I spoke to her last night. It was more of a personal call but I was chewing around an idea and wanted to know if she had any knowledge of this melodema.com web page—'

'That's not what I asked you to do,' DCI Moore interrupted indignantly. 'You know protocol. We'll deal with that as a separate incident. It's details I need right now.'

'I know. I apologise,' Thomas responded. 'Amy mentioned that a friend of Jason's had invited her to stay in Boston. She said she felt like a prisoner, she was quite low.' Thomas paused, trying to recall details. 'She also said that Scotland Yard was disorganised. They'd sent two sets of detectives round, and she ended up going through the whole story twice. Both times they expressed interest in the ring and she told me that the second time she threw the ring at the inspector – who now has it. To be honest, I didn't think a lot about it – and now I'm kicking myself.'

Another call came through to DCI Moore, so he told Thomas that he'd ring back shortly. Thomas was in the middle of explaining their chief's phone conversation to Lucy when the phone rang again.

'Boston PD missed her,' Moore said. 'She could be anywhere. They've put an APB out for her in Boston. Alderman has her ring, so it looks like the first people to visit her were the bogus detectives.'

'That's bad news,' Thomas said quietly. 'That means that they were on to her on Wednesday. But how the hell would they know?'

'That's not all. Boston PD has confirmed that Emmanuelle Sexton is also missing. She didn't turn up to give a lecture today.'

Chapter 17

Frank Duffy took the elevator down again and headed for the business centre. The business room at the MGM Grand was much smaller than he expected: an L-Shaped room with enquiry desk and a booth for collecting faxes and messages. There were five computer terminals and barely enough space to walk behind them. The computer at the far end was free. Frank swiped his credit card and logged on to the internet.

There were several resources in the UK that could help track down people – the electoral roll, marriages, births and deaths registers, and even Ebay – but he wasn't sure how it worked in the US. A simple search for Paul Hammond or Nathan Hammond gave pages of references to strangers across the world. He needed something more specific.

There were only sixteen Hammonds listed in the Las Vegas area – but no Paul or Nathan. Frank eventually found a database claiming to have personal and financial records via companies such as the United States Securities and Exchange Commission. He had to pay for information but details were accessible to banks and lawyers. He paid the sixty-dollar fee for an hour's unlimited access, using Redearth Solicitors registration as his validation, knowing too that the office back home would be able to monitor his actions. Then he began looking into the Hammond family.

Apparently Nathan Hammond had, at one time, a ten

percent share in Coopers-Herald Brokers in Boston. Frank remembered Jason telling him that he believed a brokerage firm in Boston was manipulating Brandon. He checked the records for Coopers-Herald and there were no Hammonds listed. The company was part-owned by Paul Stringham and Darren Cooper; the other major shareholders were Anthony and Nathan Stringham. He wondered whether it was a coincidence that three brothers would share the same name in a company with a tenuous, albeit registered, link to the Hammond family of Las Vegas.

Frank looked into the information held on the database about the Stringham family, but it was extremely limited. Only the past three years had been documented. Anthony Stringham was the only person registered with a full address and that was in Atlantic City.

Frank wondered what his next move should be. There was no way that he could definitely know that this was the Hammond family, but he had a gut feeling that it was. He decided to fly to Boston and booked the next flight out, which was tomorrow at six in the morning.

***

By the end of the phone conversation with DCI Moore, Thomas was numb. Lucy placed her hand on his knee, sensing that the news was bad. He explained that both Amy and Emmanuelle were now missing and that it was a priority case both in the UK and the US. The Commissioner had already demanded a full investigation and Jim Alderman's neck was likely to be first on the block.

Thomas could foresee problems for himself too; he should never have called Amy. He was scared. Not only was the chief inspector's job slipping away from him, he would now have a fight to keep his own job. Arnold Pearce was a high-profile barrister; he was likely to be the one raising the axe highest. God forbid anything happened to Amy. He couldn't begin to imagine the fallout that might lead to.

'We're in deep trouble, Lucy. We have to solve this quickly.' Thomas turned to the computer.

'Thomas!' she said fiercely. 'Don't even think of it! It's over. Hand this information to Alderman!'

Thomas didn't even look up; he ignored her and continued looking for clues on Photoshop.

'Thomas?' she pulled him towards her. The revolving office chair turned her way but he didn't want to look at her. She pulled his arm towards her and placed his hands in hers.

'Thomas, let it go.' She spoke softly.

'I'm doing this to help find Amy,' he responded. 'I could lose my job over this if the force realises exactly how far we've come. In fact we could both lose our jobs, maybe even face jail. We can't tell Alderman, or Moore, or anyone – we can't, Lucy.' He placed his lips gently on her forehead. 'I feel helpless. The best we can do right now is to try to get somewhere and hope that somewhere along the way we can help Amy. Find out if there's a reason why somebody would want her. For now, there's nothing in the clues that links Amy in any way to the money.'

Lucy looked dejected. Thomas felt guilty but he knew he was right. They were in this together now. They couldn't have foreseen the mistakes at Scotland Yard. If they said nothing for now, they wouldn't technically be withholding evidence as nothing linked the treasure hunt with Amy. All they could do was work with Alderman and Boston PD to try and find Amy.

Lucy went to make coffee while Thomas continued investigating the image. This time, he drew a blank; there was nothing he could find using his Photoshop tricks. Maybe it was 'just a picture'. Maybe the clue was in the page title: *Tell me why*. Tell me why? Why what? What was the picture of? What was its significance? Where was the next page to be found? There was no password box this time.

Lucy joined Thomas with the coffee. He was still staring at the photograph in Photoshop, trying different effect tools and adjustment features to see his he could find anything hidden within it. He even made a half-hearted attempt to try melodema.com/page3.html but the page failed. He knew that Jason wouldn't have made it that simple.

'Just a thought,' Lucy said, 'Maybe we just have to identify the picture. Maybe it's Italian, or Greek. Maybe he even took the picture himself?'

'It's worth checking an image browser,' Thomas said. He placed 'justapicture' into the search engine. Only nine results showed, including melodema.com/tellmewhy/justapicture.jpg.

'No way!' Thomas said as he clicked on the image. 'You telling me they can bypass passwords?'

The browser would not let him, in – he had a 'forbidden' message – *you are not authorised to view this page*. Thomas was relieved. He couldn't see how Jason would have let that one slip through. He returned to the web page and slowly circled the image with his mouse, to see if there was a hidden link, something that would turn the arrow icon on the screen to a hand. He paid meticulous attention to the page, as a forensic investigator would comb a crime scene. There was nothing there.

Lucy was watching over his shoulder.

'I wonder if you can find out *when* it was taken,' he mumbled to himself.

'There is a way. It depends on whether the picture comes directly from a digital camera or if it's a scan,' Lucy said. 'I don't know if you can view in Photoshop but I know some online software automatically stores the information. I've seen it from time to time.'

Thomas looked up 'embedding photographic information' online and read that digital cameras automatically store 'metadata' such as camera details, resolution, shutter speed, as well as date and time of photograph. He researched for ways to read this data. Eventually he found a forum where somebody had asked the same question. The inquirer was told that this information automatically shows up when you right-click the image and look at the 'properties' and scroll down the details.

Thomas tried and it worked. The photograph had been taken on April 10th 2005 at 18.10, using a Minolta camera 10/2500-shutter speed. The program fell short of giving GPS coordinates, which would have helped.

'OK, great. Now I suppose we need to find out where he was on 10th April 2005,' Thomas said.

Something about the date seemed familiar. 'Can you remember the date that Jason made his will?' Lucy asked.

'May, I think May the 5th or thereabouts, same day as his birthday if I recall. So this picture was taken three weeks beforehand.' Thomas had a sudden thought, 'What happened to all Jason's work stuff? We know Brandon cleared out his flat and house in Cornwall. What about the office?'

Lucy didn't know. The information wasn't documented in the file she prepared for Scotland Yard. Amy would know … but she was missing. Thomas shuddered. This was a link to Amy; if she had the information then there was a motive. He saw Lucy's eyes fill, and he pulled her head towards him. He knew what she was thinking. They were in deep trouble.

'Look, we have the address. Jason's office was in Chancery Lane. Let's go there tomorrow morning, first thing, see if we can get inside, or at least get some information. I know it's Saturday, we may draw a blank, but it's worth a shot.'

Lucy's tears left a small damp patch on his shirt. She apologised and he laughed it off. 'Of course, this photo may have no relevance at all. In fact I have a strong hunch that it doesn't. The *tellmewhy* page name probably has more significance.'

'Unless…' Lucy interrupted. 'Unless he means "tell me why he has put a photo as the next clue". It could have been *any* photo.'

They both stared blankly at the photograph.

'Just a picture… Not necessarily a photo? Maybe we need to look for a picture?' Lucy suggested. 'Maybe that means a picture on his wall, something he kept?'

'Hylas and the Nymphs!' Thomas shouted, recalling his conversation on the phone with Amy. 'She said that Jason had wooed Penny by showing her his prints of Hylas and the Nymphs.'

Lucy took over the computer and searched for images of the famous Waterhouse painting. They couldn't grasp the significance of Jason's message *Tell me why* but it *felt* as if they were on the right lines, so researched the origins of the myths. Thomas was convinced that they would find another anomaly, as they had with Artemis and Diana.

'Maybe,' Thomas suggested, 'we're looking at this upside down. Going back to the ambiguity of the last clue, maybe he means *tell me why* Artemis had an eagle on her hand, while all famous statues and painting of Artemis had her with a stag or hunting dogs.'

'That would make sense, especially as the first part of the clue also seemed ambiguous: Sallust was actually quoting Appius Claudius: *every man is an architect of his own fortune.*'

Thomas allowed himself a guilty smile. Considering the trouble they were in, not to mention the trouble Amy and Emmanuelle were in, the thrill of the chase was still enough to drive away their consciences.

Thomas was in awe of Jason. In coming to understand the person he was, he found himself aspiring to be him too – maybe in a way that seemed obsessive. He had put his job on the line for him now. There were times, over the years, when Thomas had been dealing with a particularly intelligent criminal that he had felt a psychological bond. Often he would lie awake at night wondering what it would be like on the 'other side'. Right now, he felt that he had crossed that line.

So it was hardly surprising that he crossed another line.

He asked Lucy to stay the night and, to his surprise, she agreed without hesitation.

Chapter 18

Amy scanned the cardboard signs, handmade by strangers waiting for passengers from her flight from London, but she couldn't find her name. She was tired but excited. Following the slow-moving queue at passport control had given her a new surge of energy; she was completely unaware of the chaos in London or the fact that she was in real danger.

As she left the terminal building, she heard a voice call her name. She looked to her left and was greeted by a man wearing a black suit with a sky-blue shirt and burgundy tie.

'How was your journey?' he asked with a smile, reaching to take her luggage. 'My car is round here.'

Amy smiled as she recognised the man. He had accompanied DCI Dawson only yesterday. She shook his hand and apologised that she couldn't remember his name.

'Agent Stringham,' he replied, 'FBI.'

It was the first time she had heard him speak – he had an American accent. *FBI? Wow,* she thought.

***

News of Amy's disappearance circulated fast. Liaison was trying to keep the story away from the press but the pressure was building. DCI Moore was in his office, off the clock, to help DCI Alderman's team investigate Amy's disappearance. He understood how bad this looked and knew that it could ricochet on Charing Cross's Special Crimes and Operations if Riley's phone conversation was linked in any way to her disappearance. He was furious.

Meanwhile the two detective constables who had let Amy through were being given the 'hairdryer treatment' from DCI Alderman. They explained that the driver had shown a badge and claimed that he was from Belgravia Station. The driver said that he was taking them to the station for an ID on a suspect. The bogus detective had given the constables instructions to remain at the apartment. When they radioed back to the station to give their half-hourly report, they'd said it was 'all clear' because there was no sign of any disturbance.

Neither officer could remember the names of the bogus detectives. They should have written them down to log Amy's movements. That was just one mistake in a catalogue of errors – and DCI Alderman realised how bad it looked.

The officers gave descriptions and photo-fit images were circulated around the metropolitan boroughs to see if anyone recognised the bogus detectives. Meanwhile CCTV footage from cameras en route to the airport, together with Gatwick Airports own surveillance cameras, was monitored by a team of officers brought in for emergency overtime.

Across the Atlantic, Boston PD reported that they had missed Amy. Witnesses identified her and said that she'd travelled alone, looked happy and left the terminal building. Nobody seemed to know what had happened to her after that.

The FBI was updated and immediately sprang into action to assist Boston PD. They'd been monitoring Frank Duffy for the past two days; they were aware that he had a meeting with a senior executive, Beverley Johnson, at Hurrahs in Las Vegas, but had chosen not to approach him. He was obviously doing his own investigations. The FBI considered bringing him in to see if he knew anything about Amy's kidnapping but decided to keep a watch on him for another twenty-four hours.

For the moment, there was nothing but questions: How did two bogus detectives from Scotland Yard worm their way into Amy's parents' house in such a convincing manner? How did they get hold of badges and so easily manage to collect Amy from under the noses of the police's own surveillance team? To Jim Alderman, this reeked of corruption from within the force and – even more worryingly – it was an extremely professional job involving many players. It was a high-class set up; it *had* to be about money. The department was going to be crucified over this.

***

Thomas Riley and Lucy Bridges were standing side by side, looking up as the escalator moved them slowly into the daylight at Holborn. During the week there was a frenzy of activity here. Lofty, red-bricked, glass-panelled buildings housed some of the nation's most important law firms, publishers and investment companies. An old-English pub with a sandstone front stood amongst them, dwarfed by these walls of commerce.

It was still early, not quite nine o'clock, and it seemed colder. The downdraft from the London Underground drew in an icy blast of air as they reached Chancery Lane. Jason's former office was close by. The doors were locked. An intercom system alerted the security guard and he came to meet them.

'I can't let you in here,' he told them.

'I understand,' Lucy said, flashing a smile. 'Have you worked here long?'

'About three years, ma'am,' the guard replied, his eyes fixed on the pretty woman in front of him.

'Did you know Jason Chadwick? I believe he had an office here before he passed away,' she continued.

'I knew him, yes, ma'am. A decent man he was. It was a

big shock to us all when we heard that he'd died.'

'Has his office been cleared out, do you know? Or is it still occupied?' Bridges was in control, Riley simply observed her act. She had a way with people, she would make a very good press officer, he thought.

'As far as I know, ma'am, the office has been let out to a new firm. They're moving in this week.'

'Oh I see.' Lucy looked through the door into the lavish reception area: the building had a marble floor so smooth that it sparkled. 'Do you know what happened to all his office documents?'

'I saw his secretary bringing down boxes at one time, ma'am. I assume she was clearing out his possessions.'

'OK,' Lucy said to the guard. 'I appreciate your help. Thank you.'

Thomas and Lucy walked further up Holborn, neither saying much, both thinking about how they could possibly gain entry to Amy's flat. They passed a Starbucks as it was opening. Thomas motioned to his partner and they immediately made for the door.

'We're in trouble enough,' Thomas started. 'I say we go to work, see if we can convince Moore to let us check out Amy's flat. Let's see if there was anything in Jason's diaries that gives an indication of what he was doing in the days leading up to his death.'

'I don't see we have an option. Are you ready for Moore, though? He's going to be pissed off.'

'Like you say, we don't really have an option. Every minute matters if Amy is in trouble. I can handle Moore,' Thomas lied.

He feared DCI Moore and Moore knew it.

***

Riley arrived at Charing Cross just after eleven. Lucy was to follow shortly – they didn't think it was wise to turn up together and she needed to change her clothes. Riley could claim that he had called her.

DCI Moore was shocked to see him and he could hear the sniggering of his colleagues as he made his way towards Moore's office. He hated this hell-hole as much as he wanted the chief's job.

'You need my help, boss?' Thomas's voice was quiet, an acceptance of his own defeat; he was ready for Moore's wrath. Yet he knew that his presence there – out of hours to volunteer his help – showed that he was professional enough to try and make things right.

The chief inspector motioned to Riley to close the door.

For the next ten minutes, Moore turned into a pit-bull terrier, using his words like bullets, firing reality checks into Thomas Riley's conscience. Thomas stood motionless and didn't say a word.

After a while, Moore's voice was a blur. He wasn't saying anything Thomas didn't know already. His final words were that if the investigation linked Thomas's call in any way to Amy's abduction, then the department would tear him to pieces.

'I was wrong, I have no excuses. But I'm here now. I want to help and I may have a line of investigation.' Riley's voice didn't falter but inside his conscience was shot to pieces. If this is what it was like on *the other side* then how did the criminal cope? He concluded that criminals were simply born without a conscience.

Lucy Bridges arrived in time to hear the end of Moore's wrath from outside the door and she was shaking with sympathy for Riley.

'It's probably worth looking at Jason's work diaries for the weeks and months leading up to his death. Maybe he met up with somebody. I seem to remember Amy telling me that Jason's office documents were in her flat. She was going to sort through them,' Thomas told his boss.

Moore had calmed a little now that he had vented his frustration. 'We'll need a warrant,' he said. 'Unless Arnold

Pearce agrees. Let me talk with him.'

An hour later, Thomas and Lucy were at the Pearces' house. One small consolation was that Thomas felt they were officially back on the case. Moore had cleared it with Alderman at Scotland Yard. Alderman was pleased for any help.

A distraught father opened the door and Thomas was shocked. Arnold Pearce appeared to have aged overnight. He was a giant but his body language and his voice made him seem small.

He gave Amy's key to the inspector and asked them to promise to find Amy.

'We'll do everything we can,' Lucy said.

Arnold Pearce acknowledged her words with a nod before turning away and closing the door. The detectives looked at each other. They simply had to find Amy.

Chapter 19

It was only when Frank Duffy walked out of Logan airport into the Boston sunshine that he remembered he'd not booked a hotel. He asked the taxi driver if there was a Holiday Inn in the Cambridge area.

'Of course,' the driver replied.

Boston felt very different to Las Vegas obviously, but the waterways of the Charles River that surrounded Logan airport were just as fascinating. It was hard to get a sense of direction; there was water everywhere, and they must have crossed at least four bridges.

Thankfully there were vacancies at the hotel. Frank booked three nights; he was unsure why, but felt that he needed a base. He planned out his next movements while he unpacked his holdall.

A copy of the *Boston Herald* lay on the bedside table, compliments of the hotel. Frank made himself a coffee and began to make a plan for the weekend.

***

'Did you sleep well?' Emmanuelle Sexton asked Amy, as she perched on the edge of her bed.

Emmanuelle was wearing a white dressing gown and drinking fruit tea. Her hair was wild and she looked surprisingly relaxed in these unfamiliar surroundings.

'Yes, thank you. I did,' Amy replied. She was already organised, with makeup applied and fully dressed. 'This is a lovely house.'

'I wonder who owns it,' Emmanuelle said.

Agent Stringham knocked on the door of Amy's room then let himself in. 'Girls!' he said loudly with a smile. 'Glad to see you up so early. I trust everything was comfortable for you last night?'

He sat down in front of a long, kidney-shaped table. The huge glass window framed the Atlantic; there was nothing between the house and the ocean but a luscious garden. The place looked like a country house hotel, the sort of hotel that would be used as a health farm in England – or maybe the setting for a Cluedo murder.

The previous day, when Agent Stringham met Amy at the airport, Emmanuelle was waiting in the car. The girls were told to switch off their mobile phones and hand them over to the agent. Stringham didn't pull his punches. 'You're both in danger. I'm taking you to a secure residence, just for now.'

They travelled north from Logan Airport towards Philips Point. There were a lot of police cars heading towards the airport as they set off, but the girls didn't really register them. When they reached the house, they were given a room each and told to make themselves at home.

'Grab an early night. I'll meet with you tomorrow morning,' Agent Stringham said. 'Some of my colleagues will be here by then. 'We'll talk about what's happening then.'

Amy was in bed by nine. She and Emmanuelle had talked for about half an hour; they seemed to have a lot in common besides their affection for Jason. Now, after a good night's sleep, it was time to get some answers.

'So, then, why are we here?' Emmanuelle asked.

'It's for your safety,' Stringham began. 'I'm an officer with the Federal Bureau. Professor Chadwick was an important man. Not just because of what he achieved in developing the

World Wide Web, or even his ongoing work with the tech giants, but also because of *who* he was.'

'You mean who his parents were?' Emmanuelle enquired.

'Yes. His father was a very influential man. Jason believed that his parents were murdered. We were in the middle of following up his claims when Jason died mysteriously, too.'

Amy felt tremendous relief. At last there was somebody who was willing to take control, to investigate her own doubts about her boss's death.

'DCI Dawson at Scotland Yard approached us and asked me to be present when he met with you, to see how genuine the threat to you seemed,' Agent Stringham continued, looking over in Amy's direction. 'When you received another visit from Scotland Yard, we realised that we were dealing with a high-powered criminal network. We think those other guys were impostors. Our feeling is that they wanted the ring that Jason left you.'

'Oh no!' Amy said. 'I threw my ring at DCI Alderman. He took it with him.'

'I see.' Stringham frowned. He was silent for a minute, then said, 'I think you should remain in the house for a few days. You'll be safe here. This place is owned by a senior government official. It's secure and you won't come to any harm. If you need anything, just let us know.'

'I need to be at work on Monday,' Emmanuelle said firmly.

'We'll do our best to get you there. I'll make sure your families know that you're safe and under our protection. We do have some leads but it would help if later today we could meet again. My colleagues and I need to talk to you about Jason. We need to find out more about his life, his contacts, try to piece together what we know.'

The girls agreed though Amy was confused. Why would she be in danger thousands of miles from home? It was frustrating – she was still a prisoner, but on the other side of the world. And anyway, where was the danger coming from?

'If the people following me were really after Jason's ring, they've got what they wanted. Why would I still be in danger?' she asked Agent Stringham.

'You could be right. They may well have what they need. It's possible that the danger is over, but I still think we need twenty-four hours or so to follow up our own investigations, just to be certain. It would help us to talk with you anyway, because you may be able to help us find out exactly what happened to Professor Chadwick and his parents.'

∗∗∗

Thomas Riley and Lucy Bridges had just entered Amy's flat when Riley's mobile phone rang. It was DCI Moore. 'Just had a call from the FBI – guess who turned up in Boston? Frank Duffy. He's booked himself into the Holiday Inn in Cambridge. They're keeping him under surveillance. It's our best hope yet; he obviously knows something. He may be able to lead us to Amy.'

Thomas updated Moore on their progress and spoke of their concerns about Arnold Pearce. 'I think we need to keep Amy's dad up to speed with any information, no matter how trivial, if for no other reason than to stop him from imploding.'

DCI Moore agreed.

Amy's flat was on the first floor of an apartment block that resembled a converted warehouse. Outside the back window, a car park to the rear housed numbered bays for each flat. It had a small kitchen, diner and lounge all in one. At the end of the main room, there was a double bedroom and a bathroom. It was compact, ideal for a single person or young couple. An alcove wall framing a log-effect fireplace had bookshelves either side. One was stacked with books, the other with CDs and DVDs. The bottom shelf contained boxes of files and folders; there were more of these behind the sofa.

Lucy started looking through the boxes. Each folder had the name of a university on it and the papers inside appeared to detail various lectures; they were obviously Jason's. She passed a box to Thomas and they waded through them in the hope of finding a diary. They were just beginning to plan the painstaking process of piecing together the dates from each folder, when Riley uncovered a hard-backed A4 diary. He looked inside: 2003. From the scribbles on the pages, he realised that they'd found what they were looking for: these were Jason's work diaries.

Bridges found 2005 and went straight to April 10th. There was nothing listed but Jason had given a speech at the University of Manchester on the evening of the 9th April and another lecture at Hallam University in Sheffield on April 11th.

'So that photograph was taken in the UK, probably between Manchester and Sheffield – assuming he took it himself.'

'Good work, we'll look into that later,' Thomas said. 'Let's take the last couple of years then comb through them at the station. If there's anything strange, we'll investigate.'

***

Frank Duffy sat in his hotel room. He was tired; it had already been a long day He picked up the copy of *The Boston Herald* and caught sight of a news article.

It was a single column on the front page, adjacent to the main story: **Boston PD search for missing women.** There was a small photograph of Amy Pearce directly underneath the headline. The story read:

Boston Police Department are concerned for a woman, feared abducted yesterday afternoon from Boston Logan airport. Twenty-four-year-old Amy Pearce (pictured) was apparently under police protection in London following a previous attack. Her parents believed that she was going to stay with a friend in Boston; however police have failed to make contact with either women and are concerned for their safety.

The article gave details about how the public could help, with a special helpline number.

Frank sat straight up in panic. *Dear God no! What the hell had happened?*

Chapter 20

Nathan Hammond joined his brother, Anthony, upstairs in the manor at Philips Point. He studied the piece of paper before him, trying to make sense of the notes that Paul had stolen from Thomas Riley's house in the early hours of Friday morning. Paul would join them later today and together they would try to extract as much information as they could from Amy and Emmanuelle.

Nathan had managed to open melodema.com/page2.htm. The clues meant very little to him, but he could see that Thomas Riley and Lucy Bridges had been there before him, investigating the idea of Diana being the Greek goddess Artemis. He wondered why he wasn't getting any further with 'stag' or 'dogs' or various similar passwords. He concluded that if Diana was indeed Artemis, Jason must have been thinking of a specific painting or picture of the goddess. So Nathan continued with the search engines, using his intuition to guide him.

Anthony left the house to meet Paul at the airport – there was no way that Nathan could be seen there so soon after yesterday. He had rushed back to Boston quickly from London and Anthony had worked tirelessly to set wheels in motion. The house was owned by a friend of Darren Cooper's and Heralds-Cooper managed his estate; it was perfect. Luckily Nathan had timed it right to be able to pick up Amy from the airport.

The girls were in the garden, looking out to the ocean. Nathan could see them from the window. They seemed very much alike, sharing similar passions. But Emmanuelle seemed wiser – more philosophical. He was pleased that they'd settled in quickly.

***

Thomas Riley and Lucy Bridges finally left the station at seven, both exhausted from the long day. Hours of filtering Jason Chadwick's diaries had led to very little. Most of his engagements over the past twelve months had been routine: lectures, corporate meetings with executives, seminars and lectures. There was nothing out of the ordinary. Indeed, his diary looked very similar for the months after his death too. More reason to back Amy's theory that Jason didn't seem to be in the frame of mind to take his own life.

They headed straight back to Thomas's house. The events of the past twenty-four hours had made everybody nervous. It appeared as if the whole force was being watched, or stalked. After Lucy helped Thomas cook and they'd eaten, he escorted her back to her maisonette so she could grab a change of clothes.

She had agreed to stay one more night with him. They would make a decision where to go with this case and their relationship tomorrow. Lucy didn't have the energy to fight her emotions and it seemed as if Thomas had given up the fight too. It was inevitable that nothing would ever be the same again; it would either be better, beyond their wildest dreams, or worse than they could ever imagine. Right now, they were spiralling, not knowing which direction the fall was likely to carry them.

On their way back to Thomas's house, Riley noticed the dark blue BMW again. It drove past the front of his house and carried on. He'd forgotten to check the license details on the National Police Database, nor had he mentioned the car to Moore. Maybe it was just a local man driving to and from his home - but somehow Thomas didn't think so.

'I think that we're being watched.' Thomas spoke quietly, looking forward.

'The BMW?' Lucy asked. She'd seen it too.

They reached the end of the street and crossed the road to Thomas's house. The car was out of sight.

'I think somebody knows we're looking for Jason's money,' Thomas said. 'The break-in, the car, the secrecy over Amy's abduction – it all adds up.'

'Do you think we could be in danger?'

'Not sure, but we need to be extra careful.'

When they got inside, they immediately updated themselves with 'The Hunt' as they now referred to it. Lucy was first to claim the computer. She found an online map of the North of England and studied the area between Manchester and Sheffield. The main road passed through the Peak District National Park. Lucy typed 'Peak District' into her image browser. Mam Tor – the shivering mountain –was one of the main search results. The sheer oval shale face housed a bronze-age fort. The winds from the escarpments provide excellent thermals and many of the photographs showed views of the Peak District taken by paragliders, making their descent in the valley towards the caves of Castleton.

It wasn't long before Lucy recognised the viaduct in Jason Chadwick's clue. A similar photograph was taken from Monsal Head, a viewpoint to the Monsal Dale valley from the main road to Bakewell.

'So now we know where and when,' Thomas said. 'Now what do we do?'

There was no password box on this page. Thomas suggested that they take a similar approach to the last time that there was no box. He typed melodema.com/monsaldale.html into the browser. This failed, as did /monsalhead.html and monsal.html.

'OK. Let's investigate this page name for a while and

come back to that,' Lucy suggested, highlighting *tellmewhy* with her mouse. Why Monsal Dale? She thought again about the picture, if it was 'just a picture'. The *tell me why* clue might come back to one of Jason's own pictures. Maybe something had happened to one of his pictures. Or maybe it was simply about art in general.

Lucy followed her instinct and returned to the last clue. The eagle on Artemis's hand seemed contrary to the depiction of Artemis in art during the past two millennia. Maybe this was Jason. Maybe oddities like this fascinated him. A cross-reference of 'Artemis Eagle' threw up some interesting possibilities: Artemis's head was used in a series of Roman coins. On the reverse was an eagle on a pediment. In mythology Zeus, Artemis's father had an eagle, which he used as a spy – like an extra eye. Maybe Artemis was carrying Zeus's eagle? Also, in Roman and Greek mythology an eagle was a symbol of battle, especially the onset of battle. The release of the eagle would show the warriors behind the frontline that battle was commencing. Maybe the architect at Caesar's Palace was depicting Artemis as a front-line warrior, leading her army to battle? Lucy doubted it. Thomas was sceptical, taking the level of intellectual reasoning down a level.

'Maybe,' he said, grinning, 'this was the architect's attempt to Americanise the mythology for the sake of elevating her. It's an inane twist for the sake of tourists.' He paused, waiting for Lucy's reaction.

'In English?' Lucy said, confused.

'Maybe the eagle is depicting the American emblem – the architect is trying to claim Artemis as an American Goddess.'

'No way!' Lucy said, horrified at the audacity of the suggestion. 'That's vile!' She shuddered but Thomas's theory made sense; after all – this was Las Vegas. Something like that would also enrage Jason: the perversion of ancient history for the sake of commercial patriotism. It enraged Lucy too. 'That's a gross injustice, and insult to greatness,' she said, turning back to the computer to shut out the thought.

'Could we not ask Caesar's Palace?' Thomas suggested. 'Or better still, see if we can track down the architect. Find out from the horse's mouth.'

'Good idea.'

Lucy continued her online investigation while Thomas doodled his thoughts. *Injustice*, he wrote. *Sacrilege* was more accurate.

'The architect was called Melvin Grossman,' Lucy said, interrupting Thomas's thoughts. 'I can't seem to find a direct contact. Not even sure if he's still alive. I'll email media relations at Caesar's Palace and see what they can offer.'

Lucy typed www.melodema.com/romancoin.html into her link bar and let out a yelp as a new page opened. Thomas looked up as he saw the page turn white. He dropped his notes as he lunged forward, resting his elbows on the back of the couch as he read the text. The page simply said: *You would think so but no.* Underneath it was a button: **Try again**.

Lucy looked at Thomas. She was disappointed. The excitement was in vain. To make matters worse, when she clicked on the *Try again* link, the page linked back to the opening www.melodema.com page.

'We're on the right lines though, we must be! I'm confident now that *Tell me why* is referring to the Artemis clue,' Thomas said.

They could forget about Hylas and the nymphs, or even Monsal Dale, for now. He asked her to type in melodema. com/battle.html. This gave an error page, as did /battlecry. html and /forwardbattle.html, but when she typed in / intobattle.html she got another page. Once again, it was white but this time it said: *Good theory, but no.* **Try again.**

'This is so frustrating!' Lucy yelled and stood up. Thomas watched, trying not to laugh. He went over to her and held her until she calmed down. 'I don't know how you can stomach this. I hated puzzles when I was young.'

'We're close. We'll get there,' Thomas promised.

This time Thomas went to the computer while Lucy poured

herself another drink. He tried /zeus.html and /zeuseagle. html, as well as /americanemblem.html, all without success. The 404 error page had the equivalent reaction of the computer swearing at him. It was really saying *Fuck off, loser*.

He looked at Lucy. She was sitting on the couch, her back to him, sipping her drink. Thomas left the computer and joined her. She looked depressed.

'Who are we kidding?' she asked. 'We don't really know him at all. Did anybody? We're at the mercy of his fantasy to save lives. We don't have a clue.'

'How many times does something which is potentially good turn out bad?' Thomas asked. 'If he knew what was going to happen, he would have probably given his legacy to a tramp.'

Neither of them spoke for a while. Thomas gently played with Lucy's hair as he rested his arm on her shoulders.

'I think we should tell Moore tomorrow. Maybe the Yard or the FBI can get further,' Lucy said.

Yes, he thought, it might well be the safest option, especially if they really were being watched – but they risked finding themselves in even more trouble. Deep inside he really wanted this money; it was his only chance of spending his life with Lucy without compromising his work or the driving ambition inside him. *What a mess.*

'I feel as if it's just you and me against the world at the moment,' he said, twirling delicate strands of her hair between his fingers.

The quiet of the evening seemed somehow inspiring, and he felt as if he really *did* know Jason. Something inside him that felt as if he was forming a real connection with the professor. If the obvious answers resulted in dead ends, maybe this came down to Jason's feelings. Were they on the right lines with the eagle representing the emblem? Thomas felt repulsed by the thought. Would Jason have felt the same? He tried to place himself in Jason's shoes. He was haunted by the words *Injustice* and *Sacrilege*. Something was telling him to explore them.

'Let me try something,' Thomas said, wearily levering himself off the sofa. He went over to the computer once more and typed in melodema.com/emblem, /usemblem, and /sacrilege but the computer *swore* again. Frustrated, he tried melodema.com/injustice. html

'Oh my God!'

Lucy jumped out of her seat to join him.

A message opened up from Jason:

Well done, I have to congratulate you so far on your intuition. You could have typed '/romancoin' or '/intobattle' and a page would have opened up for you, leading to a dead-end. The truth is that the architects and artists at Caesar's Palace placed twists on classic ancient mythology. It is claimed that the artist responsible for the statues at Caesar's Palace could not resist the irony with Artemis. Her eagle was a subtle but vulgar reference to the American emblem. To me, this was an extreme injustice and injustice is the one thing that enrages me about life. By all indications, Artemis did not like the eagle. The eagles in the Agamemnon were hunters of the hare, whose foetus represented the inhabitants of the City of Troy. To Americanise Artemis, in such a way that she exposed her dignity and placed an eagle on her hand was the greatest possible insult to her legacy.

Did you like the picture? Pretty, wasn't it? You will have to visit one day; they make a decent cup of tea in the café. It seems in conceivable where such a great king's legend could be set in a monk's pen so long after the fact.

This time Jason had left a password button, as he had with the original melodema.com opening page.

Thomas and Lucy read Jason's message through several times. The clue was obviously about the great king but the comment about the café seemed very random.

Their excitement was a welcome relief from the anxiety of the past twenty-four hours and it eased their conscience because, again, there seemed to be no real link to Amy. Thomas felt particularly happy with Jason's message; it was the first time that Jason had interacted with him. To be congratulated from beyond the grave was a humbling experience. And he felt that his connection with Jason was growing stronger.

'This is addictive!' he said, writing out the new clue by hand onto a piece of paper.

'I feel like Howard Carter,' Lucy agreed. 'Imagine what that must have felt like, uncovering Tutankhamen's treasures?'

Thomas placed his lips gently on Lucy's forehead. 'We'll find out ourselves, no doubt. But for now…' He handed her a copy of his written clue. 'We still have a lot of work to do!'

Lucy smiled as she sat down. They were still in trouble but there was *hope*.

Chapter 21

Paul Hammond congratulated his brother on his good work as he climbed into the waiting Mercedes convertible at the airport.

'The girls have bought it so far. They're not expecting you but we can run a story to keep our phoney investigation going,' Anthony said. 'You'll have to keep up the act a little longer, make sure they don't hear you slip into an American accent.' He chuckled.

Anthony brought his brother up to date on the girls, the story and how their investigations had progressed so far with the search for Jason's money. Paul was resolute in his determination to claim this legacy. 'We've earned it. We're this close; woe betide anyone that gets in our way now.'

'What about the detectives?' Anthony asked

'It's taken care of. They won't be a problem. Quite the opposite, in fact,' Paul replied. 'I've been discussing the new plan with Darren Cooper. I'll fill you in with new developments on the way.'

***

Frank Duffy spent the evening planning his time in Boston. The weekend office closures were an inconvenience but he knew time could be running out for Amy. He went to bed early. The room was noisy from the relentless hum and rumble of traffic outside his window. The night seemed endless but the new day saw Frank even more determined. He left the hotel immediately after breakfast.

The Coopers-Herald offices were in the heart of downtown Boston, in the centre of Federal Street. There was a single closed door with a plaque and bell in a plush refurbished building close to Post Office Square Park. It was no walk-in real-estate supermarket; this was high class. Coopers-Herald claimed their clientele were the elite: lawyers, politicians, surgeons and, of course, celebrities. It was a 'closed shop' business, with no advertising; recommendations were the backbone of the business. If somebody wanted a property, whether to live in or relocate their business, Coopers-Herald was the go-to. The company turnover was impressive – albeit the 'official' profits were questionable.

There was no sign of movement from inside the building and the doors were closed. Not that Frank had any intention of going in; he was merely hoping that there might be some clue as to where somebody would take Amy. A phonebook search of Boston had failed to give an address for any Stringhams in the area. There were several Hammonds but not a Nathan, Paul or Anthony.

Frank walked to the park then sat for a while, contemplating his options. The day was still new. The park was alive with retired couples walking their dogs, joggers, young boys throwing footballs and young children cycling around the trees.

Frank had known all week that he was being followed. Not that he particularly minded; he knew it would be official and it made him feel safer. In the park, however, his tracker couldn't be so discreet. The man, wearing navy pants and a blue shirt, carrying a newspaper and drinking coffee from a paper cup, was staring aimlessly into a tree. He caught Frank's gaze and chuckled. Knowing his cover was blown, the man casually walked over to the seat next to Frank. The two men did not make eye contact.

'It's a pleasant day,' Frank said, still looking forward.

'Nearly the end of mine,' was the reply. The man took another sip of his coffee.

'Do you know…' Frank spoke, slowly assessing his next words with the precision of a surgeon, 'where a professional person, say a lawyer or a university professor, might locate in Boston? Possibly outside of the city, somewhere with a bit of land and a decent view?'

'Plenty of professionals in Boston,' the man replied. 'They're scattered everywhere. Personally, I would head north of the harbour, Somerville or Melrose maybe.'

'Thanks. Maybe I'll head that way and take a look. Maybe find myself a decent real estate broker.' Frank ended the conversation, standing up, still without glancing in his new acquaintance's direction. 'If they hurt her, I'll string 'em up myself,' he muttered, then walked back towards the hotel, leaving the man on the seat.

✳✳✳

Great kings were numerous and a monk's pen could mean any monk that ever wrote. Alfred the Great was an obvious starting point. Limiting their search options to 'Monk – Alfred the Great' produced results which directed Thomas and Lucy to a number of articles. However, Alfred had originally aspired to be a monk and there didn't appear to be writings about him *by* a monk.

They continued their search into the night without making any connections. Maybe they needed a fresh start in the morning. They were both tired so they made their way to bed before midnight, but only after Lucy had updated their notes on the hunt and shut down the computer.

The peace was welcome after the chaos of the week and they were pleased with the evening's investigations. But the question remained: *where was Amy?*

Thomas cuddled Lucy to sleep; her warmth and gentle

breathing gave him a brief moment of contentment before he fell asleep.

***

Nathan Hammond joined the girls in the garden. They were sitting on the swing bench and appeared to be reading from a hand-written A4 notebook.

Emmanuelle looked up and moved closer to Amy, motioning to Nathan to sit down next to her. 'Jason kept a journal when he was younger. He wrote about me so Amy was just reading what he'd written.'

'Yeah,' Amy said, with a smile. 'Jason was trying to hide his wife-to-be, Penny, from Emmanuelle when she came to visit him in Boston but Penny was jealous and being awkward. Jason had written the weekend like a comedy sketch. It's hilarious.'

Emmanuelle explained, 'I've known Jason since eighth grade in Las Vegas. My father worked for Donald Chadwick. I was a year behind Jason at school and I deliberately followed him to Boston.' She looked towards the sea, smiling. 'We were good friends, though never actually went out together. But it was hard for us to be apart.' She paused briefly. 'I liked Penny, even if I was a bit jealous of her, but Jason was happy.'

Amy continued the story. 'When Emmanuelle first visited Jason in Boston, he tried to keep Penny and Emmanuelle apart and failed miserably. I don't think Emmanuelle realised how bad it was until now.' She nudged Emmanuelle lightly in the ribs with her elbow. 'Jason described his lecture from Penny, after Emmanuelle had returned home to Las Vegas as like being in the principal's office with his pants down, taking a severe whipping while a Rottweiler mangled his testicles.'

Nathan chuckled, relieved that the girls seemed so relaxed. He thought it might be worth having a look at

Jason's journals.

Chapter 22

Lucy heard the knock at the door first. It was a gentle knock, three quick raps. Thomas's arm was wrapped around her, gently squeezing his body to her back while his arm was sandwiched by her breasts, his hand resting short of her chin. She kissed his hand and moved his arm off her, which woke him up.

'You OK?' he asked.

'I think I heard the door,' she replied.

Someone knocked again, this time a little louder. Thomas looked at the clock; it was seven-thirty. There was a rattling and Thomas recognised the sound of the letterbox. He pulled on a hooded top and old jeans then went downstairs.

A brown A5 envelope was on the floor, in front of the door. Thomas picked it up and opened it slowly, standing in front of the door. Inside was a photograph of Amy Pearce. A yellow post-it note stuck to the photograph said. 'Help her. Let me in'.

Thomas opened the door slightly, enough to let his new safety chain pull tight. A man wearing a black three-piece suit stood waiting.

'Who are you?' Thomas asked quietly.

'Please let me in. You can help Amy,' the man said. He looked confident but pensive. Thomas weighed him up: quite tall, early fifties, thinning hair, deep frown lines on his forehead.

Thomas felt uneasy. He wasn't sure if his gut feeling was to run or surrender to the man before him. It certainly confirmed his fears that he was being followed.

'Please…' the man said again. His voice was gentle, almost a whisper. He was carrying a laptop case.

Thomas looked behind him; the room was messy from the previous evening. He thought of Lucy upstairs. Was she dressed?

'OK, I'll let you in. Forgive me while I disappear for a minute to get changed.'

'That's fine,' the man said taking his first steps into the room. The door shut behind him. He turned to Thomas, calmly reached in his pocket and pulled out a handgun, pointing it straight at Thomas's head.

'Oh fuck no!' Thomas said. His heart raced, his legs nearly gave way. He prepared for the inevitable.

'Be quiet and listen carefully,' said the man, still speaking calmly. 'I want your mobile phone.'

'It's upstairs,' Thomas said, instantly regretting his words. Don't bring Lucy into this, he thought.

'Good,' said the man. 'We need to collect your girlfriend too.'

Thomas walked upstairs, the gun pointed at his back as the man followed him. Lucy walked out of the bedroom and Thomas noted that she was dressed in only a shirt and knickers. She smiled as she saw him reach the top of the stairs but immediately saw from his face that something was wrong.

'Thomas?' she said, about to step forward to him. Then she saw the gun in his back and the stranger.

'I want your phones,' the man said.

Lucy looked behind her. Both of their mobiles were on the table next to the bed. She shuffled back quickly and grabbed the edge of the duvet to cover the top of her legs. She motioned to the phones as Thomas and the stranger continued into the bedroom. The man picked them up, switched them off and put them in his jacket pocket.

'Good. Now take the phone off hook and get dressed. Then we'll close all the curtains in the house and you can join me downstairs. I'll explain what you have to do to save Amy's life – and your own.'

The man watched Lucy throw on her jeans and socks, then followed her into every room while she closed the curtains. The gun was pointed at Thomas's head all the while and nobody said a word. Lucy was very conscious of the stranger's every movement and trembled as she descended the stairs. The man's gun remained on Thomas.

Downstairs, he ordered the detectives to sit down on the sofa and listen. 'We have Amy. We also have your notes on Jason Chadwick's little treasure hunt.' The man waved a copy of a print-out that Lucy instantly recognised as her own notes. 'I know you're not investigating this on police time, and I'm pretty sure two detectives from the same branch like yourselves shouldn't be spending the night together. So my hunch is that you're planning to claim this money for yourselves and fly off somewhere to live happily ever after.'

Lucy looked over towards Thomas. Yes, that was the fantasy but as much as she wanted it to happen, this had become more about finding Amy. The dream was already over. They might not be alive this time tomorrow. She tried to be professional, to assess how to deal with this crisis. Should they try to escape it or toe the line?

Thomas spoke so she took his lead. 'OK, we want Amy back, the money isn't important to us. You're right, we just wanted to be together. The hunt was a pipe dream – like a game. Neither of us even thought about the money seriously.' Thomas tried to sound confident as he assessed the power of their adversary.

'Good. So you know what we want, then?' the man said. 'You'll help us solve the clues and find the money in return for Amy's safe return. That's the deal.'

Thomas stared at the man. They had little choice but to comply. He thought quickly, trying to understand how this man and his team could have known that Lucy and he were trying to solve Jason's hunt. They couldn't have had direct access to the search history on his computer. Unless, during the break-in on Friday, somebody left a bug or camera.

Thomas looked around the room as he spoke. 'We may need information from Amy, or somebody that knew Jason.'

'We'll get anything you need,' the man responded.

'Do you mind giving us a name to call you by, any name will do,' Thomas asked, about to stand up, motioning towards the computer for permission.

The man looked up. Thomas noticed his hesitation.

'Call me Hardy.'

Hardy? Thomas looked over to Lucy who rolled her eyes. Was this the man's real name or a nickname?

'OK, Hardy, I suppose you'd like to be brought up to date then?' Thomas's tone was unintentionally sarcastic.

Thomas moved to the computer. Lucy had updated her notes from yesterday's progress but not yet printed them out. Thomas printed out three copies and gave one to Hardy.

Hardy joined Lucy on the sofa. 'We made progress last night,' she explained, pointing to the latest clue. Hardy's gun was on his lap, right hand still on the trigger. She was aware of every twitch of his fingers. It occurred to her that Hardy must have obtained her notes from Thomas's break-in the other morning. That's what the burglars were looking for.

Hardy read the new notes thoroughly. Lucy had documented their progress in as much detail as she could. The man seemed genuinely intrigued. He stared at the next clue. 'I can't understand this. My knowledge of Greek, Roman or even British history is limited. Emmanuelle is the person to ask for help.'

Hardy went on to say that he needed to find out how his accomplices were getting on with their own investigation, but that would have to be later because it was the middle of the night in Boston.

Lucy took in everything Hardy said. So his co-conspirators not only had Amy, but also Emmanuelle. At least there was a strong hope that both women were alive and would stay alive for as long as they would be needed. She hoped that the hunt would require a lot more clues.

***

It had been a long day for Amy and Emmanuelle. All afternoon and most of the evening had been spent with DCI Dawson, who had flown in from London, and Agent Stringham. They spent the whole time documenting almost everything they knew about Jason Chadwick: how they met him, the work he did, events leading up to his death, even his hobbies and political views. As much as it was tiring, it was probably a good release for both of them. Amy realised they both loved him in their own way and, if honesty were permitted, both were probably a little envious of each other's memories of him.

Amy was surprised to learn that Jason had an obsession with Greek mythology. He'd never mentioned it before, though he was the kind of man who used random quotes every now and then, and followed up her blank expression with pearls of knowledge like, 'Demetrios – he was Greek'.

Agent Stringham showed interest in Jason's journals and asked to borrow them overnight, so he could get an idea of the sort of person he was.

They were told that Jason believed his parents' accident nearly ten years ago, was suspicious. Emmanuelle told Stringham that Jason's move to Britain had been a shock. Jason's parents had always spoken of retiring to England, as Jason's mother owned property over there. Emmanuelle didn't realise that Jason was going to move with them. He had never told her why the family sold up and moved so quickly, but he said that there was a 'mafia style' gang operating in Las Vegas. Jason's father was disillusioned with the hierarchy there and it was time to move on.

Dawson and Stringham probed for information, but Emmanuelle obviously knew little or nothing about his recent years.

It was hard to assess the benefit of the conversations today, but Amy couldn't sleep. Some things were bugging her. Emmanuelle was too relaxed. She wandered around the place almost as if she knew where she was. Amy liked the woman very much. Yes, she was older, intelligent and had such elegance and grace but – there was something that made her uneasy. It was the same with Agent Stringham and DCI Dawson: there was little in the house that seemed to connect these important people with the outside world. There were obviously cars entering and leaving the house but no uniforms, no official-looking deputies or sheriffs, whatever they had in the US. Plus, Amy couldn't remember seeing a single television or radio set and that seemed very odd. In fact, the only modern gadget she'd seen was the laptop computer that Dawson brought with him, to record their interview.

Otherwise, everything was OK. Maybe she was being paranoid. In general she felt safer than she'd been in London. She had been fed well and they answered any questions that she or Emmanuelle asked. She was pleased to think that they were genuinely looking into Jason's death, as well as that of his parents. What would happen next? Would they only allow Emmanuelle to go home after they had captured Jason's killer? That could take a while. Would Amy be safe in Boston? Why would a senior Inspector from London travel all the way over to Boston?

She wished for sleep, if for no other reason than to stop her from thinking.

Chapter 23

It's amazing what you can find out online, if you're prepared to pay a little money. Frank's visit to Melrose and Somerville had given him an insight into how affluent professionals lived their lives. Long roads with properties that were spaced every hundred yards or so; two-storey buildings with balconies and pools and perfectly primed lawns. Two or three cars, sometimes boats, in each driveway.

Frank returned to his hotel and paid for an hour online. He hadn't replied to his wife's email message but did read it. He was confident that the police back home were updating her as she simply wished him luck. While browsing, he found access to release records from High Desert State Prison in Nevada.

Paul and Nathan Hammond were released in January 2004; five others connected to the multi-million dollars 'Hammond Gang' fraud were released a year before, including Anthony Hammond. Parole records showed that Paul and Nathan had moved to Boston while Anthony moved to Atlantic City. The once-weekly parole meetings were now monthly and nobody had missed a visit. They were still using the Hammond moniker. Frank wondered if the authorities knew about their use of the name 'Stringham'.

Paul and Nathan's parole officer was Trevor Mouriati. Frank found a twenty-four hour contact number and phoned him. Trevor was unable to help Frank without a formal meeting, so he arranged to meet with him Sunday morning.

Frank scoured the internet looking for any direct connection with Coopers-Herald and a property where they could have taken Amy. He also tried to find information about the Cooper branch of the company. The official website gave very little information but it did pride itself on being a 'family company'.

***

Thomas Riley was finding it hard to think under pressure. Hardy wasn't much help, not only because of the gun that he was still brandishing but also because he was impatient and unable to tune in to his and Lucy's wavelength. Thomas realised that he needed to be extra cautious. For now, at least, he had Hardy's attention and Hardy allowed him to discuss and examine the clues with minimal interruption.

Lucy had pulled up a chair next to Thomas, so they had their backs to Hardy, who was perched on the back of the sofa watching them. Thomas decided to continue the research using his own IP instead of a proxy, in the hope that it might flag up some action with the Yard's Cyber Crime Unit. He was desperate to talk to Lucy about his observations but there was no opportunity. He had to wait.

'In conceivable,' Lucy pointed out, 'is two words. Why? It doesn't make sense; it must have been spelt that way for a reason. Could it mean *conception* rather than *doubt*?'

'Yes, I was thinking that. Maybe the clue is about a place or time – maybe a year when a great king was born,' Thomas said.

'True, though that doesn't explain the monk's pen.'

'Maybe by "great king" he means Pharaoh. Did a monk write about a Pharaoh?'

Lucy explored her browser again but a half hour of searching failed to throw up anything. Lucy started from scratch with her search reference *Monk Great King* and continued to read the results, paying extra attention to the references to Alfred the Great. Suddenly she jumped. Thomas looked up; he had been writing down the clue over again, looking for anagrams under the watchful eye of Hardy.

'*Geoffrey of Monmouth.* He was a monk and the first person to write about King Arthur. He wrote a book around 1140, supposedly about the histories of kings, where he documented King Arthur as the great warrior king from the fifth century,' Lucy explained.

'Well, that makes sense. I suppose it would be inconceivable for such a great king to have been forgotten for six hundred years until this monk, Geoffrey of Monmouth, wrote about him. Maybe that's why King Arthur is categorised under British mythology rather than an official historical figure.'

Thomas typed 'KingArthur' into the password box but without success, he followed with Geoffrey, Geoffreyofmonmouth, Camelot, 1140 and even Merlin – all without success.

'In conceivable' Jason said. 'Two words. Maybe it's where Geoffrey of Monmouth conceived the story of King Arthur, as in where he was when he first wrote about him.'

The minutes and hours passed by. Neither Lucy nor Thomas had eaten or had a drink. Lucy pleaded with Hardy to let her make a coffee. Hardy agreed, but insisted that Thomas joined them in the kitchen. Thomas sat at the breakfast bar looking at his notes while Lucy raided the cupboards for something easy to eat. For a moment he forgot where he was, he forgot about Hardy and his gun, even Amy – he was on a completely different planet.

'It's where King Arthur was conceived.' Thomas stood up and hurried back to the computer.

'Hey!' Hardy yelled, waving the gun. Thomas stopped, reality slapping him in the face.

'Sorry!' Thomas began, raising his hands in a reflex action, surrendering to Hardy's power. He chuckled, as he turned round to see Hardy's irate face. 'For a split second, I forgot you were here,' Thomas confessed. 'I'll wait, but I think I have sussed this one.'

Hardy motioned to Thomas to sit down, acknowledging his honesty. He honoured Thomas with a smile and put the gun onto the small table in front of him. Lucy noted this and caught Thomas's eye. Breakfast was eaten in near silence.

'Amy is alive isn't she?' Lucy eventually asked.

'Yes, and so is her friend. For now,' Hardy replied.

'For now?' Thomas asked, concerned that plans might change.

'For now,' Hardy repeated, finishing the dregs of his coffee. He picked up the gun and motioned them back towards the living room.

Thomas returned to the computer. Geoffrey of Monmouth suggested that King Arthur was conceived in Tintagel Castle on the north coast of Cornwall. Arthur's Father, Uther Pendragon, fell for his foe Gorlois's wife, Igerna, and asked Merlin to convert him to a likeness of Gorlois. They conceived Arthur. Uther later married Igerna after Gorlois was killed in battle. Tintagel was not far at all from Jason's Cornish home. Thomas felt confident that he was getting closer. He typed *Tintagel Castle* into the password box but nothing happened. He tried *Tintagel*. 'Yes!' he shouted as a new page opened

Chapter 24

Nathan Hammond was up early. It was going to be a long day and it had to go completely as planned: they had to make serious progress. They couldn't risk the police closing in on them and the only way they were likely to get help from Amy and Emmanuelle was is if they kept the girls' confidence.

Months – maybe even years – of planning had come down to this day. All their plans had fallen into place. Who would have believed that Jason would do this? Years of manipulating Brandon had led to very little, but finding that Jason had put his fortune into the public domain was better than they could have ever dreamed of.

When the call came through from London, Nathan was ecstatic. 'Our inspector and his colleague have been very helpful,' the voice at the other end explained, with a wry chuckle. 'Get a pen and paper because they've moved on this far.'

Nathan wrote down the stages of the hunt until he was fully updated. He was satisfied, even excited, by the progress so far. 'We don't even have a use for the girls at the moment, then?' he asked.

'Not really. Isn't that ironic? These two are learning fast about our professor. They are with me at the moment – I suspect, for the sake of harmony later, it may be worth them speaking with Amy if we monitor the conversation closely.'

Nathan thought quickly. 'Yes, I agree. I have an idea. Phone me in two hours.'

'OK. We'll see how we get on with this clue.'

***

Thomas looked at the new page. It was orange, just a blank orange page. The page title was melodema.com/getyourpassport.htm.

It was difficult concentrating on the hunt while Hardy was on the phone. Thomas listened in to the conversation for clues. When he heard Hardy suggest that Amy speak to them, he breathed a sigh of relief; maybe she was all right after all.

Thomas reviewed his situation. It was obvious that these people wanted Jason's money. What were the chances of them allowing Lucy and him, or even Amy and Emmanuelle, lead their lives after the hunt was over? Amy could identify some of them, as could Thomas. The truth was that they were probably expendable. The best chance he had was to slow down the hunt as much as he could.

He and Lucy were not officially supposed to be at work today but DCI Moore was expecting them. They'd told him that they were likely to come in and help. It would only be after shift started tomorrow that anybody would get suspicious about their absence. Thomas had to find a way of escaping – he needed a way in to DCI Moore – but that could mean a death sentence for Amy and Emmanuelle.

For now, these people needed Amy, Emmanuelle, Thomas and Lucy. Thomas had to toe that line for a while longer. He hoped that Lucy realised this much too; somehow they had to feed off each other.

'Did they agree?' Thomas asked as Hardy ended the call.

'To you speaking with Amy? Yes, in two hours, but we have to make progress with this clue,' Hardy replied.

Thomas began the usual routine, starting with viewing

the page source. The page was just a background colour. There was nothing else at all, no images, no encryption and nothing at all that an investigation in Photoshop could help with. The page title was a worry: 'Get your passport,' hinted that the hunt was coming away from the Internet.

'Hardy, this is going to get complicated. I have a strong feeling he's sending us out and about,' Thomas said.

'If it wasn't for the reference to a passport, I would have thought that it was a reference to that café at Monsal Head in Derbyshire,' Lucy said. 'Jason mentioned going there some time for a decent cup of tea.'

'That's true, it must have had some relevance,' Thomas said. 'Though the internet is international, people in other countries would have to *get their passports* to come over here. So it might still be Monsal Head.'

Thomas remembered the letter to Frank. Their quest was leading to America, it had to be. The proceeds from the estate were to be sent there. He kept this to himself for now, but hoped Lucy was thinking the same.

'It's not an option,' Hardy said forcefully. 'Not right now. Let's see if we can think beyond this.'

'Why is it not an option?' Lucy asked. 'Nobody knows we're missing, nobody would suspect that we're being held hostage. It's a day...'

'No!' Hardy stopped her mid-sentence, raising his voice and pointing his gun between her eyes.

Lucy looked down the barrel of his pistol and raised her hands, trying not to show the fear inside. 'OK,' she said, her voice breaking.

Thomas stood up. 'There you go!' He motioned Hardy to the computer. 'It's all yours. I'm beaten this time.' Hardy looked horrified. 'We've solved all these clues so far by throwing ideas around. The minute you stop the chain of thought is when we dry up – and that's what has happened,' he went on forcefully, attempting to undermine Hardy and take control again. 'If you could do this without our help, you'd have done so already. So put that fucking gun away and help us – and stop being an arse!'

Hardy pulled at the safety catch and put the gun to Thomas's head. Lucy gasped. 'Thomas!' she whispered but Thomas didn't move.

'You have to trust me,' he continued. 'It's the only way you'll get what you want. Just like I have to trust you'll let us go when we've solved this.' He gently placed his hand on Hardy's hand that held the gun and eased it from his head. 'Trust me,' he said again gently.

Hardy's face was angry but he lowered the gun, replaced the safety catch and sat down. He made an attempt to regain control. 'Travelling is a final option. There's nothing on this page that suggests we know what to look for at Monsal Dale.' He pointed a finger at Thomas. 'And if you undermine me again, I'll pump you and your girlfriend with every round – you understand?'

'Look,' Thomas sat back on his computer chair, talking softly. 'You've got Amy, that's all that matters. We're not going anywhere while you have Amy. So relax, will you?' Thomas smiled as he spoke, attempting to calm Hardy. It seemed to work. Hardy put the gun back inside his jacket. The suit was so well made that the gun made little impact on the shape. It was as if the jacket was made to carry one.

'OK, firstly, we need to work out the page to open next, which will lead us to the next clue,' Thomas began, speaking as if he were directing his words at Hardy to keep him involved. 'Let's just ignore the "grab your passport" clue for a while and see what we have'.

Lucy dare not speak. The tension had peaked to a point where she'd elevated her mind to another place, a place where she could be alone with Thomas and nobody else in the world existed. That's what she wanted; she wanted life, life that she could spend with Thomas. Simply dying together wasn't good enough. She wanted to escape and run with Thomas, anywhere, and start again. If that meant that Amy had to be sacrificed, then so be it.

Guilt pulled her out of her trance. For now, there was no

escape; she had to pretend, and wait.

'Why orange?' were the first words she said.

That's a good point, Thomas thought. He raised a thumb to acknowledge Lucy's contribution then returned to the web page source file. It was the most basic web page he'd seen so far: there were merely five lines of html – the page, title and colour.

Why was it so simple? Jason liked simplicity: all his clues had required a balance of logical thinking and research as opposed to lateral thinking and cryptic puzzles. The answer could be very simple. He looked at the colour code. The orange hex code was #FE7726. Thomas typed this code into the browser search bar. There were four results that seemed to have no relevance to the hunt.

'What about the 7726?' Lucy asked. 'Could it be relevant to an account number?' She made a note for future reference. There was the 1014 or V1ct0r14, and the date 1140 that Geoffrey of Monmouth when written the story of King Arthur. The 7726 could have some relevance.

'That's strange!' Thomas suddenly recognised a connection. '1014 is a numerical anagram of 1140. I'm positive that we'll find some significance, if not now then certainly later.'

'FE could be the key,' Hardy said.

Thomas was shocked as it was his first contribution to the conversation. 'I'll check it online.'

Thomas cross-referenced every major abbreviation for FE – Federal Exchange got their minds busy. They looked at Federal Express, wondering whether there was a package with 7726 reference. Fe was the chemical symbol for iron too. They spent an hour trying to link the number to a chemical compound.

Thomas began to wonder if this had anything to do with the orange folder in Frank Duffy's office. If it was, then this was a dead end. He shrugged off the thought. He was reluctant to give Hardy any more information about the police's investigation into Vito Rolanski's murder.

He was busy studying molecular structures when Lucy had an idea. 'What would this have to do with Jason?' she asked. 'Let's get back to basics. He wasn't that sort of scientist. Let's think about the internet again.'

Thomas stopped what he was doing. Lucy was right. Hardy was looking more annoyed that nothing was happening. He had to call the US very soon and he had no news.

'Could it be even simpler?' Lucy asked. Thomas slid his chair back to make space for her at the computer. She wrote melodema.com/FE7726.html into the address bar but she just got the familiar error page.

'Try it without capitals,' Thomas suggested. He knew that web pages tended to use lower-case letters. Lucy tried /fe7726.html and a new page opened immediately. The biggest yell came from Hardy. Thomas high-fived Lucy then gently rubbed her shoulders to congratulate her. The new page was orange too but this time it had another password box. The page name gave an indication that they may be getting close; it was called, *xmarksthespot*. Could they really be *that* close?

The new page was weird. It appeared to move with the mouse curser. Tiny rollover images of symbols appeared behind orange squares; there were scores of them.

'I've seen these symbols before,' Thomas mumbled, resting his chin on his hand in concentration.

Hardy stood up and looked over Thomas's shoulder. It looked as if the symbols were in rows. Thomas continued moving the mouse. The symbols danced a Mexican wave as he glided the curser across the screen.

'Greek, maybe?' Hardy suggested.

'Greek alphabet is my guess, yes,' Thomas replied, opening the internet search once again. He found a website that confirmed their initial thoughts and printed out three sheets of the Greek alphabet. Then, starting at the top, they began the painful process of deciphering all the letters.

'I hope that the letters are in the right order,' Lucy said. They all tried to read what was written through the squares.

They wrote down every word as they identified each letter; it took a while. Once they had successfully translated each image they were left with:

'didthemotherofthealmightywarriorunderilliumcon-fusedgivethemonkslegendthismagic'.

The hunters worked backwards until the clue started making sense:

Did the mother of the almighty warrior under Ilium confused give the monk's legend this magic.

Chapter 25

This is madness, DCI Moore thought. Another incident in the crypt at St. Martins, a serious attack at Charing Cross station, hundreds of activists causing havoc in Leicester Square. Then there were their ongoing investigations, such as the stabbing at The Empire and the missing Amy Pearce. *Where were Riley and Bridges?* They'd said they would be in today. He'd tried phoning them but they were not contactable.

The Commissioner was riding DCI Alderman's back now. They'd made no real progress in their search for Amy Pearce and the inquest and analysis of the errors was slowing progress. Arnold Pearce had helped create a photo-fit of the bogus detectives from Scotland Yard. These had been sent to Boston PD and the FBI. A trace on the Mercedes used to pick up Amy led them to a stolen car at Gatwick Airport. Forensic examiners were looking over it now. Boston PD reported a witness seeing a girl fitting Amy's description climbing into a dark Subaru 4x4. Police were studying the limited CCTV footage.

The FBI confirmed that they'd made contact with Frank Duffy, who had also turned up in Boston. Frank hinted to an officer that Amy could have been taken to a more upmarket area of the city. The FBI was cross-referencing their database with known criminals in the area. They had visited Jason Chadwick's sons, both of whom were in Boston, but both seemed ignorant of Amy Pearce's whereabouts. Neither did they particularly care; both sons seemed uninterested as to what happened to their father or his acquaintances. They were still being watched though. For now, that was as far as they could get with the case. They needed a break.

DCI Moore was due the day off but he stayed in the office. He received a call from Scotland Yard shortly after midday. DCI Alderman asked if he could speak with Thomas Riley about his telephone conversation with Amy on Thursday evening. Moore explained that Thomas hadn't been in touch so Alderman was going to make arrangements to visit Riley himself.

Moore was concerned that his inspector might be in trouble. He liked Riley, he'd even given a personal recommendation for him to be promoted to chief inspector. He was shocked that Riley had been so unprofessional; he could see no logical reason why he should have contacted Amy. Moore prayed that this incident would not backfire on them all.

***

Emmanuelle walked into Amy's room to use her en-suite shower. She could see that Amy looked tired and flustered and asked if she was all right.

'I have an uneasy feeling,' Amy said quietly.

'About why we're here, you mean?' Emmanuelle asked. 'What's the problem?'

The problem was that Emmanuelle's carefree attitude presented Amy with doubts about Emmanuelle, so she chose her words carefully. 'Possibly … I mean, what if these people are the impostors? I'm not saying that they are, it's just that nobody knows I'm here. I need to at least talk to my parents.'

'Agent Stringham did say they were informing our families but yes, maybe you should ask,' Emmanuelle said, turning on the hot water. 'I need to prepare for work tomorrow too so I hope they let us out of here today,' she continued, which made Amy feel a little easier. 'I only have two lectures this week and the admin I can do from home. You'll be alright with that, won't you?'

'Oh yes, definitely,' Amy replied, with a smile. The idea of even a suggestion of normality was pleasing.

Emmanuelle took her shower and Amy stared out of the window. The playful mist was teasing the garden; it appeared to spiral up from the sea, forming a rolling barrier at the edge of the cliff. Jason used to speak of the Cornish mist. He often walked down to Boscastle Harbour at dawn and watched the new day break up the sea mist. At one time, when his mother was alive, he would take the dogs down there. He said that it was inspirational and reminded him how lucky he was. Amy had a sense that Jason was watching over her at that moment.

Half an hour later, Amy and Emmanuelle went down to the kitchen. Nathan was already up. He was reading a file, his feet up on a glass table, wearing a black suit with white shirt and navy tie. He welcomed the girls cheerfully and offered them a coffee.

'Any news?' asked Emmanuelle.

'Developments maybe, no suspect as yet, but certainly developments,' he replied. 'We'll brief you a little later, after I've spoken with my colleagues, but I'm hopeful we can get you away by the end of the day. We'll have to make sure that you're closely guarded if we don't have a suspect in custody.'

Amy was relieved. She was about to ask about phoning home when Stringham spoke again. 'I had a talk with Inspector Riley from Charing Cross. It was early so I assumed you were asleep. He was asking after you. I think he may have a few questions so he's going to phone again soon.'

'Ah, thank you. I want to get a message to my parents to let them know I've arrived OK, in case they were worried. Inspector Riley can take a message.'

'Yes, that's fine. Just be careful not to tell him where you are, in case he lets any information slip. We're dealing with sophisticated criminals here, of that we are certain. They may well have phones bugged or cameras monitoring conversations. We mustn't rule out anything at this stage.'

Nathan made the girls coffee and left them in the kitchen while they had some breakfast. When Hardy phoned from London, he was quite buoyant and pleased that they'd made progress with the clues. Nathan was content and he discussed a plan for the conversation with Amy. He asked Hardy to discuss their plan with Thomas Riley and phone back in ten minutes.

***

Ten minutes later, Nathan went back into the kitchen. He motioned to Amy, waving the phone. As Amy ran to him and grabbed the phone he whispered, 'Remember?'

Amy nodded. 'Hello?' she said into the mouthpiece.

Thomas was relieved. At least she really was alive. He followed Hardy's instructions to the letter. 'Hello Miss Pearce. How is Boston? I trust that they're keeping you well?' he said.

'I can't complain. Lots of coffee and space but I can't wait until this is over,' she said. 'Has anybody got a message to my parents to let them know I arrived safely?'

'Yes, they've been updated regularly. We're close to tracking down the impostors who have been using the police force as their access to you. Just bear with us, Amy.'

Thomas hoped his words were reassuring and that Amy would feel more relaxed, but he felt guilty, even angry with himself.

'I have just a quick question Amy.' Thomas started to feel nervous and, because he was trying to improvise, he stuttered. 'I am ... I mean *we are* trying to build a ... I mean trying to work out what happened to Jason on the weeks leading up to him making his will in 2005.'

Hardy was looking ready to intercept. Thomas raised his hands to let him know he had regained control.

'Yes,' Amy said

'Jason had two lectures in April 2005, one at the University of Manchester on a Saturday, followed by another in Sheffield Hallam on the Monday. Do you remember that?'

'Yes. I remember that well,' Amy replied. 'I was there too.'

'Did anything happen that weekend that was out of the ordinary? Any strange meetings or change in Jason's mood?'

'He was a bit distant maybe, but his usual self – it was a good weekend. I spent the Sunday with him. He didn't meet with anybody at all.'

'Did you go to the Peak District?' Thomas asked. He was beginning to worry that the hunt had finally landed at Amy's feet.

'How did you know that?' Amy sounded shocked, alarmed.

'Monsal Head Café?'

'Yes! Yes. Has that any relevance to what happened? We were alone. We didn't even make any phone calls.' Amy seemed worried.

Thomas heard the mumble of a male voice behind her and she hesitated. He panicked in case he had touched a nerve.

'It's OK, Amy. That's fine. We just needed to rule out any other meetings that day to make sure there are no holes in his diary. I didn't intend to shock you.'

'It's OK, I understand,' Amy responded, her tone more downbeat. 'I have to go, Agent Stringham needs me to end the call,' she said. 'Give my love to my parents and tell them that I'm OK.'

'I will, Amy. You take care and enjoy the rest of your visit,' Thomas said. The phone went dead but hopefully she'd heard his words.

Thomas switched off the phone and handed it back to Hardy without looking in his eyes. He kicked the computer chair and walked towards the kitchen.

'Thomas?' Hardy said, following him. Lucy sat on the arm of the sofa. She didn't speak.

'I need a glass of water,' Thomas said, without looking back. If the gun was pointing at him, he didn't care. Hardy followed him to the door. Thomas poured his water and raised it to show Hardy. 'Happy?' he said, returning to the living room, walking right past Hardy and his gun.

Thomas began to feel stronger. Behind Hardy's suit and arrogance was a weak man; he looked out of his depth. If this was a professional job, there was still a chance that it wasn't infallible. Thomas had found out a name, too: Agent Stringham. Was that a real name, he wondered.

Thomas turned to Hardy. 'Right, here's the plan. If you genuinely intend to release Amy and not kill her, then you do this much. You allow me to make one phone call to Amy's father to tell him that she's alive and well.' He looked Hardy straight in the eye as he spoke. 'We will solve this hunt. It will mean us travelling and it will also require Amy. She has information – I know that for a fact but we don't know what is needed until we uncover the next clue.'

'I can't authori...' Hardy began.

'Listen,' Thomas interrupted, raising his voice. 'Nobody knows you are here. The minute they suspect anything, your plan is in trouble. I'm sure you worked that one out yourself. So if we need to travel, especially if it's abroad, then we need to get a head start. I am not playing games with you here – it's common sense.'

'I understand but I'm not the one that can authorise that.' Hardy's voice was starting to wilt. Thomas knew he had got to him.

'Scotland Yard are hot, they'll be prioritising this case to make sure that they can limit the damage. If they know Amy is safe, it will be to your benefit too.' Thomas picked up his home phone and held it up. 'I'll phone DCI Moore's secretary and leave a message. I'll say that I received a photograph and a mobile phone – the photograph was of Amy and when the phone rang, it was Amy. I'll say that she left a message to her parents to let them know that she is alive and being treated properly. The people that have her want to prove an injustice that Jason was connected to. I'll say I have to stay in a hotel in London overnight, but can't say where yet. This will throw them off the scent for the real motive and give them a different line of enquiry. They will be concerned for me, yes, but at least they will know Amy is safe.'

'I'll need to run it past the rest first,' said Hardy.

Thomas handed the phone over but Hardy used his own mobile and made the call straight away.

Thomas looked at Lucy. They made eye contact briefly. He was willing her to read his mind.

Chapter 26

Amy was initially pleased following her conversation with Thomas Riley. At least it calmed some of her fears from the previous night. He seemed a bit strange though, as if he was nervous. Was he holding something back? Maybe something had happened to her parents and he'd been told not to say anything.

She thought of his questions about Derbyshire. That was her special day, the one she treasured the most. How would the police know about Monsal Dale? Her stomach sank, filling with acid, and she placed her hand over her it as if to stop the pain.

Emmanuelle noticed. 'You OK?' she asked.

'I'm just paranoid,' Amy explained. 'I had a feeling he was holding out on me. I'm worried that something has happened to my parents.'

'Stop doing this to yourself, Amy.' Emmanuelle walked over and hugged her friend.

A tear fell down Amy's face. 'I just want to have my life back again.'

Nathan Hammond walked back into the room. 'Hey, you two. OK?'

'It's OK, Agent Stringham,' Emmanuelle responded with a wink. 'I think she's a little homesick, that's all.'

Amy produced a tentative smile. Agent Stringham looked concerned. He left them again as a car pulled up outside and went to meet the guests.

It was Paul and Anthony Hammond.

'We may have a problem,' Nathan said, as he greeted his brothers. He explained his decision to allow the phone call. They could understand his thinking – in fact, it was a brilliant plan.

'The problem is, as she finished the conversation she mentioned that *Agent Stringham needed her to end the call.*' Nathan looked at Paul's face. There was no emotion there at all.

'That could complicate matters,' Paul said eventually. 'It might not be a bad thing but we must keep tight control. If things go to plan, it probably won't matter.'

The brothers headed towards the house. Nathan thought it best to warn them why Amy was upset. 'She's a little distressed, but I think that is part relief and part homesickness. I think she'll be alright though. It does add more substance to our story now she's spoken with somebody she trusts.'

When they went into the kitchen, Amy was in better spirits. She explained about the conversation with DI Riley.

Paul congratulated his brother after they left the girls, and the men updated each other on the progress in London with the hunt.

∗∗∗

Frank Duffy was up early. A good night's sleep had been just what his weary mind and body needed. When he awoke at six, he decided to take an early morning stroll. He was meeting the parole officer about two miles from his hotel on Fenway, not far from the University of Art. He decided to walk along the Charles River and take in the picturesque city.

It was a beautiful morning and quiet, too. He wasn't aware of being followed. Maybe the police were satisfied enough to trust him following yesterday's impromptu meeting in the park.

Frank met Trevor Mouriati at his office. He apologised for asking for a meeting on a Sunday. Trevor was tall, dark, maybe Caribbean, with thinning slate-coloured hair. He had intense eyes but was softly spoken. Frank showed Trevor his ID.

Trevor was concerned, as Frank was not from any recognised US police department. 'I don't think I can help,' he said.

'Well, if you can't answer questions, maybe you can listen and bear my words in mind,' Frank suggested.

Trevor smiled. Wherever there was protocol, there was always an unorthodox approach.

'You have the Hammond brothers on your books. I know because I found their release information.' Frank looked for any reaction in Trevor, but he kept a good poker face. 'They are probably pillars of society now. They have their new business – real estate, I believe.'

There was still no reaction at all from Trevor. Either he was extremely professional or about to lay one on him for even suggesting that there may be a problem with his *friends*.

'Go on,' Trevor said.

'Well, I believe that they've reverted back to their mother's name of Stringham,' Frank explained. 'I also think that they are responsible for kidnapping this British girl, Amy Pearce. It was in the papers yesterday.'

This time there was a reaction from Trevor. He started writing notes: 'Amy Pearce', 'Kidnap'.

Frank continued. 'Amy Pearce worked for Jason Chadwick, who we believe was murdered a few months ago. She's been followed and a man died when he got in the way of a chase. It was Jason Chadwick's father who uncovered the scam that sent the Hammonds down.'

Trevor looked concerned. 'Is there any evidence at all that links them?'

'Not that I'm aware of, just a set of coincidences,' Frank admitted.

'I can't discuss this, Mr Duffy.' Trevor seemed agitated. 'And I really hope that you're wrong. This could ricochet in too many directions.'

'Sounds like Las Vegas all over again. They dragged the Mayor into that one,' Frank commented, starting to rise from his seat.

'Their parole term ended two months ago, Mr Duffy, so I can't legally comment and I certainly can't promise anything,' Trevor said, 'but I'll see what I can find out. I hope you find your missing girl.'

'Thank you, sir, I appreciate your time.' Frank nodded a respectful salute to Trevor before turning to leave the office.

***

Nathan didn't sound happy on the phone to Hardy in London. Paul and Anthony were trying to piece together the conversation.

'Who is calling the shots there?' Nathan asked. 'Wait!'

He quickly explained to his brothers about Thomas Riley's demand to make contact with his office to get a message to Amy's parents. In some ways, it made perfect sense but it was a gamble. There was too much that could be said between the lines that could lead the police to call in on Thomas in his apartment.

'Tell him to do it but if he screws up, or if Thomas doesn't stick to his word one hundred percent, tell him you'll shoot his girl.' Paul suggested. 'They have a name, don't forget.'

Nathan relayed the message and ended the call.

***

Hardy explained the instructions from Boston. Thomas looked at Lucy. Her pretty, frightened face looked more beautiful than ever. Then he stared at Hardy in disgust and turned away.

'Thomas?' Lucy called, looking perplexed.

'Forget it. I couldn't make a call like that under pressure. Nobody could,' he admitted.

'You can,' Lucy said calmly. 'Amy's family need to know.' She left the sofa and placed her hand on Thomas's shoulder.

'No Lucy, I can't,' he responded gently.

Hardy looked at Thomas, who caught his eye and looked away again. Then Thomas looked at the clue again. He needed to take back control, or get the hell out. If the men in Boston's instructions really were to shoot, then Hardy would have the confidence to strike at any time. He printed out the clue in a large font, one for Lucy, one for Hardy and one for himself.

'Right, we need food. Let's take this to the kitchen and find something to eat.' Thomas stood up motioning towards the kitchen in an obvious attempt to prove he was not defeated enough to let the men in Boston get to him. He didn't look Hardy in the eye, not once.

The kitchen was small. There was enough space to cook and prepare a meal but not to hang around or eat – or solve one-hundred-million-dollar puzzles. They stood there though, waiting for pasta to cook while Lucy grated cheese.

'The mother of the almighty warrior,' quoted Thomas.

'Yes, King Arthur again surely,' Hardy contributed.

'That has to be the monk's legend he refers to, though it does seem a bit too obvious.' Lucy fumbled the last flakes of cheese onto the grater.

'Who was the other warrior of Camelot?' Thomas asked; his knowledge of the name related only to the lottery. Thomas wondered what Jason thought of using a British mythological figure like King Arthur as an icon for gambling.

'Sir Lancelot, I believe,' Lucy answered.

'*Under Ilium confused gave the monk's legend this magic.* Isn't Ilium an old Greek settlement?' Thomas asked. 'I'm sure we came across Ilium in an earlier clue.'

'Old Asia Minor, land of Troy, I think. Which is it now part of Turkey.' Lucy searched her memory for a link to a previous clue. 'Are we returning to Artemis's territory here?'

'Or Homer's poem,' Thomas said. 'When he met his wife-to-be, she was reading Homer's Odyssey.'

'OK, so we need the mother of a great warrior, possibly written by a monk – maybe Geoffrey of Monmouth. And we need a link to Troy,' said Hardy.

'What about confused?' asked Lucy. 'Maybe it's a twist on a Greek myth again – like Artemis and Diana, adopted into Roman mythology with names changed.'

After they ate, they returned to the living room and Lucy sat at the computer. After confirming that Ilium was a settlement, which was believed to have been built on the ruins of Troy, they broke down the search into sections, attempting to piece it together like a puzzle.

'Well, we know King Arthur's mother was supposedly Igerna,' said Lucy. 'There's plenty of information on his father, Uther Pendragon. Again, it was Geoffrey of Monmouth's original writings that documented the ancestry.'

'Maybe it's the monk's mother?' Hardy suggested, staring again at the clue in front of him.

Lucy continued searching. 'They didn't document their mothers much back in the Middle Ages did they?' she joked. 'Nope, I can't find any reference to Geoffrey of Monmouth's mother, at least on the primary biographical sites. I may have to delve deeper. Shame we can't take over a library for a while'.

'Hold on,' said Thomas, looking at the clue again. 'Logical thinking. A monk wrote of a great warrior. It doesn't have to be Geoffrey of Monmouth. Cross-reference *Troy warrior monk* and see what results you get.'

Another hour passed as Lucy searched fruitlessly to link the clues. 'This one's a bummer,' she said.

Thomas was writing his own notes again. The gunman was focussed on Lucy as she waited for that spark of inspiration. Lucy's mind raced back to Jason's original story about the ring. She wondered whether there was a connection to the Tower of London and the crown jewels. Her gut feeling was that eventually a clue, if not this one, would lead there. She wondered whether there could be a vault there, or if there was an official code for any of the jewels still housed within.

'Who was the great warrior of Troy?' asked Thomas.

'Hector, I believe,' Lucy replied, even before search results confirmed her knowledge. 'His mother was Queen Hecuba, apparently.'

She continued with the search, slowly becoming more despondent as they ruled out options.

'The only thing I know about Troy was the Trojan War itself,' Hardy intervened. 'Who was the great warrior there?'

'Achilles,' Lucy answered, proud of her recollection of Greek mythology. 'Though he was Greek.'

'OK, who was his mother?' Thomas asked.

Lucy searched, this time with success. 'Thetis, the sea nymph,' she said with a smile. 'Thetis tried to make her son immortal by dipping him in the River Styx. However, she forgot to wet the heel she held him by – thus the phrase "Achilles' heel". His heel was weak and vulnerable and according to legend that's where Paris shot him.'

She cross-referenced 'Monk' with 'Thetis' online; the results failed to uncover anything of value but Lucy made a direct hit when she cross-referenced 'Geoffrey of Monmouth' with 'Thetis'. She whooped, and Thomas and Hardy turned to her.

'According to many historians, several of Geoffrey of Monmouth's characters bore a resemblance to characters in Greek mythology. One in particular was the Lady of the Lake, who bore a resemblance to the sea nymph Thetis. Though Geoffrey only referred to the leader of the maidens of Avalon as Morgan Le Fey, later legends claim the Lady of the Lake was the leader of Avalon.' She paused briefly while reading further. 'Get this,' she continued. 'The Lady of the Lake was apparently the one that gave the sword Excalibur to King Arthur.'

'This is beginning to make sense,' said Thomas. 'And also explains the *confused*.'

'Again, it's pretty simple,' Hardy said.

Lucy looked at him, wondering if he was trying to undermine their efforts, or if he was beginning to get sucked into the hunt.

Thomas noted Hardy's buoyancy and wondered if he could use it to their advantage. 'It was Jason's way,' Thomas said, smiling over to Hardy as he spoke. 'I honestly feel that he set this hunt up for people to find his legacy and understand the sort of things that made him happy, angry or inquisitive. My intuition is telling me that he is taking this out of the computer now, though.'

'What would the password be, then?' Lucy asked, looking at Thomas for advice.

'He refers to this monk's legends, so the reference could be to Geoffrey or the sword – probably the sword itself, Try "Excalibur",' Thomas responded.

Lucy typed the word into the password box. It worked.

Chapter 27

Frank Duffy left Trevor Mouriati's office and headed back towards the river. The air was warm, the streets busy with students. Four or five young men with skateboards passed him, riding two-wheeled against the kerbside.

Within two hundred yards, he felt a tap on his shoulder. He jumped, sensing trouble, and took a sharp breath as he turned around. It was Trevor Mouriati. He handed Frank an envelope.

'I do hope you're wrong. You never met me and I'll never see you again, do you understand?' Trevor made his speech and then turned away, back towards his office.

Frank walked into a small park off Fenway. It was busy and all the benches were taken. He bought a mineral water from a hotdog stand and sat on the grass, leaning his back against a tree, and opened Trevor's envelope. Before he looked inside it, he scoured his surroundings. Either the police had given up on him, or their surveillance had moved to a safer distance. He wondered whether he had been spotted with Trevor and, if so, what they would make of it.

Inside the envelope was a typewritten note with an address at Philips Point. Underneath, hand-written in block capitals: *APPROACH WITH EXTREME CAUTION.*

Frank eventually found a cab and asked the driver to take him to Philips Point.

'At Swampscott?' the cab driver asked.

'I assume so,' Frank replied, embarrassed at his lack of geographical knowledge.

'It's about a half hour drive, maybe more depending on the traffic.'

'That's OK. Thanks.'

The cab dropped Frank at the far end of Swampscott, at the entrance to Philips Point, which was a series of farms and coastal residences. He looked at the address in his pocket; he could see Philips Manor from the roadside. The property was walled and though he couldn't see the entrance, he assumed that it was probably security gated. He wondered who lived there – surely not the Hammonds; it was almost palatial, as if royalty or a celebrity owned it.

Frank walked around, assessing the perimeter. He didn't really have a clue what to do next. *Approach with extreme caution*, he remembered. Every now and then a car passed. An older woman with two German Shepherds was sitting on the wall, smoking a cigarette, and he commented on the dogs. She was very elegant – and seduced by his 'Australian' accent. Frank let her assume she was right.

'Nice houses here,' he said. 'The manor looks impressive. Anybody famous live there?'

'Not anymore,' the woman responded. 'It used to be owned by the former president of the Massachusetts Senate. The house has been leased since then to all sorts of people. I believe the Rolling Stones wrote an album there a few years back.'

'Impressive!' Frank said, with a smile. 'High security, then?'

'You're not thinking of gate-crashing, young man?' the woman said, expelling a perfect circle with her cigarette smoke.

'Oh, no! Wouldn't dream of it, ma'am,' he responded with a wink.

'I like you,' the woman grinned. 'I could listen to your accent all day.' She called for the dogs and bade farewell to Frank. 'Enjoy the party,' she said as she moved on.

There was a small lane to the north of the property. The secluded lane dropped steeply towards the sea. Frank followed it for a while. The high wall to the manor trailed on to the beach. A small bush gave just enough leverage for Frank to look over but he could only see the roof of the manor. There didn't seem to be anybody around.

He looked around again and decided to climb over the wall. He chuckled as he landed. This was the second wall he had climbed in his adult life, the first being when he scaled the wall of Amy's parents' house. He landed awkwardly and winced a little as his ankle twisted. Then he slowly followed the wall back up the hill to get a better view of the house.

***

It was shortly after twelve o'clock in Boston when Nathan Hammond answered the phone from London. Thomas and Lucy had moved further with another clue. Nathan was relieved that Thomas had backed down from his demands to contact Amy's parents. However, time was moving on. Just how many clues were there?

Nathan was told that the latest clue hinted that they should get their passports together. It was very likely that they were close to being given a direction in which to travel. Nathan's theory was that the money was in a bank account, so the clues would have to lead towards a particular town or bank. He initially thought this was likely to be in America but the clues still seemed to be focussed on England. They needed to progress further and faster.

After Nathan had updated his brothers, Paul wondered whether they would have any use for Amy and Emmanuelle.

'I don't think it's a coincidence that Amy was left the ring,' Nathan responded. 'But at least she's here in case we need her. We'll dispose of her when the time is right.'

'You know the plan, Nathan.' Paul gave his brother a firm stare.

Nathan stood up and looked out of the window. 'The police found the Mercedes at Gatwick,' he said. 'There'll be a photo-fit of you all over the UK papers by now. You'll have to lay low until the last minute. I hate this pretence with the girls.'

'Speaking of which,' Anthony interrupted, 'the girls are expecting another meeting shortly. What's our line today? Emmanuelle wants to go home so we're going to have to come up with a pretty good reason for her to stay if she's not to get too suspicious.'

'London had better hurry up,' Paul said. 'Let's delay meeting the girls for as long as possible.' He rose from his chair and watched the two women in the garden. They seemed relaxed. 'I'll have trouble getting back into England if Jason's banked his fortune there. Let's just hope our information is good.'

Chapter 28

Thomas, Lucy and Hardy looked at the new page in amazement. This web page was completely different to the others: there was movement everywhere. The background was light purple with multicoloured letters tiled over the page. A bar of images rolled over to reveal letters when the mouse went over, with letters at the top and bottom of the page framing an animated image of even more multicoloured letters, which were moving so rapidly they gave a sparkling effect. The page address was melodema. com/gothere.

'This is going to take us ages to unscramble,' Thomas said. 'Jason wants to make us work!'

'That's it, though,' Lucy, said instantly. 'He said that in his will – something about anybody that claims his fortune would have to work for it or earn it.'

'The trouble is,' Thomas added, his voice dispirited, 'Jason wouldn't have known we would be under pressure and lives would be at risk. If he's watching us now, he must be devastated.'

'I hope he *is* watching,' Hardy said, with a sadistic smile.

'Arsehole,' Thomas muttered under his breath. Lucy heard him, Hardy didn't.

'Where do we begin?' Lucy asked, handing a pen to Thomas while she took over the computer.

Thomas started with 'gothere', trying to work out if the

clue was 'go there' or 'got here'. He sensed was that this was the starting point for the next clue. Lucy isolated the main background image. There were five rows of letters: A B C D E taking the top row and U V W X Y the bottom. It seemed as if there was a colour code, though some colours were the same; many just seemed a darker shade and many were grey. She went through each letter:

A,B,C,F,H,J,K,L,M,P,Q,T,V,W,X,Y were all grey

D, N, R, U were purple

I, S were green

E, G, O, were red

Lucy printed the information twice then sat with Hardy on the sofa while Thomas went to work on the animated image. The image was a square, with multicoloured letters moving quickly. He saved the image, which was called *link. gif*, and opened it up in his animation software. Surprisingly, for all that movement, there were only five separate frames. Thomas stared at each frame to see if anything jumped out at him. Eventually he decided to count the letters: forty-three. He counted each frame and each had forty-three letters.

'It's a jumbled message – I think it's simple. Each word is a different colour.' Thomas spoke without looking behind him.

'Let's hope,' Hardy replied.

Thomas began to write down each coloured letter from the first frame:

Red = STHRAEF

Blue = TNEMMO

Yellow = MY

Orange = HTE

Purple = MSGSNII

Pink= STRPDOUE

Black = IS

Green = THRMOE

White = MY

To Thomas's amazement, the four other frames were identical. 'I think these are just anagrams,' he said. He printed out the letters and offered the print-out to Lucy and Hardy. Hardy claimed it.

Thomas moved on to the rollover images. It occurred to him that the latest clue was a combination of all of those that had come before. Though he was writing down the letters hidden underneath the coloured squares, he reminded himself to check the images for steganographic clues, as he had done at the beginning. It was a long process, though. Underneath each rollover image, he wrote the letters out by colour; the message wasn't difficult to read or unscramble. It simply said: *all the clues have now passed.*

There were three rapid bangs on the door and they all jumped. Thomas and Lucy immediately turned to Hardy. He took out his gun and placed a finger to his lips as he made his way towards the door. Three more knocks followed.

Lucy watched Thomas for his reaction and suppressed the urge to yell for help. The most likely visitors at this time on a Sunday were their colleagues.

Thomas was watching Hardy.

There was a small gap in the side of the curtain. Hardy could see one person – a man in a suit. He looked confident, he had no case or clipboard; certainly not a salesman. He was staring up at the windows.

Hardy whispered to Thomas, 'Were you expecting anybody?'

Thomas shook his head.

Lucy moved towards Thomas. Hardy caught the movement and waved the gun in her direction. Lucy nonchalantly put up her hands but continued anyway, looking over Thomas's shoulder towards the window.

'Can you see who it is?' she whispered.

'It's a suit. Grey hair, tall,' Hardy said.

There was a knock on the door again. This time they heard a voice shout, 'DI Riley?'

'It's DCI Alderman,' Thomas whispered. 'Scotland Yard.'

Hardy released the safety catch on the gun. Alderman called again. Hardy ducked, his back against the wall holding his gun in both hands. Lucy thought it looked like a Hollywood showdown. She wanted to run upstairs. The bottom of the stairwell was only a two-second dash.

Thomas looked at her and shook his head.

Hardy saw the movement and pointed the gun directly at Thomas. His face was angry and he was clearly flustered. 'Move an inch and you're both history,' he muttered.

***

'We don't really need Emmanuelle any more.' Anthony Hammond raised the issue with his brothers. Paul was still watching the girls from the window. 'She was our tool to get Amy over here and she's played her part well but she needs to go to work tomorrow. We have to look at our options.'

'Stop worrying about her,' Nathan responded. 'I'll deal with her if we can't move with the main clues today.'

Nathan joined Paul and watched as Amy walked rapidly to the edge of the lawn. She bent down, appearing to look at some flowers and started picking at some leaves. Emmanuelle was watching her.

'Amy's the problem. I feel a bit sorry for her really, she doesn't have a clue,' Paul commented, watching her summon Emmanuelle, who strolled towards her friend.

'I just hope our plan works because I can't see how we could let her go at all now, if we get delayed much longer,' Nathan said.

'It shouldn't come to that,' Paul replied. 'She's a damn pretty little thing,' he added quietly.

'You're going soft on her,' laughed Nathan.

Paul smiled. 'I'll be softer on a hundred million dollars.'

Nathan looked over his brother's shoulder at the girls. 'What are they doing?'

'I was wondering that myself,' said Paul.

The girls started heading back to the swing bench, heads down, looking at their hands, ripping the leaves as they spoke.

✳✳✳

Frank Duffy headed back towards the lane. He knew that it was more than likely the girls were being watched so he didn't want to draw attention to himself. He had managed to catch Amy's attention but her words had confused him.

Amy told him that her hosts were the FBI and that Scotland Yard knew where she was. They hadn't mentioned any names but had said that bogus detectives claiming to be from Scotland Yard were after her. Frank told her to keep her wits about her but was unable to warn her properly.

Was Amy in danger? Trevor Mouriati suspected that the girls could be here, and he was connected to the Hammonds. Maybe the Hammonds had fed Amy lies, convincing her that the real police force was the bogus one. The more Frank thought about it, the more it made sense: the Hammonds were using Amy for information. They were after Jason's money.

He turned around, briefly wondering whether to attract the girls' attention again, angry with himself for not thinking quickler. Amy obviously knew little or nothing about Jason's treasure hunt. Frank paused, but the women were walking back to the swing bench. He couldn't risk attracting their attention again. He decided to return to Boston and explain the situation to the police; he could at least give them a location.

Frank headed towards the wall but it was too high to scramble over. He looked further up towards the house and saw a low branch that would give him a foothold. As he headed towards it, he stepped on a rose bush stub. The twig snapped and he hoped nobody heard. Panicking, he tried getting over the wall as fast as he could. Amy and Emmanuelle both turned involuntarily towards the sound.

Paul and Nathan were still watching and looked in the

direction of their stare. 'There's somebody there,' Paul shouted.

The men ran out of the house and saw the intruder disappear over the wall into the lane. They heard footsteps running parallel with them. Paul placed his finger on his lips, willing his brother to be quiet, as they kept pace with the intruder.

Frank slowed, out of breath, believing that he had escaped the immediate vicinity of the garden. The brothers chased around to the front and reached the entrance to the lane before Frank did. As they appeared round the corner they saw Frank had stopped. He was looking back, his hands were on his knees and he was trying to catch his breath. He looked up as Paul kneed him in the stomach, winced and doubled over.

Nathan went behind him, pulling his arms behind his back, straightening him up.

'Who are you?' Paul asked.

The intruder looked terrified and was obviously in pain. Paul looked into the eyes of the man who stood before him and thought he recognised him.

Recognition dawned on Frank's face too. He remembered the 'opportunistic mugging' six days ago when he was followed as he left the office and made for his car. The man had threatened him with a gun. He had asked for information about Jason Chadwick's will. Frank had told the man that there was a letter which had asked him to maintain an internet domain but at that point, overwhelmed by panic, he could not remember the domain name. He remembered that it started with the letter 'M' and that the money would be deposited into a bank account and further instructions would be left at the bank.

The man had poked the gun sharply into his back and said, 'I want to see that letter.' Frank told him that he couldn't get it until the following day when the office reopened. The man refused to agree to a pre-arranged meeting, but told Frank to go for a walk at lunchtime.

The man warned Frank against telling anybody and ran from the car park. Later that evening Frank returned to the office alone, collected Jason's orange folder and left it in his office. Thus began the chain of events that led him to where he was right now. The man before him was the man in the car park. Anything he said could hurt Amy and Emmanuelle.

Frank had to protect them, so he didn't answer. As a result, he took another punch to the stomach. The pain was horrific; he could feel his organs move to accommodate the blow and his first attempt at breathing was impossible. He panicked, his eyes widened and he produced a cough that covered his attacker in saliva, mucus and blood.

'What were you doing in the garden?'

Frank shook his head, attempting to speak, terrified that he would take another blow. The other man searched his pockets and found his wallet and British driving license. The Americans nodded to each other then grabbed Frank under each arm and dragged him back down the lane, towards the beach.

'He's that lawyer from London. I thought I recognised him,' one of them said. Frank's heart sank; he knew then there was little hope now. 'You didn't turn up for our meeting, did you?'

Frank was powerless. He tried to think but his pain and terror were too intense. There was no escape.

The men didn't even speak as they carried him. The lane descended steeply to the beach, where they threw him face down on to the ground. There was nobody else around.

'Please...' Frank whispered as he looked at the barrel of the man's gun.

'Who knows you're here?'

'I'm working alone,' Frank said, attempting to rise to his feet. The man swiped the side of his head and he landed back on the ground on his hands and knees. 'I know you want Jason's money and I know where it is,' he claimed, speaking with haste through his panic, bravery disintegrating with every breath. He was selling out: anything to buy a few more moments of precious life. Not that he could give them much. His only power was his knowledge and their only weakness was that they didn't know how much knowledge he had. He had to remain strong.

The man from the car park looked at his wallet. 'Frank Duffy. Of course. How did you get here?'

'I followed leads from Jason's instructions. He knew if there was a problem you would be at the heart of it.'

'Liar!' the other man shouted.

'The FBI has been following me all week. It won't be long until they arrive. They know what you're up to. Let me help you,' Frank stuttered making another attempt to stand up.

Paul pulled back Nathan's arm as his brother pointed the gun at Frank, and released the safety. Nathan was furious; he kicked Frank between the legs and Frank yelped with the pain.

'You liar!' he shouted. Nathan kicked Frank again, then again and again. Paul shouted to his brother to stop. If the FBI really were following him, they needed to know what the Feds knew and how Frank had been able to find the house. Nobody other than Darren Cooper knew about the place, or so he thought.

Paul tried desperately to calm his brother. They couldn't risk going too far and Frank definitely had information about the money, otherwise he wouldn't be here at all.

'Wait!' he shouted to Nathan, but something had snapped in Nathan. Paul had seen it before, but this time he was out of control. Nathan's face was distorted with rage, he was shouting 'liar' with every vicious kick.

Frank looked up at Paul with terror in his eyes. Nathan drew his gun. Paul reached for Nathan's arm to stop him from pulling the trigger, cursing as he did so, but it was too late.

Nathan shot Frank in the head. The lawyer lay lifeless on the sand, his eyes still open, looking in Paul's direction.

Chapter 29

Amy sat on the swing bench with Emmanuelle. She was confused. 'What if that man was right? He obviously risked a lot to try and speak to us. He had an English accent. What would he be doing over here in Boston? Do you think that he's the same man that tried to warn me back home?'

'It is strange but it seems unlikely. These guys don't really seem the criminal type and you've even spoken with that detective from London,' Emmanuelle responded 'If anything, it's surely a worry that this guy knew where we were. Maybe we should tell Agent Stringham?'

'I don't know. Don't you think it's odd that there are no televisions here? Not even a radio. We don't have a clue what's going on outside these walls.' Amy spoke quietly, afraid of being overheard.

'You could be right. I don't think we should say anything for now. Let's keep an open mind, see if they let us leave tonight as they planned. In the meantime, maybe we need to explore a little more of the immediate area, in case we need an escape route.'

'Good idea. We'll have to be careful, though. If the Englishman was right, we need a plan that can't fail.'

The conversations over the past two days had been therapy for Amy. She liked Emmanuelle. She had the sort of inner confidence and wisdom that Amy admired. She spoke fondly of Jason and she felt at times that Emmanuelle had felt the same way as she did about him. Emmanuelle was obviously devastated when Jason had fallen so hopelessly in love with Penny. She told her that Penny seemed distant at the beginning of her relationship with Jason but they had become good friends. Amy asked her what had happened between Jason and Penny.

'They drifted apart. His work with MIT became a priority over Penny and the kids. Any time he tried to have with them was constantly interrupted and eventually all quality time simply stopped. He always loved her but the demands of work dominated their relationship.'

'That's sad,' Amy said.

'He came to me not long before they split to ask my advice. He did love her but he could never resist the thrill of the chase when it came to knowledge and the production of his other baby, hypertext mark-up language.' Emmanuelle smiled. 'He was going to pack it in and move back to Las Vegas to save his marriage but one day Penny just moved out and took the kids. Nothing he could do or say would change her mind. Jason went to pieces and even the time he spent with his sons after they separated tore him up. Eventually Penny stopped access as his work commitments kept interrupting his time with the boys. Jason couldn't cope. He ended up burying himself, further in his work and shut Penny out of his mind. She never gave him a proper chance really. I could see it from both sides but Penny changed, she blocked out all Jason's acquaintances.'

'I can see how it happened,' said Amy. 'I could never see him holding down a relationship. That must be difficult for a man with so much passion for life.'

There was a distant crack towards the beach. They both looked up without commenting on it, then Amy looked at the house. One of the agents was sitting outside the kitchen. He was on the phone and writing notes into a file.

'That's the only thing about Jason's apparent suicide note that made it seem believable. I wonder what made him write that note. Or if he didn't write it then whoever did must have known something about him.'

Emmanuelle told Amy that she didn't know the details of the suicide note so Amy explained what she could remember the detectives from Cornwall telling her on that terrible day. Emmanuelle listened, then said, 'I don't believe a word of it.'

Amy was feeling uneasy again. If the intruder was right, could she really be in serious danger? What would anybody want from her? She didn't even have Jason's ring any more. She began thinking about her parents. They must be upset to think that she came all the way over here, only to end up a prisoner again.

***

Paul Hammond smacked his brother across the face. Nathan stuck the barrel of the gun under his brother's chin.

'I don't need a fucking lecture!' Nathan screamed. The anger on his face confirmed Paul's fears that he was going to be a liability. It had been the same when he was back in Las Vegas and his temper had alerted Donald Chadwick to their fraud. How could his brother be capable of such genius and yet be so unpredictable and irrational?

Paul knew that he had to tread carefully. He had to calm Nathan down and stop him from doing any more damage – like pulling the trigger right now.

'No lectures,' Paul said, calmly easing Nathan's gun away from his face. 'It's just that it would have been nice to delay pulling the trigger a few more minutes to find out exactly how much of what he said was true.'

'If the FBI are on to us they wouldn't have allowed him to get within a whisker of here. They'd be all over us by now,' Nathan claimed, still angry but putting the gun back inside his jacket.

'That doesn't answer the question of what he was doing here and how much he seemed to know. It's not just that, though. The lawyer said that he knew where the money was. Did he speak with the girls? If so, what did he say? Too many unanswered questions.'

'He was a liar. We wouldn't have found anything out from him,' Nathan argued.

'Well it's damage limitation right now. We have to dispose of the body.' The brothers dragged the body to the far side of the beach, away from the lane. Though the lane was rarely used, some of the locals had been seen there in the past. They certainly didn't want the body to be found before they moved out. Paul wondered how the investigations were going in London. The sooner they made the move the better.

The brothers walked back to the house via the lane rather than directly through the gardens. Both were dirty and Paul had blood splattered on his shirt. Anthony heard them enter the house and went to meet them. Paul quietly explained what had happened with Frank Duffy and made a gesture of a gun shape with his hands, pointing to Nathan as he walked up the stairs. Anthony raised his eyebrows.

'We'll discuss this after I've changed. We may need to improvise,' Paul said. 'We need news from London ASAP.'

Chapter 30

There were times when Riley was attending crisis training when he doubted himself. They were taught organisation skills under intense time pressures; they were trained to deal with potentially volatile situations, including terrorist attacks, kidnapping and hostage negotiations. These were always *potential* problems. Thomas had never been in the front line of anything serious before. He used to pray that he would know instinctively how to deal with any situation should it ever happen to him.

Be strong! he told himself now. Hardy's finger was approximately one centimetre from ending his, and probably Lucy's, life. Hardy looked scared, his hand was shaking. This could have been an opportunity to calm the situation, and possibly take control of the weapon but Alderman's presence at the front door put both of their lives in danger.

Lucy was crouched behind him with her left hand on his shoulder. Both kept low so as not to make any shadows. They could hear Alderman's footsteps; he was obviously looking around the perimeter of the house. They heard him speak; his voice was muffled but from the tone, it sounded as if he was speaking into a mobile telephone. Hardy's gun remained pointed in Thomas's direction.

Thomas felt a tug on his back pocket from Lucy. She was obviously finding it hard to steady herself. His comb fell from the pocket and Hardy looked over; maybe he thought she was trying to attract Alderman's attention.

'What the fuck are you doing?' His voice was loud and startled Lucy. Thomas looked down and saw the comb. He tried to stand up but Hardy's forward momentum knocked him backwards to the floor. Hardy lunged forward, grabbed Lucy's hair and she shrieked. He put the gun to Lucy's head and pushed her head to the ground.

Thomas wondered if Alderman had heard anything. It went quiet for a few seconds. A door slammed then a car started up and drove away.

'Let go!' Thomas shouted. 'He's gone! Let her go!'

Hardy rose to his feet, dragging Lucy up with him, and threw her towards Thomas. There was a clump of Lucy's hair in his hand. 'I have no patience with either of you now,' he said. His gun was pointed at Thomas and he was out of breath. 'Solve this thing now!'

Thomas pulled Lucy to him and gave her a hand a gentle squeeze. She looked scared and confused. Their eyes caught for a brief moment; he hoped that she could read his mind. *We need to overpower him.*

'You better hope that nobody else comes. If they do, you'll both be dead in two seconds. If I'm going down, I'm sure as hell taking you with me.' Hardy seemed to smile as he spoke. It was a nervous smile, as if he were uncomfortable playing the role of a baddy.

Thomas's concern was for Lucy. He had to keep things calm.

***

Arnold Pearce sat on a cane chair in the sun lounge. His wife was inside talking to Gerard, who had arrived concerned about his girlfriend. Arnold had met him a few times with Amy – he was a friendly enough man. Gerard felt that he should be doing something to find Amy and had suggested travelling to Boston to search for her. Arnold would have liked to go too, but he couldn't leave his wife at home to wait.

As much as Arnold was angry at the police for losing Amy, he was also confused. What on this earth could be so important for her to be kidnapped? Especially in such an organised and professional manner. Was this really something to do with Jason, as the note had suggested? Or was the kidnapping something to do with one of his own cases? Maybe there was a connection with an old case file that could link to Jason. The thought that possibly he was to blame was tearing him apart.

He phoned Scotland Yard. This was an angle that nobody had touched upon. DCI Alderman was not in the office but Arnold explained his theory to another senior officer. They arranged to meet later that afternoon at Arnold's office.

* * *

Two hours of brainpower was starting to yield results for Thomas, Lucy and Hardy. Nobody had spoken a word for ten minutes but eventually the mood lightened enough for all three to communicate again. The words from Jason's puzzles were starting to form even though the final message wasn't too clear.

Hardy worked out that STHRAEF became 'Fathers'; MSGSNII became 'missing'; TNEMMO was probably 'moment'; MY and IS and HTE were self-explanatory, and THRMSOE was almost certainly 'mothers'.

Lucy was still sore from her fight with Hardy and her scalp was raw to the touch. She was working on the background clue. She had a theory that U, D, N and R were letters used twice, as opposed to their original thought that the coloured letters were a further abbreviation, which would give the letters DDNNRRUUEGNO. Thomas was working on his puzzle; he had forgotten to check for steganographic clues.

Hardy's phone rang. It was the man in Boston, desperate

for an update. Thomas and Lucy stopped what they were doing to watch Hardy, both concerned that he might put Amy and Emmanuelle in further danger. Hardy explained that they were close and that he believed that this was the last clue, but it was complicated. The voice from Boston sounded agitated but they couldn't hear clearly enough to decipher the words. Something wasn't right, though. Thankfully, Hardy did not mention the problems they'd had with Scotland Yard.

When Hardy ended the conversation he turned to Thomas. 'Pressure's on. There's been developments. We've got to get moving – even I'm starting to worry about Amy. Nerves are fraying, if you know what I mean.'

Thomas was shocked: was that genuine compassion from Hardy? He looked at Lucy, who raised her eyebrows. Maybe it was simply a deliberate attempt to put pressure on the hunt but Thomas wasn't keen on gambling right now.

'I've got it!' Lucy suddenly announced. 'It's *underground*.'

They collated all the research so far to try and make sense of what they had: * *Is Underground * Mothers, Fathers, is, my, the, moment, missing, link, Go there * all the clues have now passed. *

'We need that pink word,' said Hardy.

Thomas started looking for anagram deciphering programs online. He was half hoping not to find any, knowing that they could have used such a program earlier and saved a lot of time. Finally they found what they needed; it cost nine dollars and Thomas used his credit card, with Hardy's permission. He typed STRPDOUE into the software and instantly the result produced, 'proudest'.

'Now this clue makes sense,' Lucy began. 'It is either – My mother's proudest moment. My father is the missing link – or the other way round.'

'Yes, probably the other way round,' said Thomas. 'The problem is, the clue still doesn't make much sense, at least for now.'

Thomas had needed the lavatory for hours, but had waited until Hardy had calmed before asking. He suggested that they all went one by one and the other two sat on top of the stairs to wait. Hardy chuckled; he was obviously feeling the effects of the coffee himself. He made Thomas and Lucy empty their pockets to make sure they didn't have any pens, screwdrivers or mobile phones.

Thomas was one step ahead. He had already written a note to Lucy and tucked it inside his sock. When it was Hardy's turn to use the lavatory, Thomas passed his note to Lucy and she slipped it into her own sock. She would find time to read it at the first opportunity.

Back downstairs, they re-read the clues and tried to make sense of them. *My father's proudest moment - My mother is the missing link.*

'Well, we know that Jason's father ran security in Las Vegas. What his proudest moment was, I'm not sure.'

'This is probably a good time to ask a friend,' Lucy suggested, looking over to Hardy. 'Emmanuelle, maybe. She would know Jason's parents.'

Hardy called the man in Boston. Lucy motioned a drink to Thomas and Hardy, who was awaiting a response. He nodded and she went into the kitchen to put the kettle on. She deliberately made as much noise as possible, clunking the cups and rattling the spoons as she got the sugar and coffee ready. She was only just out of Hardy's sight but felt brave enough to reach into her sock to read Thomas's note.

At some point we must turn this around. We will not be needed much longer. Nor Amy. We can help her from a distance. It would be better to try shortly after he has spoken with Boston, first chance.

She screwed up the note and put in the bin before bringing the drinks through to the living room. She winked at Thomas as she handed over his coffee. *Good,* Thomas thought. They were still on the same wavelength. Deep inside, he was terrified – this was going to be one of the most dangerous things he had ever attempted. He hoped Lucy wasn't feeling as bad.

Hardy ended the call. 'They're going to speak with Emmanuelle and Amy and see what they can find out. They'll phone back shortly.' He looked pleased with himself. It was obvious that the Hammonds were happy to finally be brought into the hunt.

Thomas looked over at Lucy and discreetly shook his head, warning her not to try anything yet. There was no way they could make a move while they were waiting for a call from Boston.

***

Attempts to contact Riley and Bridges had failed and DCI Moore was angry. Their lack of contact was also adding fuel to the gossip that they were developing a relationship outside the station. It was all getting too complicated.

DCI Alderman had phoned to say that he'd tried to visit Riley but there was no answer, in spite of all the curtains being closed. Alderman had been told that the FBI had lost contact with Frank Duffy. Either Frank had spent the entire day in the hotel or left at the crack of dawn unnoticed. Kensington and Chelsea police had left two officers with the Pearces, waiting for any news from Boston, but as yet there was nothing. Arnold had a theory that the kidnapping might be linked to one of his work cases; they were investigating this now. There were no fingerprints on the Mercedes at Gatwick; there were some fibres, which had been sent for testing, but results were not expected back until tomorrow.

The Computer Crime Unit had made little headway with melodema.com. They were looking for a link to Amy but hadn't found anything, although they believed that the ring, or symbol, could be significant. Since they now had the ring, maybe Amy's kidnappers would ask for it in exchange for Amy.

Alderman had toyed with the theory that Amy could have

teamed up with Emmanuelle to hunt for Jason's fortune. However, when they checked Amy's laptop computer there was no mention of melodema.com. The unit had scanned Amy's emails; there was nothing suspicious about her conversations with Emmanuelle.

Alderman and Moore were both still sure that Jason's money was the motive for the kidnap of Amy and indirectly, Vito Rolanski's murder.

Chapter 31

Paul Hammond changed his blood-spattered clothes then updated Anthony on the plan. 'We need to keep an eye on the girls. If the Englishman has spoken to them, they'll be extra cautious. They might even try escaping. Where are they now?'

'They were on the swing bench.' Anthony went to the window. The girls were still in the garden, though not on the bench; they were standing at the cliff edge, looking out towards the sea.

'We have to be extremely careful. I hope Hardy hurries up.'

The phone rang within ten seconds of Paul's words. It was Hardy. They needed information. Paul explained that there had been an intruder from England in the grounds. He didn't say what had happened to him, other than it had been sorted.

'We need more information. Let's bring the girls in,' Paul commanded his brother.

Nathan entered the room. He had cleaned himself up and had a shave. He seemed in good spirits, almost high.

'You OK, bro?' Paul asked.

'Yeah, I think so. It must be adrenaline or something, I feel totally switched on.'

'The *kill thrill*,' Paul commented, rolling his eyes. 'Don't get too used to it.' He turned to Anthony and their eyes connected as they went to the door to collect the girls.

Paul and Anthony went into the garden. The girls were nowhere to be seen. The brothers looked at each other.

'Oh, no!' Paul ran to the end of the garden, Anthony following. When they couldn't see Amy and Emmanuelle, Paul panicked. He called their names several times.

Anthony ran back to the house to see if they'd gone back inside. He chose not to say anything to Nathan. The girls were not in the house.

Paul and Anthony met up by the back door. They both had the same thought: 'The beach!' That was probably a worse scenario than the girls actually running away. Frank Duffy's body was there, hidden but not very well.

Paul climbed down the rocks with Anthony just behind him. The cliff was steep but not too sheer; there was a pathway of sorts but it wasn't used much. Anthony caught his foot on a bramble and nearly lost his balance. He cursed and Paul ran back to check he was alright.

'Hello!'

They heard a shout from below, a woman's voice. 'Anybody there?'

'Amy? Emmanuelle?' Paul shouted back.

'Down here!' came the reply.

Paul's tension didn't ease. Had they discovered the body? The brothers jumped down two more overhangs before they saw two faces, smiling up at them.

The women were sitting on a rock, close to the shore edge. Emmanuelle emptied her hands of stones, tossing them in the air so they fell into the clear waters. 'It's beautiful down here,' she said, grabbing another handful of stones.

Paul smiled at them, trying to hide his anxiety. Behind them, merely fifteen yards away, was Frank Duffy's body. Paul needed to get the girls back to the house.

'Come on, you two. It's not safe at this beach. To be honest, I'd rather you stayed within the grounds of the house. Let's get back and I'll get Agent Stringham. We can update you on the latest.'

The girls hesitated, happy to stay where they were for a

while. Paul continued smiling but ushered them again, this time with a little more severity. They looked at each other, confused by his urgency, but headed back towards the lane, as the path back up to the house via the cliff was steep. Emmanuelle looked at her hands; there was blood on them. 'I think I've cut myself,' she said and ran back to the water's edge to wash her hands.

'C'mon you can do that at the house.' Paul said, his agitation starting to show.

Emmanuelle dipped her hands in the sea and wiped them. There didn't seem to be a cut. She paused briefly, looking momentarily to her left in the direction of Frank's makeshift grave. Paul's heart sank but then she smiled as she started walking back up the hill.

Amy noticed that Paul was wearing a different suit to the one he had on earlier. She'd agreed with Emmanuelle not to mention the man who had spoken with them earlier, but she had noticed Paul and Anthony's agitation at the beach.

Inside the house they sat in a large room at the back of the house. Nathan was waiting for them. 'I thought that you might need an update,' Nathan said.

Amy smiled and sat down next to Emmanuelle.

Nathan told them that they were making progress. Police in the UK had located a 'mole' at Scotland Yard who should be in custody later that night for questioning. They hoped to find out more later. 'DCI Dawson' had notes in front of him; it was almost as if he were reading them, Amy thought.

'Can I go home tonight then?' Emmanuelle asked.

'I can't see any reason why not, but we'll await the nod from London first, if that's alright with you?'

'Great, yes, thanks,' she responded.

'Meanwhile, we're continuing our own investigation this end to see if we can substantiate Jason's theory about his parents being murdered,' Nathan explained, also looking down at his notes. 'Emmanuelle, can you remember what Donald Chadwick was working on before he retired?'

'I'm not too sure but I know that he was working with

NASA for a while. Jason told me that his father had developed some digital technology enabling a camera to zoom without losing detail. He also revolutionised the security in the hotels in Las Vegas, especially those that opened at the end of the 1980s and the beginning of the 90s. I believe Donald developed a foolproof opening system for the vaults that he installed.' Emmanuelle looked pleased with herself for recollecting a trivial conversation with her friend from so many years earlier.

'Did Jason's mother help at all?' Nathan asked.

'Violet Chadwick? Oh, I don't know. She was a proper lady, she liked her circle of friends but that's all. Violet enjoyed the easy life but in spite of her royalty act, she was a really kind and loving woman. She never took much to being an American though, she was British and proud of it.'

Nathan was taking notes. He paused as if he were looking for inspiration or another question. 'So they didn't work together at all?'

'Not that I'm aware of,' Emmanuelle replied.

It went quiet for a while. Paul looked towards Nathan, who was still writing notes. Then he turned to Amy and Emmanuelle to thank them for their help and finished the meeting.

***

Paul Hammond turned to Nathan as he watched the girls return to the garden. 'They seem very relaxed. I don't think that guy managed to get to them, do you?' he asked.

'We were lucky, I think. He was obviously lying to save his own life, the coward.'

'Or ...' interrupted Paul, 'the FBI knows more than we think they do and we're being monitored. I think Anthony should get the boat ready.'

'I agree,' Nathan said, leaving the room to update his brother while Paul phoned London.

Chapter 32

Thomas and Lucy were back at the computer. Thomas remembered how Jason had hidden earlier clues; he felt that there was more to this final set of clues than they were reading.

The .gif image that had housed the anagram clue was called *remember.gif*. He began to look for steganographic clues. *Remember what?* he thought. Each of the rollover images also had a name and he wrote them down in order *travel.jpg, wisely.jpg* and *and.jpg*. He checked each .jpg for steganographic clues but there was still something missing. He felt that the overall set of clues should read: *All the clues have now passed. Go there, travel wisely and remember my father's proudest moment and my mother is the missing link.* However, this still left the 'is underground' clue. Something was missing: maybe it simply referred to Jason's fortune – his fortune *is underground.*

Hardy's phone went – it was the man in Boston. Hardy was on the phone for a while reading out the clues. Thomas watched him writing notes but Lucy was watching Thomas, hoping for a sign that the time was right to try and make their escape.

Hardy was sitting on the back of the sofa, facing the computer. Thomas stood up in front of the computer chair; he could see Hardy's gun, it was within reach. Hardy was writing notes, the pad to his right, also on the back of the sofa and he was holding the phone with his left hand. He didn't seem to be aware that Thomas was looking at him. Thomas resisted the temptation to make a move while Hardy was on the phone. He had to time his move perfectly.

As he listened to Hardy explain the clues and continued to watch him write notes, the solution hit Thomas like a train. It all made sense. Excalibur Hotel in Las Vegas, that's where they needed to be.

The second that Hardy ended the call, Thomas moved. On seeing this, Lucy also moved in. Thomas quickly reached inside Hardy's pocket for the gun. He caught the handgrip, but not tightly enough. In a reflex action, Hardy brought his arm in towards his chest, trapping Thomas's hand with the gun.

Lucy had a resin paperweight in her hand that she'd been playing with while Hardy was making his call. She moved to hit Hardy on the head with it but at the last moment Hardy moved his head back and she struck him on the side of the face. Hardy winced, releasing Thomas's hand. Thomas continued forward and Hardy tumbled over the back of the sofa. The gun flew to his side.

The impact of the paperweight forced Lucy to let go and this also went onto the floor underneath the computer desk. Thomas landed on top of Hardy. Hardy was almost upside down, his feet up on the back of the sofa, his head and shoulders on the floor.

There was a lot of noise but no words were spoken. Lucy reached over Hardy to grab the gun. Hardy tumbled sideways, Thomas manoeuvred himself on top of him, his knees either side of Hardy's chest.

Hardy's hand was an inch from the gun as he landed. He was aware that Lucy was reaching for it and he stretched out his fingers. He couldn't grab it but found enough motion to flick the gun underneath the sofa. Lucy's arms were not long enough to reach it. As she pulled back over Hardy's face, he took a bite at her hand. She winced as she broke it free and Thomas looked up concerned.

Hardy twisted his body so that he was on his side and drew his arm in to his chest. Thomas was on top of him, trying to manoeuvre him onto his back, tugging on Hardy's arm. Hardy managed to get to his inside jacket pocket and pulled out a small canister of pepper spray. Thomas took a direct hit to the face with the spray and involuntarily screamed, letting go of Hardy and bringing both hands to his own face.

The pepper spray took them both by surprise. Thomas let go of Hardy; he was still on top of him but was finding it hard to breathe or see. He was coughing and mucus was streaming from his nose. Hardy wriggled Thomas's weight off him as Lucy tried once more to reach the gun. She put her hands to his face and he could feel her thumbs over his eyes. Hardy managed to catch her wrists before she could apply any pressure and used his weight to manoeuvre her to the floor, turning sideways. She screamed and he slammed her head hard to the floor.

Three seconds later, the gun was back in Hardy's hand. He sat with his back to the wall, out of breath, his cheek and head aching. It felt like his cheekbone had been fractured and his ribs felt as if they had sunk into his lungs. Lucy was unconscious.

Thomas had crawled to the edge of the sofa. His head was buried into the arm of the sofa and he was hyperventilating. He couldn't see anything and the only sound was Hardy's breathing and the bang and thud of his own heartbeat. He didn't know what had happened to Lucy but he feared the worst. He eventually started to regain his breath. *What had he done?* Thomas felt that his mistake had condemned them all to certain death. He tried to speak but couldn't; he could only cough. He was expecting a bullet any second.

Chapter 33

DCI Alderman examined Arnold Pearce's notes. It was hard to know where to begin. The barrister had many clients and a lot of disgruntled individuals and companies had been on the wrong side in his court battles. It was a minefield. However, Alderman had created a skeleton team from within his staff to begin investigating. They cross-referenced every individual against the criminal records database and started their enquiries from there. They called for files from Frank Duffy's office relating to Jason Chadwick too, to see if there was anything that linked up. Arnold seemed convinced that there would be a connection to the kidnapping but Alderman's gut feeling was that this was all about Jason Chadwick's money.

Alderman felt uneasy. He had been reluctant to turn away from Riley's house. He had also visited Bridges' flat but there was no answer. If they were together, where would they be? And why would Riley leave all curtains closed and his phone off the hook? Alderman concluded that either they were together in Riley's house but were worried about opening the door because their secret would be discovered, or there was a problem. He decided to dispatch an officer to take another look.

***

It took ten minutes or so for Thomas to regain his senses properly. He could just about focus on Hardy who was sitting on the floor, his head low. The gun was in his hand. Lucy was next to him; she was very still.

'Oh Jesus!' Thomas said. 'What have you done?'

'Relax. She's OK. She was stirring a minute ago,' Hardy replied. His voice was a low monotone with hardly any emotion. 'Happy now?' he asked sarcastically. 'You've both sealed all of our fates, including your precious little Amy.'

Hardy didn't stop Thomas when he moved towards Lucy. He cradled her head and she opened her eyes immediately.

'I think I need an aspirin,' she whispered.

Thomas kissed her forehead then propped her back up against the sofa. He motioned towards the kitchen. 'I should make us a drink,' he said. Hardy waved him on. He was still sitting on the floor, head still down, the gun in his hand.

Thomas returned with a facecloth, aspirin and a glass of water. He had cleaned his face but his eyes and nose were stinging and he was still coughing every few seconds. He sat down on the sofa.

'What happens now?' Thomas asked Hardy. He assumed that if Hardy wanted to kill them, he would have done it by now. This was not over yet. He also noted the *all of our fates* comment too. Hardy wasn't *with* these guys: he must be playing a role. As much as this was encouraging, it was also dangerous. If Hardy felt his back was against the wall he would definitely shoot.

'You tell me,' Hardy mumbled.

Thomas assessed the situation. If he told Hardy the truth, that they needed to travel to Las Vegas, maybe he could keep Amy alive if they convinced the men in Boston that she was still needed.

'I think I've sussed the last clue,' Thomas began. Hardy looked up at him, emotionless. 'Excalibur Hotel, Las Vegas – the clue leads there. It makes sense. I think the money is there.'

This time Hardy looked at him properly. Thomas had his

attention again. There was still a glimmer of hope they could come through this.

Thomas couldn't look at Lucy. He felt guilty, but right now he needed to keep control. Hardy stood up, staring at Thomas; his cheek was badly bruised. 'You better be right.'

Hardy phoned Boston and explained that they had worked out the clue. Thankfully he didn't mention the fight and his voice sounded normal. Thomas stood close enough to hear the conversation.

'Get the first available flight. Nobody suspects anything there yet. Bring them both with you and destroy your inspector's computer data,' Thomas heard the voice at the other end of the phone say. 'Phone us back as soon as you know your arrangements and timing. In the meantime, we'll make our own way to Las Vegas right now.'

Thomas wondered what that would mean for Amy and Emmanuelle.

At the end of the conversation, Hardy reiterated the plan to Thomas and Lucy. Thomas went to the computer to check flight times. 'There's a direct plane from Gatwick to Las Vegas, but it leaves at five past nine in the morning. There are seats available.'

'Perfect. We should book now.'

Hardy took to the computer, asking Thomas to step away so he could pay using his own credit card. It would be obvious that Scotland Yard would trace any activity on Thomas's card when he didn't show up for work in the morning. They had to delay the police for as long as possible to allow them to make the ten-hour journey. Their plane would arrive in Las Vegas just before noon, Pacific time, but it would already be eight in the evening here in London. They couldn't leave any hint that they were travelling abroad.

Thomas chose to be as helpful as possible. He could see he was annoying Lucy but deliberately avoided looking at her. Hardy kept all the printed clues with him in his case. He notified Boston of their arrangements.

Thomas suggested leaving the photograph of Amy, after

wiping any prints from it. He would write a note saying: *Amy is safe and I have spoken with her. Tell DCI Moore that we (Sergeant Bridges and I) are not allowed to make direct contact. All will become clear.* Then they'd leave the printed picture of Monsal Dale close by with melodema.com handwritten on the reverse; that should hopefully lead the police up towards Manchester and away from the airports.

Hardy agreed and Thomas set wheels in motion. After they'd printed out their e-tickets, Hardy used the command prompt on the computer to format drive c:. Thomas watched as he then typed in a code to override computer's fail-safe. Within minutes, Thomas's entire data and history was wiped from his computer. Thomas gasped, but there was little he could do. He got the feeling that Hardy knew much more about computers than he let on.

'This is all well and good,' Lucy said, 'but we have to be at Gatwick by six, which means leaving here at five twenty at the latest. My passport is at home.' Then, after a pause, she threw further food for thought. 'There's no way I'm going to be able to stay awake all night, either.'

Hardy thought for a while before suggesting his plan. 'We drive to your house in my car. You pack a case with enough clothes and toiletries for three or four days and collect your passport.' Then turning to Thomas, he continued, 'When we get back here, you do likewise, Thomas. I have a bag in my car all ready for me. We'll all sleep in the sitting room. I'll let Boston know the plan. I'll tell them to ring me at least once every hour to make sure I stay awake to watch over you. I'm really grouchy when I'm tired, so if you give me any reason to be suspicious, I swear I will shoot her pretty face.'

Hardy's stare chilled Thomas. It was an unwelcome reality check. Thomas nodded to acknowledge his orders.

***

208

The Hammond brothers went upstairs to talk. Emmanuelle was sitting at the table outside the sliding French doors of the kitchen while Amy made coffee. They could hear the girls making plans for the week, talking about the places that Emmanuelle was planning to visit with Amy.

'OK, we're all set, Las Vegas it is. Darren Cooper was right. The timing is perfect,' announced Paul. 'I'll make the calls, now. Nathan, you and I will deal with the girls. Anthony, you can prepare the boat.'

'What about the body?' asked Anthony. 'It's the only thing that can connect us to all this.'

Paul looked at Nathan, whose face dropped. 'Get some blankets. We'll have to dump it out there in the ocean.'

Paul looked at his notes again, making sense of the clues before them. There still appeared to be missing information. They certainly didn't want to find themselves in a situation of knowing where Jason's money was and not being able to access it. Yes, he thought, we may well need Amy — she could still hold some vital information — but he was not keen on taking her with them, especially with the police looking for her. Jason must have left her that ring for a reason. Paul prayed that they didn't need the ring itself to access the money. It would be a gamble if he let Amy go as he wouldn't have a way to monitor her in Boston if she was needed again.

The other problem was Las Vegas, Paul thought. The Hammond family were known there and it wouldn't be possible to keep a low profile. Luckily, they knew enough trustworthy people to help. Walking into a casino and claiming one hundred million dollars, on the day Stock was released from jail, was going to set warning bells going. It was time for their disguises.

If Nathan had not killed the English lawyer, they could have gone with their original plan. There was no way that Paul could let Darren Cooper know that Nathan had screwed up again. Paul thought for a while. They would have to buy the English detectives, and trade the girls' freedom and Vito Rolanski's killer. Amy would be happy knowing that she was safe and having her holiday in Boston.

Paul made several calls to set their own plans in motion before calling London.

Chapter 34

Outside seemed so bright. Although the best of the daylight had ended, the evening sunshine painted a surreal crimson sky. The fresh air smelled wonderful to Thomas as they ventured outside.

Hardy drove them the short distance to Lucy's flat. He escorted them up the iron stairs. Inside, there was a handwritten note on the floor from DCI Alderman, asking Lucy to make contact urgently. The three stayed together the whole time while Lucy packed her things and located her passport. Hardly a word was spoken.

Thomas was feeling better but his throat was causing him trouble. It felt as if he had eaten a porcupine. Lucy was still complaining of a headache; she had a bruise on the side of her head and her scalp was still raw from her earlier encounter with Hardy.

The gun was permanently in Hardy's hands. With every order he gave, he used the gun as an extended finger. His confidence was high, he had control.

They returned to Hardy's car. 'Oh no, pull over!' Thomas said as Hardy drove around the corner towards his house. A police vehicle was parked directly outside. Two uniformed constables were knocking on his door.

'Fuck this right now!' Hardy responded, pulling the car over and switching off the lights.

They watched the officers look through the curtains and

use their radios. Thomas didn't need this pressure, just as things were beginning to fall into place. As much as alerting the constables could have been a way out, it was also messy and too dangerous.

'I need to talk with them. They'll have been concerned that there was no contact and that the curtains are closed. It's a matter of time before they force entry. They'll see the mess and our notes.' Thomas looked directly into Hardy's eyes. 'I don't want this any more than you do. Not now. You will *have* to trust me. It is the only option we have.'

'Get rid of them!' Hardy demanded, pointing the gun at Lucy. 'She is the guarantee that you don't pull any stunts. And when I'm done with her, you can guarantee that I'll come for you, no matter what! Got it?'

Thomas looked at Lucy and she nodded and waved him on. 'You can do it. Tell them you've been out with me all day in Manchester. It doesn't matter what they think. You can tell them that you've just come from my place.' She blew a kiss at Thomas as he turned to leave.

Thomas walked down the road towards his house and the officers. He didn't recognise them – maybe they were sent from Belgravia. His heart was racing. There was no way he could let them in. Hardy would probably snap if he were put under any more pressure.

'Can I help you guys?'

'Thomas Riley?' the taller of the officers asked.

The officers had been dispatched by Belgravia Police Station as a favour to DCI Alderman. Thomas followed Lucy's line. He explained that he'd been out all day and must have forgotten to pull his curtains. He asked the officers to apologise to Moore; he would explain everything to his senior officer tomorrow. The constables radioed back to their station and were instructed to leave Thomas and attend a road traffic accident outside Victoria Station. Thomas watched them leave. A moment later he was joined by Hardy and Lucy.

'That was close!' Thomas said to Lucy, taking her in his

arms as she entered the house.

Hardy followed. 'Good work,' he said.

The man in Boston called Hardy within a minute of them returning. Hardy handed the phone to Thomas, it took him by surprise.

'Listen carefully,' the voice from Boston said. 'Move out of earshot from Hardy and just answer questions with *Yes* and *No*, understand?'

'Yes,' agreed Thomas, shifting towards the window, cradling the earpiece as if the signal were weak. 'Yes, that's better I can hear you now,' he added.

'I know that you were working on this hunt without your superiors' knowledge. Am I right in assuming this was an escape plan with your pretty sergeant?'

Thomas hesitated; he was loath to admit it but neither did he want to rock the boat, so he agreed.

'Good. You also want Amy and her friend home safely and your Polish waiter's killer caught?' the voice continued.

'Yes,' Thomas agreed.

'Well, this is what I can offer you. Five million dollars should set you and your girlfriend up nicely. Amy has a nice break in Boston with Emmanuelle and I offer you the Polish guy's killer. We want the money Inspector Riley; we are not murderers.'

'Yes, I see,' Thomas said, his confusion reaching unprecedented levels. He distrusted the voice but continued to listen. They were obviously bargaining for something.

'You're an intelligent man, Inspector. You worked those clues under intense pressure, you should be proud of yourself. Jason Chadwick's death really was suicide. He was running scared of himself. All we want is his money and we're happy to share it. So are you with us, or do we do things your way and see who else gets hurt in the crossfire?'

Thomas paused before answering. His thoughts were disrupted by the voice again.

'You do understand the magnitude of the situation? We have people everywhere, even in Pimlico now. They can help or, if needed, hinder.'

'Yes.' Thomas surrendered. 'Yes I'll do exactly what you say. I understand.'

'Good, then this is what you do.'

Thomas listened to the man's instructions and digested his words carefully. He was told about Hardy's involvement. If the voice on the phone was genuinely making a bargain, then he could see how their plans would work and everybody would indeed end up happy. It would have to work like clockwork, though.

'Thomas?' Lucy asked, as he finished his conversation.

'It's OK.' Thomas said, looking at Hardy. 'They were warning me off any funny business. They have people everywhere including Pimlico, blah, blah…' Thomas raised his eyes in sarcastic indignation. Hardy smiled. Lucy looked disappointed.

***

Amy and Emmanuelle were back on the swing bench, so that they could speak out of range of their hosts. The conversation had turned to the beach. Emmanuelle told Amy about the blood on her hands but the absence of a cut. They had both noted that the two men were flustered, even fractious, at the beach. Maybe the Englishman was right. Where did he go? Would he end up landing them in more danger by reporting their location to the wrong people? Moreover, if the blood on her hands wasn't Emmanuelle's, then could it have been the Englishman's?

'Definitely time for plan B, if they don't let us out tonight,' Emmanuelle spoke almost in a whisper now.

Amy knew this meant trying to find a way out. Whether they were really in danger at the house or outside, she didn't know. She looked up from the swing bench, towards the beach. Nothing made sense any more. 'I think we should maybe head back down to the beach,' she said.

Emmanuelle immediately jumped down from the swing bench and starting walking, linking her arms with Amy so as to appear carefree to the watching eyes in the house.

Paul Hammond was on the phone, setting plans in motion, when he saw the girls head towards the edge of the garden. They disappeared through the small gap in the fence towards the top of the cliff. He quickly ended the conversation and called his brother.

'Damn! Not again!' Nathan looked angry. Paul wondered if it was such a good idea to enrol his brother in the chase but he knew that Anthony was preparing the boat. Had he moved or uncovered Frank's body?

They sprinted to the edge of the garden and virtually hurled themselves down the cliff face. They both called loudly for Amy and Emmanuelle but there was no answer. In the distance, they could see Anthony. The boat was hooked up to a mooring on the edge of the bay. Luckily he hadn't reached the beach just yet. The brothers descended to the beach but the girls were nowhere to be seen.

'Where the hell are they?' Nathan asked. He placed his hand into his pocket and reached for his gun. Paul put his hand out towards him to stop him and motioned his brother to calm down.

'We can't trust them,' Nathan said. 'We finish this here and now. Dump them with the lawyer.'

'Shhh,' Paul interrupted, placing his finger to his lips and giving Nathan a stern stare. He could hear voices. 'Over there!' he pointed towards the lane.

The girls came round the corner. They were obviously surprised to see the men standing there. Then both girls smiled. Paul felt relieved that he appeared to have caught them in time. He didn't look at Nathan as he spoke through his smile, 'I think it's OK – don't do anything stupid!'

'Good news, girls,' he said loudly, as they approached

Nathan followed his lead. 'We were looking for you!' he smiled over at them.

'We went for a walk along the cliff edge,' Emmanuelle

explained. 'Please tell me we can go home now!'

'Yes, that's what we came to tell you. You can go home now.' Amy looked as shocked as she did happy.

'It's a bit complicated, and you're likely to be quizzed by the local police, but I'm satisfied that you're safe. The police back in England have identified your attacker. We are ongoing with our own investigations and at some point I'll update you with our progress. We believe that there are senior political figures and members of the police force involved with a corruption scam dating back many years.'

'What sort of scam?' Emmanuelle asked.

'We can't say,' Paul admitted. 'Though I do work for the Metropolitan Police, my job is international security. DCI Alderman, who you spoke with, works with us, though he should never have been assigned this case. It will be OK to talk with him, should he request a meeting.'

'So we're definitely not in danger any more?' asked Amy.

'It seems unlikely. I think you should be able to enjoy your stay in Boston now.'

Emmanuelle raised her hand for a high-five, a rare expression of excitement.

'When can we leave?' she asked.

'We can either drop you off at the station now or, if you can bear with us for about an hour and a half, one of us will drop you off in downtown Boston.'

Amy mentioned her case; it was heavy to lug around. She looked at Emmanuelle but she just shrugged.

'We'll wait for you,' Amy said.

They made their way back to the house. Once inside, the girls immediately went upstairs and started packing. The brothers heard them singing and laughing.

'Are you sure about this?' Nathan asked, concerned.

'Yes, trust me,' replied Paul, putting his hand on his brother's shoulder. 'Now, let's clean this place as much and as discreetly as we can.'

Chapter 35

It was quiet now. Thomas had dimmed the lights. He shared the sofa with Lucy, laying top-to-tail, their bodies crossed like lucky fingers. Thomas gently caressed Lucy's shoulder with his toe. Hardy was sitting on the computer chair reading his notes.

It had been quiet for about twenty minutes when Thomas spoke quietly to Hardy. 'It's true what they say – blood really is thicker than water.'

'I've always believed that,' agreed Hardy without looking up.

'He didn't mean to kill Vito Rolanski. Otherwise he would have shot him.'

'What are you talking about?' Hardy asked, turning towards Thomas, his face screwing up, showing the lines on his forehead.

'Your son, I mean. You're protecting him. He has lost his way in life but underneath he's a nice man. He would make a good father, give you grandchildren to be proud of.'

Lucy was listening but didn't comment. She was trying not to respond, so as not to send Hardy into a panic. Thomas was either making another move or about to get himself shot. She eyed Hardy, assessing his reaction.

'What are you saying?' Hardy asked. He must have been fully aware that he had been double-crossed.

'I'm saying that I know,' Thomas replied. 'I understand

what happened. He got involved with gambling, nearly got killed the last time he owed money. He went over to Atlantic City and by chance met Brandon Chadwick. When Brandon didn't pay up his debts, he lost control – you couldn't bail him out this time.'

Hardy was looking worried and fondling the gun. Lucy gently kicked under Thomas's arms to warn him but he continued.

'Your son somehow found out that Brandon's father lived here in England. I'm not sure if Jason was already dead by the time he tracked him down, or whether Brandon had said something to him, but he was after Amy's ring that day at the Swallow café. He didn't know whether it was worth something or not, but he knew it meant something.'

'Did the man in Boston put you up to this? They're double-crossing me!' Hardy stood up, gun in hand.

'Not a double-cross, they want to help. They want that money without risking jail. Leaving a trail of dead bodies won't help them. They offered a suggestion that might help everyone.'

At this point, Lucy sat up. Nobody spoke. Hardy looked like a fallen man. He was still holding the gun, but it rested on his lap.

'They said they'll give you two million dollars which you can keep for yourself or give to your son for when he comes out of jail.'

'He won't go down for this, I swear!' Hardy raised his voice and Lucy started to panic.

'It's the best thing that can happen for him. The charge would be manslaughter. He turns himself in, pleads guilty and acts remorseful. The judge will show leniency and he'll probably get five or six years, out in three – you can give him a fresh start.'

Hardy paced up and down, listening to Thomas but acting as if he were avoiding the words like a verbal assault course.

'That gun in your hand won't work by the way,' Thomas continued. He looked over to Lucy. She shook her head at him, obviously afraid, but he carried on.

Hardy looked at the gun and pointed it at Thomas, who didn't wince. 'It has dud bullets in it. Go ahead, pull the trigger.'

Hardy pointed the gun at the back of the sofa. There was a sharp crack and Lucy yelped – but there was no bullet hole. Hardy fired again and a third time; still no hole. He threw the gun on the floor in disgust.

Thomas got off the sofa and picked it up carefully, penetrating the barrel with a pencil. 'It was given as a weapon for gaining power or respect. It was never to be used. This, you see, is Vito Rolanski's murder weapon. It was unfortunate that he was killed. It now has your fingerprints all over it.' Thomas motioned to Lucy to get up, fearing an explosion of anger from Hardy, but he just sat down.

'What happens now then?' Hardy asked dejected, his eyes sunken.

'Leave now. Today never happened. Speak with your son. The promise of money and a new life when he gets out may be enough to convince him. I'll give you a twelve-hour head start. Please don't mention the treasure hunt to anybody because I still need to get Amy home safely.'

'What's in it for you?' Hardy asked.

'Money,' Thomas answered, 'plus peace of mind. Their people are organised, they have contacts all over London. If I grass, or you for that matter, we'll end up pushing daisies, of that I'm certain. So we need Amy and Emmanuelle home safely.'

Hardy stood up and walked to the door. 'We have no option but to trust them, but how? I was supposed to get a million – enough for my son to lay low for years. They've double-crossed me. Let's just hope they're telling the truth this time. I don't trust them at all. You shouldn't either,' he muttered. 'I doubt my son will turn himself in now. I fear he'll just become angrier.'

'Let's hope for your sake he does,' Thomas responded. The murder weapon still perched at the end of his pencil.

'So will you bring back my money?' Hardy asked sarcastically.

'You have my word, I'll make sure you get it,' Thomas replied. He didn't think Hardy believed him.

'I won't wait up. For what it's worth though, good luck and I hope Amy comes home breathing.'

Hardy slammed the front door behind him. Lucy burst into tears and hugged Thomas tightly. Then they were both in tears.

Chapter 36

Amy could hear the agents cleaning up downstairs. She commented to Emmanuelle how clandestine the whole weekend had been. They felt like they were characters in a James Bond novel.

Amy felt relieved. Obviously her hunch about her hosts was wrong after all and maybe the frustration that she had sensed was merely concern. For a second she wondered if she and Emmanuelle were to be taken somewhere and killed, but she closed her mind to the thought. After all the paranoia of the last week, that was one step too far. *I'm a nervous wreck*, she thought.

After packing their clothes, they tidied the room and carried their bags and cases downstairs. The other agent – Amy still didn't know his name – helped lift them into boot of the car. Then the girls wandered back into the garden to pay their last respects to the swing-bench that they had occupied for most of the weekend. Amy contemplated mentioning the man in the garden but didn't feel that it was necessary any more.

'We'll have a proper drink to Jason tonight,' Emmanuelle promised and linked arms with Amy as they looked out onto the ocean.

'I could get used to this lifestyle though,' Amy commented, content that she felt actually free at last.

***

Paul Hammond watched the girls while wiping the cupboard doors and taps in the kitchen. He was thinking about the conversations that Amy and Emmanuelle were likely to have with Boston PD and the FBI. He thought about Frank Duffy. Even if the FBI were not shadowing him, this lawyer from London still managed to find a way to track them down. How? For now, they had to make sure Duffy had well and truly sunk to the bottom of the bay. He figured that Emmanuelle would probably be able to lead the police directly to the house. They had to hope that there was no evidence left to link him and his brothers to the place. Paul was concerned about any photo-fits. Their plans to disguise themselves began at Las Vegas. They had to get there with minimum of fuss so they had booked their flight from New York instead of Boston.

Paul was looking forward to seeing his brother Stock again. He was the mastermind of the family; he had hatched the original plan more than two years ago with the help of Darren Cooper. But Stock never dreamt that Jason would make things so much easier by putting his fortune into the public domain by launching an internet treasure hunt.

So many things fell into place for this plan to work. Paul chuckled at the irony. Even the accidental killing of the Polish waiter became a tool that they could use to their advantage because it brought in Oliver Carsley, who would do anything to protect his son. When it was obvious that 'Diana' was a Greek goddess and not, as they had thought, a pet name for Amy, things still worked out right because Amy was lured to Boston and held at ransom.

Yes, Amy might well still be needed, Paul thought, but doing things this way leaves options open. It's either going to happen smoothly and with little fuss or there's going to be a race against time. Either way, we're going to claim that money, he promised himself.

Paul phoned Darren Cooper and updated him on their progress. Darren's own investigations had led him to believe that the money would be in Las Vegas, he just hadn't worked out the details. Darren would try to monitor Amy and Emmanuelle's actions in Boston through his own network of contacts.

A little while later, Anthony was ready to take the girls. Paul instructed him to drop them off close to Emmanuelle's house then meet Nathan and himself at Malibu Beach. The girls thanked them before leaving.

Paul and Nathan had one last clean up. They collected the cleaning bag, together with their bloody clothes and some blankets, and headed to the beach. Frank's body was a horrific sight; it had already been attacked by nature's parasites.

They manoeuvred the body into the blankets, dragged it onto the boat and headed away from the shore, journeying south into the deeper waters of the bay. About a mile out, they weighted Frank's body then dumped him, along with all the other evidence, into the blue waters of the Atlantic Ocean. They took a few minutes to make sure the boat was clean before heading back west into Dorchester harbour. They docked and took the short walk to Malibu beach. Anthony was already there.

The brothers set off towards New York.

✳✳✳

Emmanuelle lived on Kelly Road, not far from Central Square and Anthony had dropped them off on River Street, a stone's throw away. She was shocked when they arrived at her house: There was a black and yellow 'BPD' sticker on the door. The police had forced entry into her home.

Emmanuelle let herself in, opening the door wider to accommodate Amy and her case. The house had been searched and her computer was missing. They were both surprised that there was no police presence in the immediate area because the house didn't look secure.

Emmanuelle threw herself onto her green corner couch and let out a sigh of relief. 'Well, at least I'm home again,' she said. She motioned to Amy to join her on the couch. 'God knows what's happened here, we better call the police.'

Amy agreed and sat down, while Emmanuelle made the call. The house looked strange; it resembled a museum and yet seemed homely. Two giant brass pharaohs framed the fireplace and above, on the wall, there was a fresco of the great pyramid with a hieroglyphic ring border. It was a perfect circle, brown and a crimson red with a black border and hieroglyphics in red and gold. The floor was stained and varnished and cream rugs formed a patchwork effect. Amy loved it.

The voice at the other end of the phone sounded euphoric when he realised who he was speaking to. They would send somebody round immediately.

Emmanuelle poured Amy a glass of wine and they drank to Jason Chadwick, Vito Rolanski and better days.

Chapter 37

In spite of the detour, Riley and Bridges called in to their station at Charing Cross. They knew that DCI Moore would not be on duty until eight o' clock but they left a package and a carefully written note for him with the night duty staff. The package included the picture of Amy and the gun, which had been placed inside a freezer bag to keep Hardy's prints on it. They also included the picture of the viaduct at Monsal Head in Derbyshire.

From the station, they drove directly to Gatwick. The flight to Las Vegas was eleven hours and the journey seemed endless. Neither Lucy nor Thomas could sleep. After the weekend they'd experienced there was so much to talk about. Lucy's head was still tender to the touch. She was still frightened and aware that they remained in danger; the men from Boston would not want to share the money when they got it. They might well decide to 'tie up loose ends' and kill them both.

Thomas told her about the phone conversation with Boston. He felt it was a very professional set up. The best bargaining chip they had was their knowledge. He also had something else – the missing part of the clue. To avoid putting Lucy in danger, he hadn't told her that he knew it. He would only pass it on to the people from Boston when he felt they had earned it. They needed to know that Amy was safe. Lucy was relieved that they still held some power, but was still anxious.

***

When Moore arrived in the office, he was inundated with news. DCI Jim Alderman from Scotland Yard had left a message to contact him immediately. Alderman explained that both Amy and Emmanuelle had turned up safe and well at Emmanuelle's house, unaware of the fuss and manpower that had been involved in their search.

DCI Moore was still on the phone to Jim Alderman when he spied Lucy Bridges' note and package. His day became even more complicated as he read out the note to DCI Alderman and explained about the gun and pictures. *What the hell was going on?* The note was written by Bridges:

Amy is alive and well in Boston, Thomas has spoken with her, she is with Emmanuelle and should be in touch today. Please let Amy's parents know ASAP. Vito Rolanski's killer should also confess today, the enclosed gun is the murder weapon. We are on the case and heading up north. We won't be back until Wednesday at earliest. Can't explain at the moment, but <u>trust us</u> even if you take us off payroll – it's complicated – read between the lines. All will be become clear. Sorry, Lucy

DCI Moore wasn't sure whether to be angry or worried about his detectives. How could he read between the lines? He certainly didn't like the idea of being short-staffed for the week.

Had Bridges and Riley somehow managed to do a deal in return for Amy? They must have had direct contact with the kidnappers.

'Damn, I shouldn't have walked away yesterday,' DCI Alderman confessed. 'They were probably there after all.'

'Trusting them isn't a realistic option, sounds like they've traded themselves for Amy.'

'You're probably right. I'm loath to move in case we put them in danger though. Look, we know Amy Pearce is safe, let's trust them for now and give them twenty-four hours. Send someone with the package here, let us look into it. I'll need to talk to our Super.'

Moore pondered for a few minutes after the call. What was the reason behind the photograph of the bridge? Were they behaving in the same manner as Frank Duffy was – leaving him clues to investigate internally? He had to trust them and wait.

***

Oliver Carsley sat quietly in his office, Pattinson and Parkes in Battersea; it was early Monday morning and no staff had arrived at the solicitors' practice yet. He had summoned his son, Ashton, to meet him there.

Oliver's mind was fogged with worry. Ashton had never been in trouble until after he graduated from Cambridge University eighteen months previously, when he'd developed a gambling habit. He owed money and Oliver kept bailing him out – until one day he refused. The debt was only a thousand pounds but he called his son's bluff. It had been a terrible mistake; Ashton was beaten up badly. His face was slashed and he spent three weeks in hospital. Afterwards, however, Ashton fought his demons. He avoided gambling and began to get his life back on track again.

Then Ashton went to America for a holiday. His trip took in New York, Chicago, Washington DC and finished up in Atlantic City. While he was there, he met Brandon Chadwick. Brandon was a hustler but Ashton got the better of him. By the end of the three days in Atlantic City, Brandon owed Ashton one hundred thousand dollars. All hell broke loose when Brandon refused to pay: there was a fight and Ashton spent the last night of his trip in a cell. He was seething, but a stranger who called himself Tony Strong had bailed him out in time for him to catch his flight home.

The man told Ashton that Brandon owed him money too. Brandon had apparently told Strong that his father, Jason, lived in London and had agreed to pay off all his debts. Tony gave Ashton as much detail as he could and asked Ashton to track down the man and report his movements.

At one time Ashton had an encounter with Jason briefly in Starbucks, near where he worked, nerves and adrenaline getting the better of him. He was planning to make a more controlled approach to Jason when he heard that he had committed suicide. Ashton was cursing Brandon but had to let the matter go. However, he received a call from Tony explaining that Jason's secretary, Amy Pearce, had a ring, the value of which was worth far in excess of the money Brandon owed.

Ashton tracked down Amy and followed her for several days. Tony had a plan. He arranged for a man called Paul to meet Ashton and give him a gun, and instructed him to dress down and mug Amy for her ring. Ashton was told not to use the gun; it was merely to scare her into handing over the ring. The gun was to be returned the next day, together with the ring and Ashton would be given his money.

Something went wrong. Amy spotted Ashton and panicked. Common sense temporarily abandoned Ashton and he chased after her. A Polish waiter was killed in the pursuit that followed.

Ashton had come to Oliver in tears, explaining everything that had happened. Oliver was shocked and disappointed but he helped Ashton lie low. A few days later he received a visit from Ashton in the early hours of the morning, together with the American, Paul.

Paul explained about the treasure hunt. There were two detectives who were of paramount importance to the hunt and Oliver had to hold them hostage. Paul explained that they planned to coax Amy away to Boston but she would remain safe. He would receive one million pounds. He was sure that they could pay the detectives off after the money had been claimed.

Now everything had changed. Oliver had to tell Ashton to give himself up and he couldn't see how either of them would avoid jail. Maybe jail was the best thing for his son after all. Oliver hoped that Amy would be OK. He hated his macho act with the detectives. 'Hardy' was an old nickname from school, a moniker that seemed ironic for the circumstances.

Ashton arrived, full of hope that he had succeeded and the plan was coming to fruition.

'You're going to have to turn yourself in, Ashton.' His son looked shell-shocked. 'We've both been double-crossed. But they've made an offer, which I think they will stick to as there's too much riding on it.'

Ashton was furious. 'I'm not going down for this, not for any money! They've lied once, they'll lie again. We don't stand a chance!'

'The police have the gun, Ashton. It's a matter of time before you're found. There's no way round this. Hand yourself in, plead regret, act the responsible citizen and behave. When you come out there's two-million dollars security.'

'No. Just, no!'

'Ashton. You've killed a man. I've nearly got myself killed to shield you from your own demons. There's no choice, but doing it could be the difference between manslaughter and murder.'

Oliver had never seen his son so irate, his face was screwed up and his fists tightly clenched. Ashton scowled at him then left the office, slamming the door behind him.

Oliver feared the worst.

Chapter 38

Thomas watched Lucy as they approached Las Vegas. The plane had descended a little to show the view over the Grand Canyon and it was breath-taking. Thomas caught her excitement and smiled.

By the time they landed, they were both tired. It was lunchtime in Las Vegas but it would already be late evening back in London. Thomas wondered how DCI Moore had reacted to their note. He would either be concerned or tearing his hair out with anger. Hopefully Hardy would have convinced his son to confess to the killing of Vito Rolanski.

The arrangement with Boston was that they would meet in Starbucks at the MGM Grand Hotel at seven o'clock in the evening. They didn't want to go to the Excalibur Hotel too early. After a long wait at customs and baggage reclaim, they finally left the airport. The scorching heat shocked them as they waited for a taxi.

It was two o'clock when they finally arrived at the hotel. Thomas didn't want to use his credit cards, so he offered sterling, and paid for three nights. As soon as they entered the room, they dived on top of the nearest bed and held each other close before drifting to sleep.

***

It was a smooth flight to Las Vegas from New York. The Hammond brothers had been able to land and get through airport security with minimum fuss. Paul looked at the familiar sights. It felt good to be back in his hometown. Darcy met them at the airport. She was a rock, the backbone of the whole family. Their mother's younger sister, Aunt Darcy knew everything but knew nothing. She'd been on trial for the Hammond fraud but had been acquitted. Darcy was still respected within the community; she had a reputation of being as hard as nails with a vicious temper, but she also had abundant warmth and compassion. She looked after her own, helped with the community and never missed church on Sunday morning.

The house hadn't changed much and still had a smell that was unique to Darcy, a mix of detergent, skunk and Marlborough Lites which mingled with smells from the oven. She was obviously pleased to see them; she'd been nagging them for weeks to be there for Stock's release from jail.

The brothers unpacked and spent the afternoon with Darcy, catching up on news and gossip. She knew that they were up to no good again but didn't ask questions, especially when Nathan came down with his head shaved, trying to adjust a toupée which made him look a good ten years older. Anthony helped his brother before ascending the stairs for his own transformation. Darcy chuckled; she'd seen it all before.

'Nothing changes.'

'I know Darcy. It's all good,' Paul said with a smile, reaching out to hug his aunt, placing his lips gently on her forehead.

'You just take care,' she replied.

'It's the only way we can get into a casino here, Darcy. You know that,' Paul responded.

Paul fixed his face, put on his suit and joined his brothers. 'Ready then?'

***

Thomas awoke first. He gently lifted his hand from under Lucy's shoulder to look at his watch: it was nearly six o'clock. He kissed the back of her neck to wake her. The sleep had relieved some of his fatigue but he would have been happy to stay under the covers and settle for the night.

He left Lucy to slowly come to while he took a shower. He was relieved to be meeting these guys in a public place and hoped they'd continue any future meetings in public, or where surveillance cameras could possibly monitor what they were doing. For now, it was a good starting point.

Lucy entered the bathroom as he was shaving. 'I have a bad feeling,' she said nervously. 'Would these guys really give up such a large sum of money, knowing who we are and what we know about them?'

'We have no option but to trust them at the moment. We don't even know if Amy is safe yet,' Thomas answered. He wondered about making a call to London to get the latest but DCI Moore would have left the station by now; it must be the middle of the night back in London. 'They're not going to try anything stupid in public. We can assess the situation after we've met with them.'

Lucy gave him a look as if to say *I hope you are right*.

They headed into the main casino area. Starbucks was not far from the elevators. They made their way past banks of slot machines and joined the queue, half on the lookout for a table but also for any men that might be trying to catch their eye.

They ordered coffee. Luckily, a table cleared as they were waiting to collect their drinks. Lucy rushed to claim it and smiled to Thomas when she sat down successfully. A man stood next to Thomas, as he waited for his drink.

'Nice accent. English?' he asked.

'I'm afraid so,' Thomas replied, attempting to make eye contact. He felt a light tug on his jacket as the man walked away with his latté.

Thomas sat down with Lucy and checked his pocket. His suspicion was confirmed: the man had dropped a note:

Amy is safe in Boston – check the news. Room 27/216 in half an hour.

'There must be a business room here,' Lucy said. 'We can check the news online.'

They made their way to the lobby and were directed towards the business room where there was a spare computer terminal. They immediately checked the news in England. Sure enough, Amy had turned up safe and well. The article claimed that Amy was unaware of the international police operation to try to find her. Moreover, in other news, a man was being questioned in connection with the murder of Polish waiter, Vito Rolanski. He had walked into Westminster police station and confessed.

'Wow!' said Lucy, with a relieved gasp.

'I would have loved to have been a fly on the wall in Moore's office today. He won't have known what hit him,' Thomas chuckled, putting his arm around Lucy's shoulders. 'OK, then we have to trust them this far,' he continued. 'Let's go, but stay aware.' Lucy nodded in agreement.

Their hearts were beating faster as the elevator doors opened on the 27th floor and they went down the corridor to Room 216. Lucy rubbed her palm against Thomas's palm to let him know that she was nervous. He returned the rub to tell her that it would be all right and that he loved her very much.

Chapter 39

The man that Thomas had seen in Starbucks opened the door to Room 216. There were two other men inside. Each one politely shook Thomas's hand and pecked Lucy on the cheek. They were much older and more elegant than Thomas expected.

'I trust your journey was pleasant?' the dark-haired man asked, returning to the table by the window. There was a magnificent view north towards Wynn, the Vegas Hilton and the Stratosphere tower in the distance. From his voice, Thomas recognised this man as the person he'd spoken to on Hardy's phone. He wondered which one was Amy's *Agent Stringham*.

'It was, thank you, though very tiring,' Thomas said.

The man reiterated the deal. He explained that they had done their part so far: they had released Amy and Emmanuelle and handed over evidence for Vito Rolanski's killer, proof that they intended to keep to their side of the bargain if Thomas and Lucy would help them solve the final clues.

'So, you have something for me, I believe?' he stated, rather than asked.

Thomas knew that he meant the final piece of the clue. He had to trust them. 'Yes. The black bars that framed the rollover images were separate images to the main background. Jason had used his steganography trick again. One said *"what we are"* and the other said *"the prize"*. I think the final clue should actually read: *"The prize is underground. My father's proudest moment and my mother is the missing link. Go there, travel wisely and remember what we are. All the clues have now passed.'*

'Good work, Mr Riley,' the man said as the others nodded, all looking in his direction.

'So that's the clue. We just need to work out what we do with it now,' Lucy joked, trying to bring herself into the conversation.

The third man, who had perched himself on the edge of the far bed stood up and motioned for Lucy to sit down then he joined Thomas and his brother at the table.

'Excalibur Hotel has to be the where,' said Thomas, following the earlier clues backwards, referring to the 'xmarksthespot.htm' page and the 'getyourpassport.htm' clues.

Eventually all five of them ended up huddled round the table. Each had been moving a little closer as Thomas wrote out and broke down the clues. One of the men plugged in a laptop and logged on.

There was surprisingly little information about Donald Chadwick online, just references to Las Vegas security and the odd court case he had been involved with. They cross-referenced *casino security inventions*. Eventually, they came across an article which was written in the *Las Vegas Herald* about evolving security systems, 'some of which were adopted by casinos and banks in the early 1990s'. They read on:

Most of the casinos in the early nineties adopted computerised bank vaults systems that could not be opened by keys or a single person. A nine-digit numeric code would have to be entered at source and this would generate a separate numeric code. This new code would then be typed in manually at a separate security office to open the vaults. Casinos would not commit themselves to routine times of the days either. The new casinos were virtually theft-proof and most still operate this system today.

I wonder if this was Donald Chadwick's invention, his proudest moment, Thomas thought. It occurred to them that if they had the wrong code for Jason's vault then it would be difficult not to draw attention to themselves. They had to be one hundred percent sure that the numbers were right.

There were too many unanswered questions and though the pathway led to Excalibur, there didn't seem to be any logical clues as to what to do next. Lucy suggested a walk to Caesar's Palace to take a look at Artemis's statue. They all agreed.

By now it was dark and Las Vegas dazzled. The men in suits watched the two detectives enjoy the sites. Thomas wondered how familiar they were with Las Vegas. Had they seen it all before? How could they not be overwhelmed, like he and his partner were?

They found Artemis in the centre of the Forum Shops and stared at her. She was indeed a warrior. She looked powerful and, in spite of the eagle's attempt to dominate her, she gave the impression of being resolute and in control. As they all stared at her, Thomas thought about Jason Chadwick. He didn't stand here and feel in awe of her like this, he saw the injustice. To him the eagle was sacrilege: how could they condemn her to become a product of the American ego? Artemis despised eagles – they were a threat to the small animals she adored. She was naked too, bar her bathing robe – this was Actaeon's vision of her before she killed him. Thomas looked down at her feet. Her toes were set on a block of counterfeit marble. Something caught his eye; just to the left of her toe was a number. It was engraved discreetly where her foot adjoined the base. Surely it wouldn't be a serial number? They couldn't manufacture these statues in bulk, he thought. It must be a manufacturer's stamp or mould, or it could be a year. He made a note, 1014. 1014 had come up earlier in the hunt; Thomas tried desperately to remember when.

Paul Hammond watched him as he made a note. 'Do you have something?' he asked Thomas.

'I'm not sure yet, I need to look back through the clues later,' Thomas replied, pointing at the code at Artemis' foot.

Lucy nudged him, hearing her partner's conversation. 'Victoria'. Thomas looked up. The 'folly sky' was magnificent. It was as if the clouds had been painted on a huge cotton sheet and stretched into a dome shape. It really did look like sky and it gave the effect that you were focussing for miles rather than feet. It was truly remarkable.

Yes, he thought v1ct0r14 – 1014.

Passing the food-court at Caesar's Palace, Lucy suggested collecting food to go but the smell seemed to arouse everybody's appetite so the men suggested that they sat down for a while and ate. Thomas explained his findings from the sculpture of Artemis.

'According to that article, we would need a nine-digit code to access any security vault. I wonder if any of the other clues also could be alpha-numerical?'

Lucy suggested, writing down *3xc4l1bur, 34913* and *T1nt4931* for the Excalibur, Eagle and Tintagel clues. 'That narrows things down a lot, doesn't it?' she laughed sarcastically.

Thomas looked again. The good thing about alpha-numerical numbers was that it restricted the numbers to 0 (o), 1 (i), 3 (e), 4 (a), 5 (s) and 9 (g) so nearly half the numbers were redundant. He wondered if 1014 was significant as far as the full code – or if it had some other relevance. The clue was baffling. Jason's mother was the missing link to what? *And remember what we are* had to have some logical relevance. He wished that he could visit Monsal Head now, maybe find the café that Jason had mentioned. Maybe there was another numerical clue there. He shuddered at the thought of having to go back.

Finally Nathan began exploring theories. 'OK, what we

know, or at least suspect, is that Jason's money is underground at the Excalibur. It requires a numerical password. We have all the clues in our hands; what we need to know is this: How do we get the hotel security to allow us downstairs to the vault – or security box – whatever it is? Do we maybe need two sets of passwords: one to allow us access to the vault, the other to open the vault?'

'Good theory,' Thomas agreed. 'We need to get our heads together and work out some sort of plan, even if one of us has to venture into The Excalibur and actually "ask". We are not trying anything illegal. We shouldn't feel guilty about it.'

Chapter 40

Detective Chief Inspector Moore was still exhausted from the previous day's developments. He had received a call from Savile Row police station: a young man had walked into the station and confessed to killing Vito Rolanski.

Moore had spent the afternoon interviewing Ashton Carsley. He broke down, confessing that his life was a mess. He'd been following Amy because he was being paid money owed to him in exchange for her ring. 'I only had the gun to scare her. The killing was an accident, a split-second thing. I went to push the man out the way but the gun hit the waiter's head.'

Moore quizzed Ashton about Amy's disappearance.

'I don't know anything about her kidnapping. It's nothing to do with me!' Ashton protested.

Moore was puzzled. He relayed this news to Scotland Yard; they promised to update the FBI.

Even stranger was the news coming back from DCI Alderman at Scotland Yard, who had been talking with Boston PD. They had questioned Amy and Emmanuelle about their disappearance. The women were oblivious to the search for them. They said they'd been taken to a house near Boston and looked after well. Their captors had made no attempt to hide themselves and released them without any reason for them to feel suspicious. The FBI was investigating, trying to locate the property where Amy and Emmanuelle had been taken.

The FBI was also concerned for the solicitor, Frank Duffy. They were trying to retrace his steps on the days leading up to his disappearance. More frighteningly, Frank appeared to match the description of the man who approached Amy in the grounds of the house and warned her that she was in danger.

Then there was Riley and Bridges: they still hadn't made contact. Amy confirmed that she had spoken to Riley. Everything that had been mentioned in their note to Moore had happened exactly as they had promised. Should he trust them? There was no reason not to, other than a hunch that they had somehow been sucked into something against their will, possibly trading Amy for themselves.

Alderman suggested that they make their search for the detectives an internal matter for twenty-four hours to see if they could locate them. But he was curious: what was the significance of the photograph of the bridge that was also left inside the package?

There was also an internal investigation at Scotland Yard. Nobody seemed to be aware of DCI Paul Dawson at Scotland Yard nor an Agent Stringham who worked for the FBI. Moreover, it appeared to the hierarchy that there were serious problems within the internal structure of the police for something like this to happen. It occurred to them that either inside information could be seeping out, or high-level corruption was surfacing. Even if they were dealing with imposters, how did they know so much to get to Amy the way they did?

***

Amy couldn't help the tears. The stress of the past week was too much to bear. She had a long and emotional call with her parents back in London. She couldn't ever remember her father crying before. Even her on-hold boyfriend Gerard was so concerned that he had camped out in London to wait for her. He was about to book flights to Boston to help.

Amy didn't know whom she could trust. She wanted to go back home. Right now, she cursed Jason Chadwick. What the hell had he done?

The FBI was supposedly coming to see her to ask more questions. All she had had for the last day or so were questions. If only she hadn't stopped at the Swallow café. A moment in her life had resulted in murder and kidnap, all because she stopped for a coffee and Danish pastry.

The day had already begun for most people, including Emmanuelle. She had made Amy a coffee, kissing her friend on the cheek to wake her up before she left for work. Amy was in awe of Emmanuelle, she could just carry on, in spite of what was happening around her. It was the same back at the manor – Emmanuelle just accepted things without question.

By the time Emmanuelle returned from the university around one-thirty, Amy had barely moved. Emmanuelle was concerned; Amy had been so happy when they had arrived here last night. She sat on the edge of the bed, and stroked Amy's hair. 'Are you OK?' she asked gently.

'I will be all right. It just needed to come out,' Amy said, attempting to smile. Her voice was husky. 'I'm here now. Though I'm not looking forward to going with the FBI to try and find the house we were kept in. Let's get today out the way and then I can enjoy the rest of the week.' She reached forward her hand and squeezed Emmanuelle's hand.

Chapter 41

Thomas had deliberately avoided asking for names until now but it was frustrating trying to get an individual's attention before he spoke. Eventually, after they had returned to Room 216 he asked the men to introduce themselves properly.

'It's probably better for us not to exchange names,' said Paul Hammond.

Thomas was not sure if that was a good thing or bad. On the one hand, not knowing names suggested that they were more likely to keep to their part of the deal. To know their names might lead them to consider him and Lucy as another 'loose end'. On the other hand, such a lack of knowledge also signalled distrust. He understood that still he had to keep his wits about him. He looked over at Lucy, who was sitting on the bed with a pocket notebook and pen, writing. The man he still thought of as the voice from Boston was watching her too.

'What are you on to, Lucy?' he asked.

'Just looking to see if we had missed anything,' she replied without looking up.

'I'm going!' announced Nathan. He looked agitated and Thomas could feel the tension in the air. The other two men looked at each other as he left the room.

It was getting late though, especially for Thomas and Lucy who were still shattered from the long journey. They agreed to meet up in Room 216 tomorrow at ten o'clock. The two remaining men allowed them to leave.

Thomas was overwhelmed by a strange feeling. They could have stopped the elevator at the twentieth floor, which was their own floor, but Thomas hit the lobby button. When Lucy asked why, Thomas muttered, 'Trust me'.

The casino floor was much busier than it had been earlier. They walked the perimeter. Thomas was looking for the three men but he couldn't see them. Where was the Starbucks' man going? He had seemed agitated. Was he intending to follow himself and Lucy to see what they did next? Or were the men not actually staying in Room 216? Maybe they had somewhere else to go. It added weight to his theory that these guys knew Las Vegas – almost to the point of not really *seeing* it any more.

After half an hour, convinced that they were not being followed, Thomas and Lucy returned to their own room and much-needed sleep.

***

Nathan Hammond had returned to Darcy's house less than half an hour before Paul and Anthony arrived. Paul was angry; this time he had no patience for his brother's actions. He picked him up by the collar of his jacket and threw him against the wall.

'You fuck this one up and it will be the last thing you ever do! You hear me?' Paul lambasted his brother. Nathan smiled and spat on the ground to show his defiance. Paul put his hand to Nathan's throat, holding his head against the wall. This time Nathan took notice – his eyes were almost bulging out of their sockets.

Paul finally controlled his anger, threw Nathan to the ground and placed his foot on his brother's chest. He bent down and casually placed his elbow on his own knee.

'We do this totally by the book. I am not risking going

back inside. This money is in the public domain and we're entitled to it. If we have to pay some of it out in order to claim it properly then that's our right.' Paul bent down further, adding more weight to his brother's chest and more weight to his argument. 'The minute we give those detectives any reason to doubt us, they'll go in alone and we'll have everybody on our backs.'

Nathan tried to maintain a degree of defiance but Paul knew that his brother was defeated. 'We'll get there, but it will take time. They won't do anything stupid. For now they are still working with us. DO NOT screw it up!' He eased his foot off Nathan's chest.

'We don't need them any more. We're capable of doing this ourselves,' Nathan claimed as he started to sit up, still wincing in pain and holding his throat with his hand.

'Yes we are, but they are already involved. If we give them the money then they'll keep quiet. They'll not want to risk jail themselves. If we don't give them the money, then we have to kill them and then we'll be on the run the rest of our lives. What's the point? I want to get back what we had before – the power and respect – just like you,' Paul said. 'Stock got his revenge on Donald Chadwick from the inside. This is a fresh start for us all.'

Paul offered Nathan his hand to help him on his feet. Reluctantly, he nodded.

'Donuts anybody?' said Darcy's cheery voice. It was midnight and she had heard the whole argument. Trust Darcy. Bless her, once a rock always a rock. Even Nathan smiled.

***

In the car Emmanuelle looked confused. The FBI agents took them for a ride around Swampscott but they didn't recognise any of the properties. When they'd first been brought here, they had not really taken in their surroundings.

Amy was getting increasingly angry. She found herself speaking in a sarcastic tone to the agents and Emmanuelle had to pull her up.

'We're honestly trying to help, ma'am,' the agent said placatingly.

'The only help I need is getting my life back,' Amy retorted 'As far as I'm concerned, these people you're looking for treated me well. They did exactly what they said they would and looked after us. To me, they're the only people whose actions have made any sense recently.'

They were driving north towards Marblehead when Emmanuelle shouted to stop. 'Over there, we turned out of that road.'

The agent turned towards Philips Point. Suddenly the road became familiar to Amy as well. They both pointed to the manor and the agents stopped the car.

Amy and Emmanuelle waited in the car as the men walked up to the front gate. They could see that there was no response from the intercom. The agents walked back, both talking into their phones.

'We'll take you back now and get Boston PD to check this over,' the driver said, with an encouraging smile before starting the engine and driving the girls back to Emmanuelle's house.

Chapter 42

Nathan Hammond sat alone, looking out of his window. The distant lights of Las Vegas twinkled. He was still bruised from his fight with Paul. He was angry too; being the older brother did not give Paul the right to lecture him. But Nathan knew that his own temper was fragile and he knew that his actions had already let the family down. He had become greedy.

The Hammond Organisation, the family's security firm which Stock controlled, was once well respected. They had been in charge of personal security for VIPs coming into Las Vegas, and for sporting events, especially the boxing. They had also overseen the recruitment of croupiers and dealers for the majority of casinos in Las Vegas. The company worked alongside Donald Chadwick's security firm.

One night, Donald Chadwick had seen Nathan fight with a dealer at the Bellagio. Out of curiosity, he had looked back at the CCTV tapes. Nathan had not approached the dealer at the table but had spent nearly an hour watching him. When the dealer left the table for a break, Nathan walked beside him. The dealer pushed Nathan aside and Nathan retaliated.

This incident had started a chain of events. Donald Chadwick looked further into the dealer and followed the table patterns. Shortly before the fight, someone had walked away from the dealer's blackjack table with more than five thousand dollars in winnings. A little earlier still, at the Monte

Carlo Casino, the same man had walked away with five thousand in winnings from another dealer. This eventually led to an investigation and Donald's team uncovered a pattern using particular dealers, going back many years. At one point during the day, someone walked away from each dealer with around five thousand in winnings.

Donald realised that the Hammond Organisation had recruited all the dealers; they obviously had a good thing going. They had their people hit four or five casinos a day for five thousand dollars a time. The dealer and punter got a cut and Stock pocketed five million a year.

A high profile case was drawn against the Hammond organisation. Stock was a man who was used to getting his own way and he was incensed by Donald Chadwick. Eventually, he drove him out of town before the long trial began. The damage had been done though and the Hammond brothers and several dealers were jailed.

Nathan had had his part in the family's downfall on his conscience for the past twelve years. His brothers had stood by him but deep down he knew that they were not happy. He was worried about how Stock would be with him after his release. Nathan had visited his brother several times in prison and Stock had always been good to him, even pulled him up one time to say that he wasn't to blame. Later today, however, Stock would be released. Nathan wanted to make good; he concentrated on the clues – he wanted to solve this one himself.

Nathan had printed off a screen capture of every page. It was a colourful spread of paper before him. Jason Chadwick's mother – the missing link? Could it be a family link? He wrote down Violet Chadwick's name against the rest of the clues: Victoria (v1ct0r14), Eagle, Injustice, Tintagel, Excalibur and now Violet Chadwick. He tried anagramming the first letters VEITEVC – it looked as if it should be an anagram, but it wasn't. Maybe the first letter's position of each word in the alphabet had significance – V = 22 (twenty second letter of the alphabet) – this gave the number 2259215223, which became nine digits if the 'Chadwick' was not necessary. It wasn't impossible that Jason could have done something like that but Nathan thought there would probably be a way of confirming this – and making sure the numbers were put in the right order.

If this was the nine-digit code, then what else was needed so that they could access the vault or security box?

***

The day started with some alarming news for DCI Moore. Boston PD had failed to lift a single fingerprint from the manor at Philips Point in Boston. The place had been thoroughly cleaned. They had brought the police dogs in too, but with no success. There was, however, some blood on stones at the beach; the forensic examiners were trying to establish whether it might have a connection to the case. There was still no news from Riley and Bridges.

Moore set the wheels in motion to try and locate them. He contacted police departments in the major northern cities and circulated the photograph that was left behind, to see if anybody recognised it. Sheffield police rang back almost immediately, identifying the photograph as Monsal Head in Derbyshire. They contacted Derbyshire police who would go there and investigate.

DCI Alderman phoned a little later. The FBI had requested DNA to cross-reference the blood found on the beach with Frank Duffy's. Boston PD had received a call from the Holiday Inn to say that all of Duffy's possessions, including passport, clothes and money, had been left in his hotel room.

By noon, Moore had requested a warrant to enter Riley and Bridges' homes to see if there was any indication of where they had gone. He was overwhelmed with a feeling that they were both in danger.

He phoned Amy at Emmanuelle's house, to see if she'd heard anything from them. It was early morning there; she didn't sound too happy to receive the call, but she was also concerned for the detectives when he explained that they were missing. Moore also asked about the man that they saw in the grounds of the manor and asked her to think carefully about anything he had said or done. She told him that after his warning she had heard him scaling the walls to the left of the property and that he had made a noise, but she didn't think that anybody else heard him.

As the day went on, Moore became increasingly worried. He looked at the file from Devon and Cornwall police on Jason Chadwick's suicide. According to Boston PD, the people that held Amy told her that they were investigating Jason's parents' death on his behalf. He called Devon and Cornwall again to ask if they had any details of the car accident that killed Jason's parents. He was put through to Superintendent Doug Massey.

'I remember that accident, it was on the A34 not far from Launceston, I was a uniformed inspector at Bodmin at the time, must be over ten years now.' He continued: 'If my memory serves me well, it was early morning. No other vehicles were involved. The car left the road, down an embankment and rested upside down and caught fire. The poor buggers burnt to death.'

'Did you ever discover what happened?' asked Moore.

'I'll have to check but I think that it was inconclusive. There was no obvious tampering with the car. I seem to remember a lack of skid marks, just deep drag marks at the edge of the road. It's possible that the driver fell asleep at the wheel. I'll try and dig out the file and let you know.'

'Thank you. Oh, while you're there,' Moore continued, 'can you check the file on Jason Chadwick and see whether there's any recollection of there being a laptop computer. I noticed on the scene photograph that Jason had a wireless router.'

'I'll check. Nobody has mentioned a laptop to me.'

***

Thomas awoke to find that Lucy was not lying next to him. His first thought was that she must be in the bathroom but when he called out there was no answer.

He went in to the bathroom. Lucy wasn't there, but it was obvious that she was up. Her clothes were missing and the sink and her toothbrush were both wet. He dressed quickly; after the week he'd had anything could have happened to her. Without shaving or even combing his hair, he grabbed his door key and left the room. As he reached the elevator well at the end of the corridor, Lucy stepped out, holding two Starbucks cups and a brown paper bag precariously pinched with her little finger.

'Coffee?' she asked with a warm smile.

After they finished their makeshift breakfast, they headed off to Room off to 216. The door opened immediately.

'Here is the plan for today.' Paul Hammond took control of the conversation before Thomas and Lucy had even fully entered the room. Thomas noticed that the beds were still made up: either the men had made them perfectly themselves, or they had not been slept in. The Starbucks' man was missing.

Paul and Anthony seemed agitated. 'We have to be somewhere shortly, so we'll get together again this evening back here at eight o'clock. We have to trust each other: We have to trust that you're not going to try to claim the money without us, just like you are going to have to trust that we'll give you your own share. However, if the former should happen, you won't leave Las Vegas alive. And Amy won't leave Boston alive. We are everywhere, you understand?'

Lucy looked at Thomas, who nodded, so she also nodded. She realised that both the men's gazes were directed at her.

'We wouldn't be here unless we trusted you,' Thomas said.

'Good. We have an understanding. You're an intelligent man, Riley, so you know how it works. The one thing about Las Vegas is that the eyes in the sky are always watching you.'

Paul opened the door for them to leave. 'Eight o'clock, back here tonight. Enjoy Las Vegas for the day and keep thinking!' he said with a smile.

Lucy didn't say a word to Thomas until they were in the lift, heading towards the casino lobby, rather than their own room. Yes, there were cameras everywhere, even in the elevator, Thomas thought. The eye in the sky – among Donald Chadwick's proudest moments.

'They don't deserve Jason's money,' Lucy said. 'Do you trust me?'

'Of course,' he said, entwining his arm with hers as they entered the casino area.

'Good, then keep walking and listen.' Lucy laughed, as if she were playing a game and Thomas kept a smile on his face for the eye in the sky. 'I trust that they'll give us the money. The more I think about it, the more it seems that they've done everything in their power to claim this money in such a way that they can legitimately walk away with Jason's legacy and live their lives. They know we won't grass them up.'

'Yes, I figured that out earlier. I feel that also could get us leverage to ask for a bigger cut.' Thomas's words appeared to tear right through Lucy and she released her grip on his arm and looked at him in the face,

'No!' she shouted. 'That's not what I'm getting at.' She walked away. Thomas caught up with her.

'What is it then?' he asked, confused.

'At the end of the day they are just thugs. That's why they don't deserve the money. Why do we have to do a deal with the thugs?' Lucy stopped. 'Do you trust me?' she asked again.

Thomas was worried. Was she likely to do something really stupid? He had to think quickly before agreeing. He didn't doubt her love for him and knew she had a conscience, so whatever plan was going through her head was likely to have been carefully considered.

'Yes I do, I'm sorry,' he said, pulling her gently towards

him and planting a kiss on her forehead.

She smiled, took his hand again and they headed back towards the elevators.

***

'Where the fuck is he?' Paul Hammond asked his brother. Nathan had left Darcy's house early in the morning without even a note. Paul and Anthony were initially worried that he might have tried to harm the detectives, especially after his outburst last night. They were relieved when Riley and Bridges had knocked at the room. Now their thoughts turned to The Excalibur. Surely Nathan wouldn't try and get the money solo?

Stock was being released at three o'clock today. They had to leave at one-thirty to make sure they met him from High Desert State Prison at Indian Springs. They had no option, they had to go to the Excalibur and keep a low profile.

A series of bridges and walkways connected the hotels on the south side of the strip like molecular structures. Paul and Anthony made their way to the Excalibur Hotel. A long moving walkway brought them into the building, into the casino.

As soon as the brothers reached the top of the moving walkway, a tall young man in a centurion suit and sword smiled at them. He was standing next to Guinevere, a petite, pretty blonde girl wearing warrior dress and carrying a shield and wide smile. They welcomed the brothers into Camelot and offered to have their photographs taken with them. Paul smiled as he politely declined the offer and carried walking on. They headed straight for the concierge and lobby area in the hope of finding their younger brother.

There was no sign of him there. They toured the casino, keeping an eye on the roulette tables as they passed them. That was Nathan's area of expertise – he had a system based on maximising his winning bets and limiting losing bets, so that he was only gambling long odds with winnings. He was usually successful. Nathan would often visit Anthony in Atlantic City and blitz the casinos there with a lot of success.

Upstairs there was a shopping and eating area. They ventured up the escalators in the hope that Nathan might have been tempted to sit and plan his attack over a coffee. He wasn't there but they decided to stop and have a drink and a donut while they thought about their own next move.

Paul's phone rang, it was Nathan. 'Where the hell are you?' Paul asked, before waiting to hear his brother speak. He looked over towards Anthony and raised his eyebrows.

'I've made headway with the clue. I need to meet with you.'

'We're upstairs in the Excalibur.'

'Wait there. I'll be ten minutes.'

When Nathan arrived, his brothers didn't recognise him. He was wearing jeans and casual top and Converse baseball boots. Paul laughed and Nathan returned the laugh. 'Yes, yes, I'm incognito. I bought most of this stuff en route. I'm trying to be inconspicuous.'

'Why exactly?' Paul asked, bewildered.

'I stayed up most of the night thinking. I got this theory about the first letter of each clue being related to the number of the alphabet, in which case I now had a nine-digit code number. I realised the only way to try and get information was to enter Excalibur, explain about the hunt to the security, showing them the original clue.'

'So you were trying to claim the money yourself?' Paul looked at Anthony.

'Look, I didn't. I wanted a shot before seeing Stock. Just as well though, because at least I know the system. We were right: the money is here in the hotel. Donald Chadwick installed all the vaults and a series of internal safes within the series of vaults, which were either rented out or bought. Jason Chadwick's safe is box 1014. I was asked to type the numerical code onto a keypad. The security guard accompanying me explained that when the light turns green on the unit, it means that the security office has entered the generated key. The safe didn't open though, the code was wrong. The guard told me that he could only allow two attempts per visit. I tried again, to make sure I had keyed the correct number but it also failed.'

Paul Hammond didn't know whether he should feel happy or angry with his brother. On one hand, they had much more information and finally knew that they were close. On the other hand, Nathan had tried this alone. Would he have just disappeared with the money? Paul found it hard to trust him.

'I told you, we do this together. No heroics.' Paul pointed at Nathan, with an authoritative stare. 'Let's get back.'

Chapter 43

To Thomas's surprise, Lucy said nothing about her plan. Whether it was something that she wanted to put into motion later on in the day he didn't know, but she had the clues out again and was writing notes. Lucy listed every clue in order even the sub-clues that helped lead to each page. Maybe that was her plan – solve this together themselves and get the hell out of there before eight o'clock. Either way Thomas was happy to let Lucy take control for a while.

'We need access to the computer,' she told him.

They made for the business centre and found a free computer immediately.

'Tell you what, you go and get us a coffee – make yourself useful,' she demanded, with a smile. He chuckled, agreed and left the centre for Starbucks. He liked her in this mood; she was never a control freak but he loved her confidence and her adorable bossiness.

When he returned, Lucy was still writing and looking a little flustered.

'You OK?' he asked.

'Yes,' she replied without looking up at him. 'Yes, I'm OK. I think I've found something. It may be nothing but it's interesting.'

She wrote down: Redearth Solicitors, Orange folder, Yellow melodema page – the orange colour code clue, green page, blue page, purple/pink page – she couldn't really tell whether the final page was pink or purple, it sat somewhere between the two – the fact that in his letter to Frank Duffy, his domain username was 'Indigo'. Then there was the missing link – Violet Chadwick.

'I think it's a colour code,' she suggested. 'What are the official colours of a rainbow?'

Thomas started *singing a rainbow* – 'red and orange and pink and green – orange and purple and blue – I can sing a rainbow too…'

'Close,' she said. 'I think you'll find the official colours are red, orange, yellow, green, blue, indigo and violet'

'Whoa. Of course.' Thomas stood back so quickly that he spilled coffee over his hand. 'That's it, it's got to be.' He started licking the coffee, now running down his wrist. 'The missing link.'

'So now we just need to find out what to do with this new information.'

Thomas kissed the back of her neck; he was proud of her. If there were a way to tie in the clues that became an obvious code for Excalibur, then he might be tempted to cut and run with the money. He looked at the clock and it was two o'clock. They had another six hours.

* * *

Paul and his brothers were waiting for Stock, along with Darcy. The desert heat was blistering and by the time the authorities had processed Stock for release it was close to four-thirty.

Stock was thrilled to see them all waiting. In a roadside café just outside Indian Springs Paul brought him up to date on all the gossip without mentioning the hunt: it wasn't for Darcy's ears. Stock seemed to go out of his way to make Nathan feel at ease. Nathan looked embarrassed by the 'little brother' comments and the various compliments on his business ventures in Boston.

The brothers eventually returned to Darcy's house. Paul finally managed to get a few minutes alone with Stock and briefed him on the search for Jason's money. He also told him about the deal with the detectives from England. Stock was concerned that they could be trusted; the last thing he wanted was to return to jail. There was one more thing: Nathan. Paul was about to tell Stock about Frank Duffy when Nathan walked in. He chose not to mention it just then, fearing that Stock might not be ready for worrying news.

'We don't have much time,' Paul explained. 'We have to meet the detectives. I'm sure you'll get on, they seem to be on our wavelength.'

'I look forward to meeting with them,' Stock said.

∗∗∗

After a Chinese meal at the MGM Grand, Thomas and Lucy headed towards Excalibur to get a feel for the place. They also turned down a photograph with Lancelot and Guinevere but they liked the atmosphere in the casino.

As they entered the building, they were half on the lookout for a rainbow. They saw the door to the safe box room, to the right. Thomas almost expected to see three familiar faces carrying cases of money out of it. Thomas had never really gambled in his life but often played card games at the station during coffee breaks. Lucy sat next to him to watch him play Blackjack. To his surprise, he won again and again. Half an hour later, he had turned his fifty dollars into four hundred. After a couple of losing hands, Lucy managed to pull him away. He was still three hundred dollars up and felt like a millionaire.

They headed back to their hotel.

'So are you going to tell me your master plan?' Thomas asked

Lucy smiled. 'You'll just have to trust me.'

'Well, at least tell me whether we tell them about the

rainbow clue, or not.'

'Good point,' she said. 'We'll maybe hold back on the rainbow clue until later in the day.'

'OK – as long as you know what you are doing. Meanwhile have we got anything for them?'

They both thought hard: they needed something to tell the men. 'Maybe we should remind them at least of the orange colour clue. Let's see how long they take to figure it out. I think it's been forgotten or at least overlooked,' Lucy suggested, grudgingly.

They spent the remainder of the afternoon exploring The Strip, while discussing the clues. They eventually made their way back to the MGM Grand. Lucy was sceptical about whether or not the men would be at the meeting. She had convinced herself that the men had bought themselves time so that they could claim the money and leave town.

At eight o'clock, as arranged, they knocked on the door to Room 216 but there was no answer. They camped on the landing outside the door without saying much. A housekeeping assistant asked if they'd locked themselves out but they explained that they were waiting for friends.

They sat outside the door for about twenty minutes before they heard voices they recognised. The men apologised for being late, they had been caught in traffic.

There were four of them this time. Lucy couldn't help noticing that they all had the same eyes. Surely they couldn't all be brothers?

The atmosphere was lighter. Stock called for room service, a double magnum of champagne: 'a starter for the main course,' he said. Lucy was beginning to feel that the men had already accomplished their mission. Stock raised a glass. 'Tonight, maybe tomorrow, we will toast to Jason Chadwick. He will have returned our money, with interest!'

The men laughed and Lucy and Thomas joined them in raising their glasses. It didn't feel right though. What had Jason done to these guys? Everything Lucy had learned about the man so far had been positive. He was inspirational, intelligent, funny and caring – even the fact that he'd put his fortune into the public domain showed character. She was repulsed by the four men but tried her hardest not to let it show.

A good hour or so later, Paul came over to Lucy. 'You OK?' he asked.

Lucy and Thomas nodded with a smile.

'Did you make any progress today or use the time for sight-seeing?' he asked.

'A bit of both really,' Lucy responded. 'We think the colour code hex-clue might have more significance and may have been overlooked. We also think that maybe Jason's mother being named Violet could be the missing link.'

'Interesting theory. That makes sense.' Paul nodded before turning around to broadcast the news to the others. There were more toasts; there was a party-like atmosphere in the room, everybody having cross-conversations and raising their voices to be heard over the next one. Odd.

The men joined Lucy and Thomas on the bed. Lucy felt uncomfortable; she was a pretty girl in a room with drunken men, mostly strangers and possibly killers. She felt uneasy. And what was this about the new man's toast? No, she needed to get out of here.

She kept a smile on her face but then belched into her hand. 'Uh oh!' she said sitting up sharply. 'I feel sick.'

She ran to the bathroom shut herself in. Outside, the men were amused, joking that women couldn't take a drink.

She heard Thomas say, 'I better go and check on her.'

'You sure do!' Stock replied.

Thomas knocked gently on the bathroom door and Lucy opened it, quickly locking it behind him. He put his hand on her shoulder; she made a retching sound and winked at him.

They spoke in whispers. 'Are you OK?' he asked.

'I needed to get out. I was feeling claustrophobic in there.' Lucy explained. 'The way they spoke of Jason made me angry,' Lucy said.

'I know, it sounded like they had a grudge rather than

simply wanted his money for the sake of it.'

'Do you think we can get out of here?' Lucy asked.

'We can try,' Thomas said.

He left the bathroom and she locked the door behind him. 'I may have to take her back. She thinks it's the Chinese we had earlier, rather than the drink. She was complaining of feeling queasy when we were waiting for you,' he said.

'You mentioned about the colour clues,' Paul said.

'Yes,' Thomas replied. 'There was a colour clue earlier, the orange page, which lead us to believe that Violet Chadwick was the missing link with the colour violet. Possibly there's a connection to a rainbow? Is there a rainbow at Excalibur? That was our next line of thinking.'

'OK, that makes sense. We'll investigate that. You better get the girl back then.'

Through the door, Lucy was relieved to hear this. Paul continued, 'We did find something out today. 1014 is the number for Jason's security box. Whether by design or coincidence, I have no idea. We were going to check any connection that Jason might have had to anybody called Victoria.'

Lucy retched again, they all heard.

Thomas knocked on the bathroom door. 'I'll take her back, then I'll return and help,' he said.

As he escorted her out of the bathroom, she apologised to everybody.

'Hey don't worry,' said Paul. 'Actually, Thomas, let's meet back here tomorrow at ten o' clock. We'll take it from there. Let's see if we can wrap this up tomorrow then we can all be on our way.'

'If that's all right with you, then yes,' Thomas replied, relieved. 'I don't like the idea of leaving her too long tonight, to be honest.'

The men nodded and smiled and wished Lucy a speedy recovery. Thomas and Lucy hit the '20' button in the elevator and made straight for their own room.

'Was that your master plan, then?' Thomas asked as soon

as they entered their room.

'No, not at all but I wanted to get out of there before the drinks took hold. I don't trust them,' Lucy explained. 'But it was a good delaying tactic – you played you part well.'

She pushed Thomas onto the bed and landed on top of him, lips first.

Chapter 44

No laptop had been reported at Jason Chadwick's house. A man at the forefront of computer technology, with a wireless router in his house and no laptop – that seemed wrong.

Boston police paid Brandon Chadwick a visit. Most of the possessions that he'd cleared out of his father's house had been sold, but there was no laptop taken from either his house in Cornwall or his flat. Brandon denied any knowledge of Ashton Carsley and refused to be drawn in to any blame for what had happened to Vito Rolanski.

DCI Alderman interviewed Ashton Carsley. He changed his story a little after realising that they had spoken with Brandon Chadwick and claimed somebody else had alerted him to Jason Chadwick and Amy's ring.

'As far as I know, it was a man that Brandon also owed money to. He was American and I only knew him as Tony Strong,' Ashton said. 'I didn't want to mention him before because I was afraid of him. Tony set up a meeting in London with another man – I didn't know his name, I met him at the Waterloo pub under the arches. He also had an American accent. This guy gave me the gun. I was only supposed to scare Amy into giving me the ring. The gun had blank bullets. I was supposed to meet with the man the following day near Waterloo station but because of what had happened, he never made that meeting.'

DCI Alderman was sure that Ashton Carsley was holding back information but Ashton swore that he had no knowledge that Amy was being lured to America or who might have held her in Boston. As far as he knew, Tony Strong lived in Atlantic City. Alderman was confused.

Derbyshire police called to say they had sent two officers to visit Monsal Head café in Derbyshire. They questioned the owners and showed them photographs of the two missing detectives but nobody recognised them.

DCI Moore was also uncomfortable with the progress he was making. Reasonable doubt was building all the time against the idea of Jason's death, or the deaths of his parents, being suicide or a car accident. The blood on the stones at Philips Point matched Frank Duffy's DNA – though it may well be that he'd cut his foot on the beach or had a nose bleed. The circumstances of his disappearance and the sighting by Amy had led to a full-scale police operation in the area. They retraced Frank's steps and found that he had used his credit card to investigate names online. The FBI was following this up.

Moore's concerns grew for Riley and Bridges by the hour. There must have been a reason to leave the picture and inform the police that they were travelling north.

***

It was déjá-vu for Thomas Riley. Again, he awoke to find himself alone. Again he called out to Lucy, in case she was in the bathroom, and again there was no answer. He looked around: her clothes and handbag were missing but most of her other belongings were still scattered around the room.

As he climbed back into bed and waited for her, his thoughts turned to London. Over there, it was Wednesday, late in the day. DCI Moore would be concerned. They hadn't really considered contacting him from Las Vegas because they didn't want to be traced, but the week was turning out slower than Thomas had thought it would be. He needed to book extra time at the hotel if they were to stay longer; he was grateful for the cash he'd won yesterday as it would save him having to use his card. No matter what happened today though, they needed to contact Moore.

Thomas contemplated how much of the truth he could tell him. So much depended on whether the hunt would prove successful and how quickly they could complete it. He had deliberately resisted the temptation to fantasize about what he would do with the money but if they got their five-million dollars, it would be enough to set up a private investigation company… But it would have to be done carefully. Technically, they were still on police time.

He couldn't help but feel that they'd wasted yesterday. If they had put their heads together and concentrated, they might have been able to grab all the money and leave town quickly. Though he didn't like the idea of living on the run, with that much money they could easily afford quality security. But would the men go after Amy out of spite? He certainly wouldn't like that on his conscience. He just wished that he knew more about these men. They were obviously well organised and well connected. He couldn't help but think that the sum of money that Jason had left was simply extra pocket money for them because everything about them reeked of prosperity. It wouldn't surprise him if he found out that they were staying in the penthouse suite.

He was just beginning to wonder about Lucy's plan when he heard the key swipe in the door. She had returned with cappuccinos and apple fritters. Thomas thought he could get used to this way of living. If all went to plan, he probably could.

Lucy's first words shocked him. 'We're in deep trouble.' She opened the cabinet doors that covered the television and switched it on. 'I caught the news as I was walking past a shop.' She flicked channels until she found CNN News channel and pressed the menu buttons to look at the headlines. 'Here!'

Thomas read the story:

Police in Boston are concerned for the safety of a British lawyer, Frank Duffy, last seen on Sunday. Boston PD said that they had found traces of blood at a property at Philips Point that matched Frank Duffy's DNA. A full-scale operation is underway, including police divers and tracking equipment, to check the surrounding coastal area. Police believe that this may have a connection to the mysterious disappearance of British tourist Amy Pearce at the weekend.

'Oh shit!' Thomas said. His heart sank. This changed everything. 'We need to get out of here fast. We'll have to draw a line under the hunt for Jason's money for now and return home to DCI Moore. We have enough information to help.' Lucy looked flustered. 'I don't want the third degree from Moore if we phone him. I think we should email him, and tell him we'll be returning straight away. We'll work our story for him on the way home.'

Lucy agreed, 'Let's pack then go and find out the next available flight and if there are any seats.'

Luckily it was still early, just after eight o'clock so they had time to work out what they had to do before meeting with the men from Boston. They packed their cases but left them in their room while they ventured downstairs to the business area and a computer. The next flight back to London was at 3.15pm, which would mean they had to be at the airport around half past one. That created a real dilemma: did they meet the men as arranged and try to leave, or did they clear out now and risk being chased? There were seats available on the flight so Thomas booked them and returned to Lucy.

'I've emailed Moore,' she said. Thomas was a little shocked that she'd taken on the task herself. 'I told him that we were OK, we have important information and that we'll be back in London tomorrow morning. I wasn't sure whether we should mention Las Vegas or not, so I didn't.'

'You're probably right. I'm not sure at this stage. We need to decide what to do now.'

They left the business centre and took another trip to

Starbucks, hoping that the caffeine would provide inspiration for their escape plan.

'I don't think they would let us go anyway,' Thomas said. 'They've obviously been doing their own investigations because they found out that the security box number was 1014.'

'I thought that too.'

'You know, I believed them. I honestly thought they would honour their part. They would not have let Amy and Emmanuelle go, at the risk of being identified, unless they were serious.'

'Do you think Frank could be alive?'

'I'm hoping he left a blood trail as a clue and has gone into hiding, but I fear the worst. We can't risk it though, we *have* to go now.'

'We can't meet up with them today. We have to lie low, or head straight for the airport now and spend the day inside the departure lounge. They won't be able to get us there.'

'I agree. Come on.'

***

Paul Hammond opened the door to his brother's room and pounced. He placed his hand around Nathan's throat so hard that his thumbnail pierced his brother's skin. The sight of the blood shocked him and he immediately released his grip again. Nathan, who was asleep up until the second that Paul made contact, could see the fear in his brother's eyes. He put his hand to his neck and looked up at Paul.

'What the hell?'

'You blew it again!' Paul said. He was frustrated and close to tears. 'We planned everything. This was our chance. Everything worked perfectly until you killed that lawyer. The police found blood on the beach and traced it to the guy. It's on the news now.' His voice was breaking as he explained. He was a defeated man. He hated his brother so much – blood ties no longer meant anything. He had to tell Stock too: Stock would crucify them both. Nathan's neck wound was bleeding. He placed the pillow to it as a temporary bandage. Paul worried that his brother would need stitches. It was all going so wrong.

Stock Hammond came into the room, took one look at Nathan then raised his eyes and walked out, slamming the door behind him. What if the detectives have seen the news too? They were capable of putting two and two together. They might decide to leave town with the money too.

Paul made a hand gesture of a gun at Nathan, before leaving to explain himself to Stock.

Stock was drinking coffee. He didn't even look at Paul as he entered the room. 'Don't tell me,' he said. 'I don't want to know'.

'You have to know, bro. I'm sorry, he screwed up again,' Paul started to explain but Stock interrupted.

'And then you screwed up by half killing him yourself!' Stock shouted, waving his hand in the direction of Nathan's room. It was a look of disdain. Stock was right: Paul had lost control for a second of madness, as his brother had done at the beach with Frank.

Stock looked at his brother. 'Don't tell me the details, tell me what the damage is,' he demanded.

Paul looked down, dejected. He knew that unless they could grab the money, clear out and lay low, they were looking at a long term, if not life, in jail when the English lawyer's body was found. It was a matter of time. Paul was enraged but had little fight left in him. He explained to Stock briefly what had happened and today's developments.

Stock sat with his head in his hands before getting up from his chair, moving to the cupboard, casually taking out a gun.

Paul panicked. 'Stock?'

Without saying a word, Stock stuck a cartridge in his gun then walked into Nathan's room. Nathan was up, looking in the mirror, still stemming the blood from his wound. He turned round to look at Stock and saw his brother raise the gun.

Paul called again 'Stock?'

Paul's panic alerted Darcy. She ran from the kitchen to Nathan's door just as she Stock raised the gun.

'STOCK, NO!' she screamed.

Chapter 45

Oliver Carsley heard the news on television. He had left work early, feeling sick; he just wanted to hide away from the outside world. He had turned villain and was filled with self-hatred. The news that Amy was safe and well brought some release but then he heard that a man had confessed to the killing of Vito Rolanski.

He paced up and down his sitting room. It must be Ashton. Would his son tell the truth and land Oliver in it? Why had he not received a call from the police? He couldn't think what to do next.

Oliver Carsley held his head in his hands.

***

Thomas and Lucy finished their coffee. The decision was a simple one but the direction from here on was complicated. Thomas hoped that they would have done enough in DCI Moore's eyes to justify their absence; they could lay the blame on the men from Boston and claim that they traded themselves for Amy. In a roundabout way, that's what they had done.

Deep inside Thomas was disappointed; he had wanted Jason's money. It was a chance for him to be with Lucy, without having to compromise their work. They could be partners in all senses of the word, using their skills to complement each other within their own investigation business. But it wasn't worth risking their lives for. Their only hope would be if the villains were caught before claiming the money. Maybe he and Lucy could wait a few months, even a year or so, and claim it when everything had quietened down.

For now though, he resigned himself to the failure of his dreams. He had to focus on damage limitation.

They headed towards the elevators. Thomas wondered what Lucy was thinking. He hoped that she was still trying to solve the clue – one last chance before heading back home.

'Hello, you two,' came a voice from behind them.

Thomas jumped and Lucy gave a nervous giggle.

'We were just on our way up to see you,' Thomas lied. *How the hell are we going to get out of this one?* he wondered.

'How are you feeling today, Lucy?' Paul asked. There was only him today; Thomas wondered where the others were.

'Not too bad, just weak, I was throwing up half the night. I think it was a dodgy Chinese meal,' Lucy replied. 'Where's the rest of the gang today?'

'They'll be with us later.'

The three of them went in the elevator to the 27th floor and Room 216. The maids had worked their magic; there wasn't a trace of last night's celebrations. Thomas didn't think that anybody had spent the night there.

Thomas looked at the man he thought of as 'the voice from Boston'. He could take him on, then just cut loose and flee. The thing was, even though he didn't like to admit it, he had developed respect for this guy. The voice had been true to his word throughout; in Thomas's strange fantasies over the past few days about being a fugitive, this man was his ideal criminal. He felt like he and Lucy were almost part of the gang.

That was until last night, when it suddenly didn't feel right. This man, the voice from Boston, was not in control last night. The new guy's personality had overpowered him and he suddenly seemed like a puppet. Today's news undermined Thomas's respect still further. A true mafia style execution of Frank Duffy would not have left any clues. This little unit suddenly looked unprofessional. They certainly didn't have a focus on solving the treasure hunt.

Lucy expanded on yesterday's theory and Violet Chadwick being the missing link in the rainbow, though how to tie in 'rainbow' with the rest of the clues they didn't know. Maybe there was a 'pot of gold' or gold, being another colour, presented another link. The man suggested the alphanumeric interpretation of 'rainbow', using each letter's position in the alphabet as a number, but they came up with 18191421523 which was eleven numbers – too many. They tried that same principal with Monsal Head, Victoria, Artemis, Tintagel, Arthur, Troy and even Eagle but there wasn't any clue that landed nine numbers.

The only part of the clue that they couldn't understand was the '… and remember what we are'. Nobody had been able to find any significance in that.

Thomas and Lucy became more agitated as time went on. There was no respite from Paul, no chance to grab a few seconds to discuss what to do next. They must have seemed edgy because he asked if there was a problem.

'No,' Thomas said. 'I have brain ache. I feel we're so close, it's frustrating.' He took a gamble. 'Do we know for sure that Jason's treasure lies in this 1014 vault?' he probed.

'Yes. We sent somebody in. They were directed to the security area and asked to plug in the code. He had orders to type any random number. Of course it failed, but it did confirm the procedure.'

This was some relief to Thomas, assuming the voice from Boston was telling the truth. At least the men hadn't made an attempt to claim the money without them. He looked at Lucy but she raised her eyebrows slightly. No, she didn't believe it either.

Thomas could hear voices outside the hotel door; he recognised them, and they seemed to be fractious. A few seconds later the door opened and in walked Stock and Anthony. Nathan was missing. They seemed more jovial than Thomas was expecting from the tone of their voices outside the door.

'How are things here today?'

Paul updated them on their progress so far. Lucy mentioned lunch, she was hungry, having spent the night throwing up, and she was feeling particularly empty.

'You're trying to avoid me aren't you, pretty one?' joked Stock.

'Awww, just bad timing,' she replied with a smile, placing her hand on his arm flirtatiously.

'OK. Shall we meet back here in an hour?' he said.

'That's fine. We'll see if we can finish this today,' Lucy proposed.

Thomas and Lucy left Room 216 and headed straight for their own room. It was one o'clock and, to their horror, the maid was inside. They did a quick check to make sure that they'd not left anything important then headed downstairs with their cases. Then they ran to the taxi stand.

***

'We have to move fast,' Anthony stated the moment Thomas and Lucy left the room. 'News is that the police have frogmen out at the bay. It's only a matter of time before they find the lawyer.'

'We're all in this now. We have to get this money and run. It's the last thing I wanted for you, Stock, but we have no choice. Someone directed the lawyer to the manor. If it was Trevor Mouriati, like I suspect, then he'll crack as soon as they find the body. We need to solve this today, no excuses.'

'What about the deal with the detectives?' Anthony asked.

'They have a conscience. When they realise the lawyer is dead, they'll put it all together. You won't be able to pay them off,' Stock announced.

Paul looked glumly out of the window. 'It's a shame, I like them,' he spoke, resigning himself to the inevitable. 'C'mon it's gonna be a long day. Let's get ourselves some food.'

As they headed downstairs and through the lobby towards the Starlane Walk food court, Stock and Anthony filled Paul in on the dumping of Nathan's body. They had driven him to Death Valley and left him under some rocks so that he wasn't visible from the air. They should be long gone by the time he was found.

Darcy was the problem; she was devastated and she wanted them all to leave within twenty-four hours. She had been waiting for Stock to get out for twelve years, and the very next day he shot her nephew, in her own house, right before her eyes. It was the worst kind of betrayal. As she screamed and cried, Stock wished that he had stayed in jail.

'What the heck?' Stock pointed outside the main hotel doors. Thomas and Lucy were at the taxi stand, together with their suitcases.

The brothers started running. The hotel staff had put up ropes to make sure the queue was orderly and they had to stop briefly, to puzzle out the zigzag maze before them.

Thomas spied them first and Paul saw him nudge Lucy. They abandoned their cases and sprinted down the ramp. As the brothers took chase, Thomas and Lucy turned right onto Tropicana Avenue. Thomas held on to Lucy's sleeve, almost dragging her with him.

The brothers were quick but they were not gaining ground. The detectives reached The Strip and turned right, heading north along the busy boulevard. Anthony motioned to his phone and ran up the stairs to the bridge from the MGM Grand to New York, New York; he would have a better view from up there. Paul and Stock continued the chase.

Anthony could see Thomas and Lucy hurrying through the crowds to the right. As he phoned Paul, he watched them head up towards the Planet Hollywood Hotel. Paul and Stock Hammond followed, even though they were both exhausted. Anthony said he didn't see them reappear from the other side of the path – his vision was obscured by construction work. Paul kept on walking as fast as he could, talking to Anthony on the phone, while Stock ran a little behind to catch up. Just then, they saw the couple reappear in the distance, running up the concrete stairs into Planet Hollywood.

Anthony started making his way up the Strip while Paul and Stock continued the chase. They waited for Anthony on the steps outside the Planet Hollywood Hotel, trying to catch their breath.

'They have an advantage over us – they're younger and much fitter,' Anthony claimed. Paul agreed but reminded him that they had their own advantage in that they knew Las Vegas well and the detectives didn't. They went inside the hotel.

Paul was amazed to see that the detectives had stopped by the high roller section and were leaning against the wall, talking. They were looking around but Paul dodged out of view and pulled his brothers aside.

The brothers made for the detectives, using banks of slot machines to hide behind. They reached the last row of slots and were ready to make a move. Paul had one last look, poking his head around a slot machine. Thomas and Lucy were moving towards them. As they approached, Thomas obviously caught sight of the brothers because he pulled Lucy sideways and they started running again. The security guards watched the action and radioed for backup, suspecting the chase was related to the casino.

The brothers were intercepted but Paul shouted, 'We're police!' and flashed a badge. Stock and Anthony carried on running and the security guard gave in to Paul, opening the door for him to continue the chase.

They could still see Thomas and Lucy. The path was busy and they were running north on the road to avoid the pedestrians but this kept them in view. They disappeared before they reached Paris Casino.

The brothers stood still; for a moment they thought they'd lost their prey. Then Paul spied them over the road, running towards the Bellagio Hotel. 'They're on the walkway – we can head them off!' he shouted.

The long walkway to the Bellagio ran parallel to Bellagio Drive. The brothers pulled up just short of the walkway exit and moved towards the wall. Thomas and Lucy were already at the bottom of the escalators. They had stopped, obviously wondering which way to go next. They turned right, towards the brothers, who stayed close to the wall. As soon as Thomas and Lucy were in reach, the brothers pounced.

Stock put his arms around Thomas. 'Good to see you,' he said. Thomas panicked. 'Run!' he shouted.

Lucy started off but then slowed and looked behind. 'Run! For Christ's sake!' She wanted to run, but her legs wouldn't let her; she couldn't condemn Thomas to death at the hands of these thugs.

'Run! Lucy, please run!' Thomas pleaded, his heart sinking.

She couldn't. Paul and Anthony approached her. The watching crowd looked on, uncertain as to whether to intervene. Paul showed his badge. 'Police!' he shouted, 'The party's over.'

Paul grabbed Lucy's arm and they walked on.

Chapter 46

The mirror framed a picture of sadness. Oliver Carsley didn't even recognise his reflection. The house was empty. His life, which had been so full of promise, now seemed empty. His conscience was crucifying him and the only thing he wanted to do was take away the pain. He thought of his son and the bravery he'd shown by turning himself in to the police. He thought of Frank Duffy, a fellow solicitor whom he had respected, who had probably died trying to help Amy. He thought about Thomas and Lucy who had fought hard to overpower him; they were certain to meet the same fate when Amy's captors no longer needed them.

He opened the cabinet door and looked at the ultimate pain-killers.

***

As they walked south down Las Vegas Boulevard, Lucy was close to tears.

'Today was not the day to try any funny business,' Paul said. He had his hands on Lucy's arm and back, handling her in the same way that she had been trained to handle criminals. He must have had some police training, she thought; he was very professional.

Anthony made a call on his phone. When they reached the

MGM Grand, the valet brought a Black Subaru four-by-four out to the front and Thomas and Lucy were pushed inside.

Lucy was petrified. There seemed no escape now. She felt sick; her heart was beating fast, and she was shaking and sweating uncontrollably. She tried to speak, to ask where they were going, but she couldn't.

'What do you think happened to our cases?' Thomas asked.

'You won't need them anymore,' Paul said.

Stock reached into his pocket for his gun and nonchalantly pointed it at Thomas. Lucy gasped and instinctively tried to grab it, but he slapped her across the face without saying a word.

'Well, unless you can get there fast enough to stop them opening it, you can kiss your money goodbye.' Thomas looked down the barrel of the gun without blinking. Lucy realised in an instant what he was doing. She sat up, cradling her throbbing face with her hand.

'You what?' Paul asked as it dawned on him. 'No fucking way! You didn't? Jeez. Turn the car round quickly!'

Stock replaced the gun in his pocket and put a hand on Thomas's knee. 'I liked you. My brother would have honoured the deal, you know. It didn't have to be like this. He told me that I could trust you and that you wouldn't just take the money and run and I believed him.'

'I trusted you, right up until I saw the news this morning. The missing solicitor from London, you killed him,' Thomas said bitterly. 'Then I lost all respect. You're just a thug.'

'That was Nathan,' Stock said. 'That stupid half-wit brother of mine – He screwed up, like he always did.'

He was using first names and Lucy realised that this was a bad sign. There was no way they were likely to get out of here alive.

'I told you the truth, Mr Riley, all the way, I told you the truth,' Paul said. 'If you hadn't tried to split, I would still have honoured my deal with you, even if it meant that we had to live on the run. I'm not a thug but I am a man of principle and I always keep my word.'

'We didn't know that,' Thomas said. 'We had no choice and no time to think. We had to make our move … and pray!'

Stock laughed and handed his gun to Paul. 'The money is not in those cases, is it?' he said. He reached across and grabbed Thomas by each ear, pulling his head down. 'No more games. I won't just fucking kill you, I'll rip you and your girlfriend to pieces. I'm done with these fucking mind games.' He snatched the gun back and smacked it on the back of Thomas's head before turning to Lucy.

Licking his finger, Stock stroked her cheek. She gasped in disgust, Thomas looked up, panic in his eyes. 'Enough!' he shouted, 'For crying out loud, stop this!'

Paul motioned to Stock to calm down. 'You don't have the money do you?' You wouldn't have returned to the hotel. You would be gone before now.'

Thomas hesitated. They both watched as Stock played with the gun. He didn't answer but it didn't matter.

'I'm done with this,' Paul announced solemnly. 'It's too late now, too much damage has been done. Let's forget about the money. We'll dump these two in the desert and clear out before the police or feds move in. Nathan's dead, Darcy's heart-broken, we couldn't have done any more damage if we tried. I can't believe it ended like this.' He sounded dejected.

Dump us where? Alive or dead?

The car approached the MGM Grand, the driver coughed.

'Drive on, we'll head south and get rid of these two.'

'You don't have to do this,' Lucy shouted.

Paul seemed to have little fight left. 'Yes we do. This is the end of the road for you two now. At least you'll die together.'

'No,' Lucy said, desperately trying not to show the fear in her eyes but despite her efforts, tears started to pour down her cheeks. Stock just smiled and pouted his lips in a kiss.

Thomas looked over towards Lucy and motioned to the door. He reached for the handle but it wouldn't move. He took a violent elbow in the ribs. Lucy shrieked, 'No! Leave him!' Thomas continued to take more frenzied blows. There was no letting up; he was likely to be killed right then and there. She surrendered her knowledge, in a final act of hope. '*Waterfalls!*' she shouted. 'It's *Rainbows and Waterfalls*. It's the final clue. Just let us go. Even if you just drop us off a few miles out, and give yourself head start.'

Anthony was ordered to pull over. Thomas was still wincing in pain.

'How does that work?' Paul asked.

'Trust me, it is waterfalls. I think I know what to do,' she said.

Thomas looked up. Lucy knew that he was wondering if she was playing a last-ditch game in an attempt to delay the inevitable or if she had really sussed out the clue – and if so, how long she had known the answer.

Stock looked even more flustered. He tightened the grip on his gun and pointed it at Lucy so she carried on.

'It's Rainbows and Waterfalls. Victoria isn't a girl's name, it's a waterfall. Jason visited Victoria Falls on holiday, and he often went to Niagara Falls. In a letter he left with his solicitor, he quoted the username as f0rc3 (Force) which is another name for a waterfall. The simple things that gave him so much pleasure were rainbows and waterfalls.'

Chapter 47

It was late in the day but it was all happening too fast for DCI Moore. Not only had the FBI confirmed that it was Frank Duffy's DNA at the manor, but Amy and Emmanuelle seemed to be missing again. Boston police had been trying to contact them but nobody knew where they were. Then he received Lucy's email and he realised that his detectives were in serious danger. There was no way he was leaving the office that night.

DCI Alderman had a call from Agent John Peters from the FBI.

'A boat has been found in Dorchester harbour in Boston. There are traces of blood on the outside of it. We're carrying out DNA tests but I think we can expect the worse.'

'I'd better notify family,' Alderman relied solemnly. 'Have you got divers out there?'

'We have high-tech surveillance boats trawling the harbour and bay. The house and boat were both owned by a man named Jack Lithgoe, an eccentric entrepreneur. He seems unaware that the property had been used. Boston PD have got a lead, though. Darren Cooper, a man with a mafia-style reputation throughout the north-eastern states, reportedly sometimes used the manor for meetings. Though Jack Lithgoe denied any knowledge of the kidnapping, he did confess to being friends with Darren Cooper to the point of the pair of them having a monthly golf tournament – with a side bet of ten thousand dollars a hole.'

'Nice.'

'I'd say. Darren Cooper is bad news. He has connections everywhere. People have been taking his falls for the past twenty years, but we've never been able to finger him directly for any crime. It seems people do time for him and then appear to live a life of luxury when they come out of jail.'

'Fall guys. Do you think he is responsible?'

'Trevor Mouriati, a parole officer from Boston, has offered information. He looked after some of Darren Cooper's disciples to make sure they stayed straight after they'd done their time. He said Darren Cooper didn't deal in murder: his exploits were heists, laundering, contraband, embezzlements and fraud. He had a conversation with Frank Duffy on Sunday, and seems convinced that Darren has gone too far this time. He came forward to Boston police, trading information about his meeting with the London solicitor for a promise of a transfer out of Massachusetts.'

'I don't blame him.'

'He has named three brothers from Las Vegas that Frank had mentioned. They reverted back to their mother's maiden name and relocated to Boston. We're following up on them now but they all seem elusive. Frank had suggested to Mouriati that these guys could have a connection to Jason's parents' accident too.'

'OK, this is starting to make sense. Keep us up to date. We are still looking for our missing detectives.'

DCI Alderman filled Moore in on his conversation with Agent Peters. He was worried. This had suddenly turned into an international manhunt – and was rapidly becoming international news.

It was midnight when the inevitable happened. DCI Moore found out that a body had been found about a mile off the coast at Dorchester Bay in Boston. It was yet to be identified but the preliminary report indicated that the person was male, late fifties, with a gunshot wound to the head.

Then Moore received news that a couple of British tourists had been seen fleeing from three men in an incident at the MGM Grand Hotel in Las Vegas. The tourists' cases were abandoned but Las Vegas Police Department were called. A passport left at the scene belonged to Lucy Bridges.

'Las Vegas?' Nothing made sense now. Why would DS Bridges' passport end up in Las Vegas? Her email had explained a lot about what was happening, and even suggested that the motive for the kidnapping might be connected with Jason's money, but there was no mention of Las Vegas.

Moore's stress levels were reaching an all-time high. He had all available staff try and track down their colleagues' movements to find out how they ended up in Las Vegas – especially as Amy was supposedly in Boston. He contacted the FBI and asked if they could investigate Frank Duffy's movements in Las Vegas in case his detectives were on the same trail.

He wondered about the connection with Monsal Head. Either Thomas and Lucy were trying to divert attention from their departure from England or there was a clue that needed following up.

***

Anthony Hammond was asked to pull over into Mandalay Bay.

'If you want to live then you better be right,' Paul said to Lucy as they left the car for the lobby. They entered the plush hotel with its marble ceiling and gold carvings and booked a suite, using the name Stringham.

Once in their rooms, Paul looked at Thomas who still appeared to be in pain. Stock said very little; he looked angry. Only Anthony seemed composed.

'Now Lucy, explain how we might get to a nine-digit code from your new theory,' Paul said, throwing the gun to Stock.

Stock pointed the barrel in the direction of Thomas's groin. 'And think quickly!' he added.

'Don't shoot him!' Lucy pleaded. 'Just give me a few minutes and a pen and paper. I haven't got anything with me – I dropped my handbag at the taxi rank at the MGM Grand.'

Stock looked as if he was taking pleasure from threatening the couple, as if nothing mattered any more, but Lucy was distraught. Paul worried that she'd be unable to think straight, so he motioned to his brother to stop. Instead, Stock pulled back the safety catch.

Lucy screamed.

'No!' Paul motioned again to Stock to stop, but he just smiled,

'Tick, tock, tick tock,' he chanted. The barrel of the gun was now six inches from Thomas's groin.

'Pack it in!' Anthony went to Stock to take the gun from him but Stock smacked the handgrip heavily onto his brother's wrist then turned the gun on him.

Paul realised Stock was losing control. Maybe the years in jail had messed up his mind; the calm, intelligent older brother he once knew now seemed to be devoid of conscience, and uncontrollable.

Things couldn't get any worse. Paul didn't like his lack of control. He was in too deep. Though he hadn't killed anybody himself, he was an accessory to two murders now and even if he walked away with the money, he would be on the run forever. He was almost resigned to failure; if there was any way of letting the detectives go right now, he would release them. But Stock wasn't going to give up the gun.

Paul's voice softened as he turned back to Lucy. 'Use my pen and write on this.' He handed her a leaflet, which was blank on the reverse.

Lucy's hand was shaking as she wrote 'Rainbows' and 'Waterfalls' 'r41nb0w5' 'w4t3rf4ll5'; there were only eight numbers. She attempted the alphabet number code too and neither worked.

'Unless it's quite simply Rainbows and Waterfalls,'

Paul suggested, as calmly as he could, 'That would give us 'r41nb0w5 4nd w4t3rf4ll5' – 410544345.'

'It's worth a try. We have nothing to lose,' Lucy replied.

Paul held out his hand for the gun. Stock smiled and pointed the gun to Paul's head. 'Are you sure, Paul? Are you sure you want it?'

'Give me the fucking gun!' Paul demanded, showing no fear at his brother's bullying tactics.

'I tell you what,' Stock said. 'You take the princess down to Excalibur and claim the treasure. If you don't phone me back in forty minutes, to let me know you were successful, then I'll execute Prince Charming. If you're successful then I'll leave him here alive and you send back the princess to rescue him. Deal?'

'No!' Lucy shouted. 'We're close, but this might not be the one!'

'You better make sure that it is then. Tick, tock, tick tock.' Stock grinned at Lucy, and then pointed the gun back at Thomas.

'It's a deal. You back out of it, Stock, and the next bullet fired will be in your direction. That's a promise,' Paul responded, leading Lucy to the door. He motioned to Anthony to join them but he said he'd rather stay and make sure Stock was all right. He was brave, Paul thought.

As they walked towards the escalators Paul stopped and turned to Lucy. 'Listen, whether you're right or not, I will phone him and tell him it's here. Let me deal with him, OK?'

Lucy nodded, wiping away her tears.

'This isn't me. This is not how things are done. My brother Stock, the one with the gun, he taught me good principles. I don't know what's happened to him. I don't recognise him anymore.'

The walk to Excalibur seemed to take a long time, but eventually they were heading down the escalator towards the security area.

The head of security commented that there had been a lot of interest in 1014; they were now required to take the name of everybody who asked to access it. Lucy had no ID on her; they took her name and address and noted that she was accompanied by Paul Stringham.

'Have we met before?' the guard asked Paul

'Not that I can remember,' Paul replied but Lucy had the feeling that he was lying.

They were escorted downstairs and the security guard plugged a hand held electronic device into a socket on the wall plug numbered 1014. Lucy was told to type in the security code and wait for the red light to turn green. Trembling, she carefully typed in the numbers 410544345. Part of her knew what to expect but things had changed so much that she didn't know what she wanted any more. Just to be alive tonight would be everything.

The light went green. The security guard pushed the button and walked them into the customer security vault. It worked. Lucy gasped as she opened the safe. The door was about three foot by three the safe itself was about five feet deep.

And it was empty.

Chapter 48

'This is crazy!' Paul Hammond shook his head in disbelief and stared into the empty vault.

Lucy burst into tears. They'd been gone nearly forty minutes. She pleaded with him to call his brother. 'Please tell him the number was correct and that you're in the safe. You won't be lying to him.'

Paul blinked and took a deep breath. 'Okay.'

He summoned the security guard, who opened the cage to let them out. Paul made the call to Stock as soon as he had signal.

'We got inside,' he said quietly. 'Bring the car round to Excalibur and we'll meet you at the main reception desk.' He switched off the phone and turned to Lucy. 'There. You go now, get your boyfriend and leave on the first plane out of here.'

'I'm sorry,' she said. 'I know you didn't want it to be like this.'

As she turned to leave they were surrounded by armed men.

'FBI.'

Paul's eyes filled with tears. It was over.

He watched Lucy being handcuffed and led to a side room. He was marched out of the building and placed in a black unmarked police vehicle and taken away. While waiting to turn at the junction he saw his brothers' car approaching.

Don't pull in, he said to himself.

***

As soon as Paul was out of sight Lucy spoke. She was about to explain who she was and what she was doing when an agent leaned forward and removed her handcuffs, which took her completely by surprise.

The agents introduced themselves as John Peters and Joe Farley.

'Thank God!' she said!

'We know who you are, Ms Bridges, and what you're doing here,' the agent said. Lucy took a deep breath: yes, she wanted to know how the FBI had found them but more importantly, she had to rescue Thomas.

'Good. Then we need to get Thomas, he's at the Mandalay Bay. Paul's brothers will be driving around to the front within the next few minutes. They have a Black Subaru four-by-four.'

Lucy filled them in on what she knew about the men that had held them in Las Vegas as they took the brief journey by car to Mandalay Bay. They reached Suite 445 room and knocked on the door. When Thomas didn't answer Lucy knew something was wrong.

'No, No! Thomas!' She banged ferociously on the door. Peters asked the manager who'd accompanied them for the key, released the lock and pushed open the door.

Lucy ran over to the bed. Thomas was lying on the floor, head against the wall – and he was bleeding. Both knees had been shot and he had another bullet wound in his abdomen. He was holding the wound, trying to stop the blood flow. He couldn't speak but held out his other hand for Lucy. She hugged him, in tears, while the FBI agents called for paramedics.

***

Anthony Hammond was driving with Stock, approaching Excalibur, when he saw a flurry of police activity. He suggested to Stock that they go round the block; he was feeling uneasy.

Stock tried ringing Paul but his phone was off. He had a really bad feeling. They continued down Tropicana and, as they slowed to turn left behind the hotels, a black BMW M5 passed them. Paul was in the back, looking straight ahead.

'It's the fucking Feds!' Stock shouted, enraged.

For Anthony, this was the last straw. He was repulsed by the way his brother had callously shot the English detective without even the slightest hesitation.

They continued west, trying to think of a plan. Anthony wanted to dump the car and run, but didn't rate his chance of outsmarting a bullet. For now he was a captive, with no choice but to fall in line with his brother. He suggested travelling back to Darcy's, changing cars then heading towards Los Angeles. It was easier to get lost there.

Stock agreed.

When they pulled into Darcy's drive, every one of Stock's possessions, together with every photograph of him, was boxed up on the garage floor. Darcy saw them pull in and disappeared upstairs. She obviously wanted nothing at all to do with him.

To Anthony's amazement, Stock handed him the gun. 'You load up, bro. If I don't say goodbye to her properly, it will kill me.'

'Go away! I don't want to see you! Just leave me!' Stock heard Darcy's heartbroken voice as he knocked on her bedroom door. He sat down on the landing with his back to her door. Of all the people in the world, the one he admired most was Darcy. She was the last person in the world he wanted to hurt. For twelve years, she had visited him once a month without fail. He never dreamed that he would do anything to hurt her. He had destroyed the spirit inside her and some sort of karmic retribution had taken him by the scruff of the neck and crucified the person he thought he was.

He longed for her to open the door. He knew he could enter but still had enough respect for her to let her make a move. Time stood still, or so it seemed. Twenty minutes later, he composed himself enough to ask one more time, 'Please Darcy? Let me say goodbye. Let me look into your eyes and tell you how sorry I really am.'

'Just go, Stock,' she said, gently.

'Take care, Darcy,' he told her, as he descended her stairs for the very last time.

'Come on, let's go.' He motioned to Anthony and they got into the car. Stock looked up at Darcy's window as they pulled out of the drive. She held a handkerchief to her nose, her face streaming with tears. She raised a hand, a small wave. He saluted her and they pulled away, heading southwest.

* * *

DCI Moore's team was working with Las Vegas PD and the FBI. News was coming in fast. There were reports of a chase though Las Vegas. Security cameras at Planet Hollywood identified Thomas and Lucy being followed by three men. One man had claimed to be from the police but they were not recognised from any FBI database and it was suspected that these men were the Hammond Brothers. Other witnesses said that two people were seen being escorted down Las Vegas boulevard by three professional-looking men.

The FBI confirmed that the men were after Jason Chadwick's money, which was in a vault in a Las Vegas hotel. They had initially assumed that this was why Frank Duffy had travelled there; they'd been surprised that he left for Boston without even getting close to the money.

Almost all of Moore's staff came in voluntarily to help. They found out that Thomas and Lucy had travelled to Las Vegas early on Monday morning on tickets booked by an

Oliver Carsley. Surely this must be a relation of Ashton Carsley?

DCI Alderman was on his way over to interview the man himself.

Chapter 49

As Lucy travelled with the paramedics to hospital, Thomas was drifting in and out of consciousness. She didn't stop talking in the ambulance, trying to keep him awake. Agent Peters remained with her while the medical staff took Thomas to the operating theatre. She tried to give the agent as much detail as she could about everything that had happened since the minute Thomas opened the door to Hardy. So much still didn't make sense.

Peters told her that they believed it was the Hammond Brothers that had held them. He explained about Jason's father, Donald Chadwick, putting them in jail; that was why they probably felt it was their right to claim his money.

'That makes sense. I realised they were brothers. Stock made an acrimonious toast to Jason; I wondered at the time what his story was,' Lucy said.

'Boston Police found a body north of the harbour. It hasn't been identified but it's likely to be Frank Duffy's.'

Lucy was saddened but she already knew. It was hard to feel any sympathy with her captors.

'Stock made a reference to his half-wit brother Nathan. I realised then that Frank had probably been killed. Sounds to me as if their plans went very wrong. I can't really fault how Paul and the other brother were towards us especially at the hotel. They both tried to diffuse the situation with Stock – though Paul was prepared to dump us in the desert.

In fairness, he did let us go when he had his chance, so his bravado might have been a show.'

'Miss Pearce and Miss Sexton said pretty much the same.'

'I didn't like Stock from the start. I even faked food poisoning last night to get out the room.'

'Stock was only released from jail yesterday.'

'Really? That figures then. It would account for his unrestrained behaviour, he seemed to be devoid of any conscience.'

The conversation drifted. It was hard for her to concentrate enough to relive the hell of the day when Thomas was in the next room with a dozen surgeons, fighting for his life.

Agent Peters left her alone with her thoughts for a while. He phoned his office to get the latest developments and fill in his colleagues with the information he had from Lucy.

***

DCI Moore was exhausted after a night he would rather forget. He felt helpless. At least he had names and a motive now, but why had Riley and Bridges been dragged into this mess?

He was just packing up to leave the office when the bombshell dropped. Alderman rang to say that the FBI had arrested one of the men that held Amy but Riley had been shot three times and was having emergency surgery. Lucy Bridges was safe and was helping the FBI with their enquiries.

It was a dark day indeed. Moore made difficult calls to Thomas Riley's parents and to Lucy Bridges' family too. He'd been dealing with dejected family members all day. Frank Duffy's and Amy Pearce's families had rung the station a dozen times or more.

He left the station head down, dreading tomorrow.

***

Stock Hammond's rage was out of control; he had never experienced anything like this before. For years he'd planned the things he would do when he was released: a new home in Boston, being part of the family business again. Now Donald Chadwick had turned the screw on him. He'd had the last laugh from beyond the grave.

What now? Stock wanted revenge, he wanted the money and he wanted somebody to pay.

He and Anthony travelled towards Los Angeles on Interstate 15 and stopped at Baker, a small town at the foot of a mountain pass.

Stock could tell that Anthony was loath to stop but they were both hungry and thirsty. They pulled into the parking area of a roadside café. Anthony had placed the gun inside the glove compartment.

'No!' Anthony said as Stock reached for it. 'You won't need it, we're just stopping for refreshments and then we'll be on our way.' He glared at his brother.

'OK,' Stock muttered reluctantly. As they were leaving the car and his brother's back was turned, he reached for the gun again. They went into the busy restaurant and ordered food.

Anthony excused himself and went to the men's room; he was still there when the food arrived. Stock became more agitated as the minutes passed by. Eventually he thumped his hand on the table so hard that his brother's plate bounced upwards and crashed back down on the table, spilling his pizza to the floor. Everybody looked around.

Stock felt crushed by the weight of his rage. He pulled the gun from his jacket. 'What's up?' he shouted, staring in no particular direction. 'Never seen a psycho with a gun before?' There were several screams as customers dived under the tables.

Stock went to the restroom. It was empty; Anthony had

escaped through the window.

When Stock re-entered the restaurant, all eyes were fixed on him. He waved the gun around and held it briefly to the belly of a little girl, blowing a kiss to her mother before leaving the building. He ran towards the town. After ten minutes he abandoned the hunt for his brother. He'd heard police sirens heading for the diner, so he knew that he had to get away quickly.

A blue Ford was approaching fast, hip-hop music blaring from its speakers. Stock stood in front of it, forcing it to swerve before grinding to a halt. The young driver shouted abuse at him, but he grabbed his collar and yanked him out of the car through the open window. He pointed the gun at the kid in the passenger seat, who put up his hands and hastily climbed out of the car. Waving them both aside with the gun, Stock got into the driver's seat and roared away.

He headed on towards Los Angeles. He knew he was out of control but he just couldn't stop.

***

Anthony Hammond sat exhausted on a bench at the far side of town in the middle of a small industrial estate. He'd been running for fifteen minutes and was struggling to get his breath back. His heart didn't seem to be slowing, even though his legs had stopped. He thought of his options: the last thing he wanted to do was to go back to jail. Nathan had killed the lawyer in Boston; Anthony could claim that he helped his brother dump the body because he was scared. He could claim that Nathan had lost control. He was pretty damn sure that Paul would be taking that line with the FBI.

It was obvious that Stock had lost it. Anthony feared for his life, remembering how Stock had killed his brother and probably the detective. The only way Anthony could expect a break was if he turned himself in right now and helped the police catch Stock.

He walked into an industrial unit and asked if there was a police station or sheriff's office in town. The man before him could see that Anthony was scared and had been running. 'Yeah, you need me to call? What's happened?'

'Please do, they might want to hurry.' Anthony sat and waited while the call was made.

'The police are busy dealing with an incident at the diner on Interstate 15. They will be here as soon as possible,'

'Yeah, that's what I feared. I'll wait.'

Twenty minutes later, a deputy arrived. Anthony stood up. 'My name is Anthony Hammond. My brother, Stock, has killed two men today. I was scared and ran from the diner. I want to help you catch him.'

The deputy didn't cuff him and Anthony was happy to go down to the station. The FBI was first to get there. Anthony briefly explained to the agent what had happened during the week, including what had happened to Frank Duffy in Boston.

'We've spoken to your brother Paul. He also seemed very concerned about Stock.'

'He has a gun and little in the way of a conscience. I think he will head for LA and get off the main roads as soon as he is clear of the mountains.'

'We've radioed for backup and roadblocks. He hasn't taken your car but an Escort estate was stolen about half hour ago.'

Anthony was searched then detained locally while the police looked for his brother.

***

Lucy waited. Two hours had passed and there had been no news. Neither had there been a hurried rush of personnel from the theatre where Thomas was undergoing emergency surgery. Lucy didn't know if this was good or bad. She hated the smell of hospitals. She'd been in too many as part of her job, questioning victims after they'd been attacked. This was the first time she'd been on the other side, Thomas was a victim and so was she, by association.

Lucy was thirsty but didn't want to leave the waiting area in case she missed the doctor. Her mind left Thomas and, for a second, she felt deep sympathy for Jason Chadwick. She prayed that he would not be looking down on them from whatever heaven there might be to see the hell he'd left behind.

A doctor left the operating theatre, and came over to her.

'How is he?' she asked. The doctor led her to a side room.

'Stable, for now but impossible to assess the long term damage. The bullet in his abdomen fortunately found a path which avoided doing too much damage to Thomas's organs. However, the bullet came to rest in his spine. They were waiting for a specialist surgeon to arrive and assess whether they should remove it or leave it. Obviously the other two bullets have done serious damage to his knees, which will take time to heal. He is certain to be wheelchair-bound for many months.'

'What's the worst-case scenario?' Lucy asked, holding back her tears.

'We can't assess the long-term damage to his spine until after this specialist has examined him. He could have up to one hundred percent paralysis, but that really *is* the worst case scenario.'

Lucy's eyes filled. 'Can I see him?'

'Not now, we are awaiting assessment.

For Lucy, the worry was almost unbearable. Thomas might well survive but whether he would have a life, she didn't know. It was hard to know whether she should be relieved or in mourning. Things would never be the same again.

Chapter 50

Arnold Pearce was on the war-path. This time he wanted answers. DCI Alderman had phoned because Boston Police needed to speak with Amy urgently and they didn't know where she was. Arnold had been trying to contact her for forty-eight hours. Emmanuelle didn't turn up for a lecture on Tuesday afternoon. In the early hours of the Wednesday morning, the FBI had entered Emmanuelle's house. There was no sign of either girl.

Arnold's fears grew. There was no way that Amy would have remained out of touch for all that time, so something must have happened.

He followed the news stories and phoned through to Alderman and Moore every hour or so for news. The man arrested in connection with Vito Rolanski's death was Ashton Carsley, son of a solicitor, Oliver Carsley. Arnold knew of Oliver and had met him as he lived locally. He had a feeling that maybe Oliver had information since he was supposed to have spoken to DI Riley. Maybe he could explain some things off the record easier than he could explain them to the police.

Arnold phoned his secretary for a contact number. Despite ringing repeatedly, nobody answered the phone. After an hour of trying, he ventured out of the house and headed for where he believed Oliver Carsley lived. It was a quiet cul-de-sac off the Kings Road in Chelsea. The houses were modern detached two-story buildings with garages. Arnold hoped he would recognise Oliver's car.

He saw a silver BMW parked in the drive of one of the houses, pulled over, parked and went to the front door. When he rang the doorbell, there was no answer. He knocked loudly on the door then took a few steps back looking for any movement in the upstairs windows. Daylight was fading but there were no lights on in the house.

Arnold peered through the letterbox. There was an open suitcase on the floor. A few clothes were hanging over the edge, as if the case had been rummaged through, and then left.

'Oliver!' Arnold shouted. 'Oliver, I need to talk with you. Amy is missing again. I need your help!'

There was still no response. Arnold walked around the property, looking in each window. Nobody was there. Maybe Oliver was visiting his son. As Arnold passed the kitchen window, he froze. On the table, there was a large black and white photograph of Amy. Arnold stared. It looked as if it was a candid photo, taken without her knowledge. It was the sort of photograph that a private investigator might take. *What the hell was Oliver up to?*

Arnold called Alderman from his mobile.

'I've just come away from interviewing Ashton. I believe his father purchased the flight tickets for the missing detectives. I was about to come over.'

'Yeah, it's definitely Amy, Oliver must know something.'

'Stay there if you can and wait for our officers, I'll come and see for myself.'

***

Stock Hammond lost control of the Ford and ditched the right hand side into gravel before correcting himself. The road was quiet as he travelled through the mountains on Interstate 15.

He was so angry. He smacked his hand hard on the steering wheel every time he thought of Anthony and Nathan. He had to speak to somebody. For twenty minutes or more there was not a single building. Eventually he came to a small village at the foot of a barren hill which looked like a dry wasteland. There were three or four houses, a convenience store and garage. Stock pulled over, composing himself before he used the public telephone. He phoned Darren Cooper. Darren was not happy either. He had been following the news all week and wondering when somebody would call him. Stock screamed his anger down the phone and Darren listened.

The Hammonds were related to the Coopers via Stock's mother. His uncle, Nevin Cooper, was Darren's father. Nevin had passed away ten years earlier, while Stock was in jail. The Coopers were well respected throughout the eastern states and Darren Cooper held the family together. He was greedy, devious and manipulative; he had a great mind and was a natural adrenaline junkie. He got his fix through scams that sometimes took years of planning. Somehow he always ended up on top, and clean.

Stock had competed with him at one time. The Hammond Organisation was Stock's attempt to rival Darren. Stock had to concede his position of superiority to Darren while he was in jail, but they respected each other and still managed to hatch up plans from between the walls. Darren was the only person that Stock trusted.

Darren Cooper knew the FBI was after him and that Trevor Mouriati had grassed him up. He was keeping a low profile and denying any knowledge of the mansion at Phillips Point being let out to his cousins. He was looking for a new fall guy. Stock pleaded with Darren for help but there was nothing he could do, unless Stock could make it to Chicago, where Darren was hiding out.

Stock slammed the phone down. In the distance, he saw a convoy of police vehicles. He got back inside the car and drove around the back of the garage. A young woman in the convenience store opposite had been watching him. She had left the store and was looking in his direction. He left the Ford and ran over towards her, flashing his gun at her. She froze as he approached.

A small green car, possibly a Honda Civic, was parked to the side of the shop.

'Is that your car?' Stock shouted, looking towards the convoy.

'Yes,' she cried. 'Don't hurt me!' She was shaking as she fumbled for the keys.

'Get inside!'

'No, I mustn't leave...'

Stock didn't have time for arguments. The limits of his patience had already been breached. He picked up the woman. She was small, childlike, and Stock was surprised how light she was. He threw her back towards the store. Her long hair obscured her face and that made it easier for Stock to pull the trigger. The woman crumpled to the floor.

Stock started the Honda. He looked to his right; the convoy about to enter the village. He drove off slowly at first, hoping to be out of sight before the police were close enough to realise that he was driving. The road took a slight bend and as soon as the police were out of his rear view mirror, he put his foot down.

Stock wanted to turn off the Interstate at the first opportunity, if he could just make it to the next main town. He felt a great rush of adrenaline as and his anger temporarily changed to laughter. But his laughter didn't last long. Coming towards him was another convoy of vehicles.

As they approached, Stock tried to focus ahead, looking at the road as six, seven, eight police vehicles rushed passed. He kept an eye in his mirror, while chanting: *Don't turn around, don't turn around.*

The last two police vehicles slowed, made a one-hundred and eighty degree turn and then started following him.

* * *

Arnold Pearce was sitting on Oliver Carsley's doorstep when a police van arrived. Four uniformed officers spoke with him as he explained why he was there and showed them the photograph of Amy through the window.

After knocking on the door and getting no reply, the officers forced their way into the house. It was very quiet. Arnold went into the dining area of the kitchen and saw several other photographs of Amy on the table.

The police officers searched the house. There was a shout from upstairs and Arnold followed two officers up the narrow open staircase.

'We need a paramedic up here now,' one of the officers shouted back to his colleague. He stopped Arnold at the top of the stairs.

'You should go back down. We may have a crime scene here.'

'What's happened?' Arnold asked.

The officer told him that there was a man on the floor in the bathroom.

'Oh God no!' Arnold returned downstairs.

This was a bad omen.

* * *

Stock put his foot down to try and put as much distance between himself and the police vehicles as possible. The road was winding down the mountainside. As it started to straighten, he could see the valley below. California's desert sands started to show more greenery and he could see lush forest in the distance. There was an entirely different feel about the surroundings.

He kept picturing the young woman he had shot and was distracted, enough to forget about the chase for a few moments. When he looked in his mirrors again, he saw the police were approaching fast. This time their lights were flashing. Then, from nowhere, a police helicopter appeared, almost directly in front of him.

This is it now! Stock thought. He didn't want to go back to jail but the fear that he could die right here was another option that he couldn't stomach. He drove faster. The police helicopter stayed with him, swooping low on occasions, forcing him to swerve.

An armed police officer had a rifle aimed at his car but Stock just kept going. He was numb, with no plan, no hope of escape. In the distance, another convoy of police vehicles approached from in front of him.

This is the end of the road.

Stock drove faster.

Chapter 51

Amy and Emmanuelle returned to Boston feeling elated. They were completely unaware of the chaos in Vegas. They tried to phone DS Bridges, tell her the good news but couldn't contact her.

It hadn't taken long at all for them to figure out the last clue. When Lucy Bridges had phoned, explaining about Jason's treasure hunt and the progress that they'd made with the clues, they couldn't believe it. She explained how the men who held them at the manor had been both probing for information and at the same time making sure that they were not involved in the hunt for the money themselves.

DS Bridges told Amy that she deserved the rewards of his hard work much more than these bullies did. She said that she hoped that Amy would be able to solve the last clue and claim it as quickly as they could get to Las Vegas – and prayed that she would beat the men to it. She told her she would try to delay the men for as long as possible.

Amy recognised the picture at Monsal Head immediately, and she immediately recalled her conversation with Jason.

'That's what we are,' he had said to her, 'rainbows and waterfalls.'

It hadn't taken her and Emmanuelle long to understand how the last clues worked. Emmanuelle laughed at his references to the injustice towards ancient culture. She was with him that day when they first discovered Artemis at the

Forum Shops. He had returned to Las Vegas about three years after his move to England for a conference. He was discussing the fact that Artemis had an eagle with the hotel manager of all people. Emmanuelle explained her theories about Zeus's all-seeing eagle and protector, and suggested that Artemis was leading a battle; the eagle was a symbol of the onset of battle.

The manager had chuckled and said, 'Yes, of course you are right, but this is Las Vegas. Wouldn't it be ironic – especially being the emblem of the United States of America?' Jason's face had dropped and he walked out of the hotel, ashamed to be American. It rattled him all week!

They were lucky, they didn't have to wait long for their flight to Las Vegas. Amy couldn't believe it when the vault was opened. The money had been neatly stacked in bundles of hundred-dollar bills. The security staff helped her carry the cash to her hotel and the hotel had transferred the money into her UK bank account. The instructions had all been left inside the vault. Ten million of the ninety-five was transferred to Emmanuelle – that was all she wanted to take, even though Amy had offered her half. The hotel even dealt with the IRS. She gave them a hundred thousand dollar tip – it was hard to believe she could even contemplate doing something like that.

Jason had left a note with the money and that was another reason that she wanted to track down Thomas and Lucy. She decided to phone London as soon as they returned to Emmanuelle's house.

There was so much money and so many things that she could now do with her life. A memorial for Jason would be first priority. Ideally she would make a clearing at the base of the waterfall in Monsal Dale. Possibly put a bench there, or maybe even a paved area, just a few square metres with Jason's infamous words *Rainbows and Waterfalls*, inscribed on a plaque.

When they got back to Emmanuelle's house, two officers from Boston PD were sitting outside.

'Miss Sexton? Miss Pearce?' one of them asked.

'Yes, what's going on?' Emmanuelle looked confused. Amy feared trouble. Was this money going to put her in more danger?

The girls heard the police officer radio that they had returned and were home safe and well. It was all too familiar. *Surely not again?*

***

Police vehicles formed a barricade on the road and armed officers stood behind the cars with rifles. Stock was hurtling towards them with no sign of slowing. The officers on the ground started to scatter as he approached – he obviously wasn't going to slow down. Two hundred yards, one hundred yards…

An officer in the helicopter fired shots at the front of the car. The semi-automatic rounds penetrated the bonnet and the roof but Stock's motion was relentless. Fifty yards, thirty yards…

Bullets shattered the windscreen. Stock involuntarily swerved but could no longer see the direction he was travelling in and couldn't keep hold on to the steering wheel. The car went sideways and there was a massive bump.

Stock was aware that he was flying. He retched, as if he were on a rollercoaster. Suddenly there was a massive thud and he felt a blow to his head.

And that was it.

***

DCI Jim Alderman arrived at Oliver Carsley's house shortly after the paramedics. It was too late. Pill bottles were strewn on the floor and Oliver's neck was in a noose, made of silk ties and tied to the bathroom cabinet handle. Oliver's weight had ripped the cabinet off the wall but the knots were tight enough to restrict his airflow.

There was a note in his bedroom. It read:

'I do not trust anybody and I trust myself even less. I am sorry I let you down, Ashton, but money alone will not cure your problems and I cannot live a lie for the rest of my life, especially knowing that people have been killed. I am so sorry.'

Alderman met Arnold Pearce downstairs. He was sitting on his colleague's sofa with his head in his hands.

'More unanswered questions,' Arnold muttered as he left the room and prepared to go home.

Alderman stared at the photograph of Amy on the table. Nothing made sense. It was as if there were pieces of several jigsaws before him, all having the same picture but with different shapes.

***

Lieutenant Harry Leeson arrived at Emmanuelle's house within minutes of his colleague's call. He explained to the girls that they had been reported missing again.

'We weren't missing, we had to leave quickly,' Emmanuelle explained. 'I should have notified the University but got overwhelmed.'

'You say you went to Las Vegas?'

'Yes, we found out what all the fuss was about, but you must know that by now.'

'Ma'am,' Lt Leeson interrupted. 'I'm glad you've returned safely. Amy, you will need to phone home – your parents are worried. Especially since this is a multiple murder investigation.'

Amy gasped. 'What do you mean?'

'There was a body found off Philips Point that has just been confirmed as the missing British solicitor, Frank Duffy. There's also been a shooting in Las Vegas of DI Riley. They're still awaiting news on his condition.'

Amy burst into tears; another person had died because of her and another one was seriously injured. She suddenly felt as if Jason's gift to her was blood money. Guilt and shame mixed with the knowledge that she had rightfully claimed his money; it was like finding out you were responsible for your best friend's death on the same day you win the lottery. It was hard to take; only an hour before she had been so happy.

Lt Leeson continued softly. 'Two of the men have been found, including the one that had claimed to be DCI Paul Dawson. We understand that the man that called himself Agent Stringham has been murdered by his own brother, Stock, who had just been released from jail for masterminding a major fraud operation in Las Vegas. Jason's parents had helped put them all behind bars.'

'I remember the case well,' Emmanuelle said.

'Unfortunately Stock is still on the run, heading for Los Angeles, but we are confident that we'll find him.'

The girls explained where they had been and why they had left so suddenly. They had been completely unaware of the news during their brief trip. The lieutenant was relieved. 'I'll leave you now to call home,' he said as he turned to leave.

Amy phoned immediately; her parents had been put through their own hell this past couple of weeks. After the heartbreak of the past two weeks, it was heaven to speak to them. Her father couldn't hold back his tears – but this time they were tears of joy. Amy could hear her mother crying too. Gerard was with them. Her father told her that Gerard had been a rock during the last few days. He had tickets to fly to Boston in the morning and help look for her. They all wanted Amy home as soon as possible now.

After the call, Amy leaned against Emmanuelle on her

deep sofa. She was numb. So badly did she want to enjoy the happiness of Jason's treasure and drink to him and yet there was so much sadness.

Emmanuelle reassured her. 'You have to understand Jason again,' she said. 'For him to leave the money to you would have been an admission of his own feelings. Because of his parents' death he wouldn't have wanted to risk putting you in danger. He did the next best thing; he set this out after leaving the biggest clues inside your head. If you loved him, like you did, you would find the money. He must have been overseeing this from above because you ended up with it anyway, in spite of having no knowledge that it even existed.'

Amy blushed. 'Maybe. It's just that I find it so hard to accept that people have died as a result.'

'Jason once said to me that fact tends to deal more twists than fiction,' Emmanuelle said. 'This is an example. I can imagine Jason playing out the hunt in his head, fantasising about what might happen. The reality is that the ending was the same but the story wasn't the adventure he planned. It was a horror story, far worse than he could have ever imagined.' She held Amy's hands and looked at her. 'But he wasn't to know that. You shouldn't feel guilty. Enjoy the money and do good things with it, OK?'

Amy smiled and nodded. From that moment on, it all seemed so clear. She read Jason's note again:

Congratulations! I set out this quest with one or two special people in mind but if you've found this by true means then you are special to me too.

I have learned one thing in life: you can never make your dreams happen on your own. People along the way help you, advise you, show you where your errors are and put you back on the path to success. For you to find my legacy, some people must have helped you on the way. You know who these people are, so let your conscience decide their worth.

Chapter 52

Lucy looked out of the window onto the River Thames. It was a beautiful day. London looked magnificent: the early morning sunshine was just low enough to reflect majestically from the river, silhouetting the landscape of the tall and sometimes odd shaped towers of the capital.

'To us!' announced the voice behind her. Thomas handed her a glass of champagne.

'And Amy Pearce,' she added, bringing his wheelchair around so that he could look at the spectacular view from their new office.

Rileys Investigations sounded so much better than Riley and Bridges. Not that they needed an excuse to get married. Thomas was getting fitter by the day, the strength in his legs was growing and he was able to stand now; he would undergo a programme of exercises to help him walk again very soon. The bullet had been removed from his spine. It was a six-hour operation that required the precision of a robot hand to make sure the bullet left at exactly the same angle it had entered. One millimetre either way and he would have been paralysed for life.

Amy Pearce had flown back to Las Vegas after just one day with Emmanuelle in Boston. She had stayed with Lucy, holding her hand throughout the long operation. When Thomas pulled through, she flew back to England again leaving Lucy and Thomas with a cheque each for five million pounds. She told them it was Jason's wish.

When Lucy told Thomas about Amy's gift, he cried. Watching him for all those days in the hospital, she knew that no matter what, she had to be with him now; she wasn't going to let him out of her sight. The job didn't matter, regardless of Amy's money. He asked her how Amy knew about Jason's money.

'Well, let's say I wasn't just in Starbucks in Las Vegas getting your early morning coffee. I told you to trust me,' she boasted with a wink. 'I also told DCI Moore a little of what was happening. I had to gamble, I just regret not telling him where we were in Las Vegas. Deep inside, I knew we wouldn't see the money from the Hammond brothers.'

Roland Moore, now Superintendent, wasn't exactly proud of them, though he apportioned no direct blame for what had happened. They both received official reprimands and then handed in their badges. They had abused so much protocol that there was no way they could stay in the force. But they were both brave and it was common knowledge that Amy had gifted them money from Jason's legacy. She had even shown Moore Jason's letter.

Amy decided that the proceeds of the sale from Jason's house in Cornwall should go to Frank Duffy's family and the proceeds from his flat to Vito Rolanski's family. They had made the ultimate sacrifice for Amy.

Emmanuelle explained a legend that had been adopted by many civilisations throughout the history of mankind, which said that those who sacrificed their lives for others could be granted the gift of light after death, if those who they died for lit a torch for them. So Thomas and Lucy, together with Amy and Emmanuelle, agreed to light a candle every week for the men who had died.

The file on Jason Chadwick's death was closed. His laptop was found in Amy's flat amongst the contents of the clear-out from his office. Though Amy couldn't remember bringing it home, she could never rule out the possibility that it had been there all along, especially as Gerard had helped her clear out the office. Maybe Paul Hammond was right and Jason really was running scared of himself – or maybe he truly believed that he could oversee the 'adventure' from above and help guide Amy to his fortune.

* * *

In 1929, the great walls of the Vatican City were erected to assert its sovereignty and settle the Roman Question that had strained relations between the Italian government and the Bishop of Rome. The new state of Vatican City became the official papal residence and the global capital of Catholicism.

The Melodema Stone was taken from the Sistine Chapel by order of Pope Pius XI. There were many myths about the stone. It was a siren to evil; the virtuous could touch the stone and hear angels; others claimed to hear 'voices in tongue' when they approached it. The stone was placed at the base of an external south facing wall without knowledge to the citizens of Rome.

Jason Chadwick could never remember why he first drew the symbol. It was just a quirky way of writing the letter M. Eventually he adopted it; when he signed his name, he would draw the symbol next to his signature.

The dream he had about stealing the crown jewels and getting caught because he had dropped his distinctive ring, played on his mind for weeks. Jason decided to have a ring, with his symbol, made up at a local jeweller and called it his Ring of Conscience.

In the box underneath the padding for the ring, he noticed there was a handwritten card saying 'melodema' on it. This meant nothing to Jason Chadwick until his honeymoon in Rome with Penny in 1984. A taxi dropped them off near the Vatican and they walked down Via Paolo VI, following the external wall. Jason noticed a chipped stone with a carved motif, which looked very similar to his ring.

He placed his hand on the stone to touch the symbol.

As Penny watched in amazement, he stood still. 'Wow! Do you hear that?' he asked.

Penny couldn't hear anything.

When he stood up, the choir in Jason's ears faded away.

Years later, he found out the full story of the Melodema Stone. Jason believed that his adoption of the symbol was some sort of sign and that the ring protected him from doing wrong. It became his 'Ring of Conscience'.

****

Amy and Emmanuelle stood there in the rain, looking at the Melodema Stone as Emmanuelle told Amy the story. Amy took the ring off the chain around her neck and kissed it before gently placing it in Emmanuelle's hand.

'Here,' she said. 'Jason gave it to me so that I could find the first clue but I'm sure that the ring was always meant for you.'

A tear trickled down Emmanuelle's cheek. She put her arms around Amy and they walked away. It was a new beginning for both of them, a new bond created from the ashes of Jason's memory.

EPILOGUE

The beginning of the end

Darren Cooper sat alone in his Boston office. The light was off and there were just the ambient lights of the city for illumination; he often did his thinking in the dark.

Where did it all go so wrong? He had planned meticulously and all the right doors opened for them along the way. He had relocated to Boston and asked his cousin Paul to befriend Jason's son, Brandon. He even stage-managed Brandon's losses and debts so that he could test Jason, see to what level he would go to help his son.

Jason's suicide in England was perfectly executed. It was his nephew who had done the business for him once again, just as he had with Donald Chadwick and his wife's 'accident' ten years earlier.

After Jason's will was disclosed and it became obvious that he'd left no real money for his sons, Darren called on his nephew again. He had managed to uncover Jason's secret after hacking into his laptop.

His nephew even got as far as page one of the strange domain and found Jason's initial clue. He also discovered from IP activity on the domain that somebody else was hunting: Thomas Riley and Lucy Bridges. From there on it looked so easy. Paul and Anthony had done everything to the letter.

If only Darren had dealt with Nathan after the Hammond Organisation was brought down. Stock was back behind bars again, this time for life. He had nearly died after his car overturned in the high speed police chase through California. He wasn't the man he used to be and Darren certainly couldn't rely on him any more.

No, Darren thought, the Coopers were all he had now. His cousins had failed.

Paul and Anthony would be out of jail in three years; the judge was surprisingly lenient with them. They had both claimed that Nathan and Stock were so volatile and irrational that they'd feared for their lives and been bullied into being accessories to murder.

Darren Cooper still wanted his money. The Hammond brothers had agreed to pay him a twenty-percent cut for his own part in the plan for Jason Chadwick's millions. Somehow he had to think up a new plan.

He called his trusted nephew again. It was late in England, midnight he reckoned, but his nephew knew him well, it was the Cooper call.

'Gerard!' he said. 'How is Oxford, this lovely evening?'

AUTHOR NOTES

December 2013

Ring of Conscience is a work of fiction that uses real places and landmarks to help the story's authenticity. It has been an immensely exciting project to work on.

The world and the internet have evolved since 2007 when I first created a sample **melodema.com** page to check that the clues and tricks work. Las Vegas has also changed: the newly built *City Centre* and *Cosmopolitan* complexes have altered the landscape of *The Strip*. Even the structure of the Metropolitan Police has changed. It will be interesting to look back in another six years to see what else has altered.

The hunt portrayed in this book works and melodema.com exists. If you're feeling adventurous, you can follow the clues and try to solve them before the characters do. I have also set up a separate treasure hunt with different clues on **www.melodema.net** Even though the prize might not be Jason's millions, it still has value.

The *Ring of Conscience* also exists. Jason's story is my own. I wrote a song about it when I was nineteen and my sister had the ring made for me. I still wear it to this day.

*The next mystery for Riley's Investigations, **A Parallel Trust**, is being written and will hopefully be released by the end of 2014. The novel is already as exciting to write as Ring of Conscience, and my personal empathy and connection with the central characters is stronger than I've ever felt before.*

JAMES STODDAH

James Stoddah grew up in Kent and was educated in Cumbria before settling in Lancashire with his three sons. He resisted higher education in favour of following a passion for music writing. For a number of years he worked in the music industry as a writer-performer – successful enough to earn a living without being burned by the media spotlight.

James has always been fascinated by mystery. Much of the creative inspiration for his books stems from games he created to entertain his children as they were growing up. Treasure hunts with clues to treats in the house expanded to physical clues he would leave over hundreds of square miles for day trip adventures.

Feel free to add/follow/question and keep up to date with James Stoddah online

www.jamesstoddah.com
www.facebook.com/JamesStoddah
www.twitter.com/JamesStoddah
http://melodema.tumblr.com/

and of course don't forget **www.melodema.com** and **www.melodema.net** to have a go at the hunt yourselves and try and claim your own treasure.